P9-DNN-417

SCHAUMBURG TOWNSHIP DISTRICT LIBRARY

3 1257 01680 2505

Schaumburg Township District Library
130 South Roselle Road
Schaumburg, Illinois 60193

BITE THE MOON

A MOLLY MULLET MYSTERY

BITE THE MOON

DIANE FANNING

FIVE STAR
An imprint of Thomson Gale, a part of The Thomson Corporation

THOMSON

GALE

Detroit • New York • San Francisco • New Haven, Conn. • Waterville, Maine • London

SCHAUMBURG TOWNSHIP DISTRICT LIBRARY
130 SOUTH ROSELLE ROAD
SCHAUMBURG, ILLINOIS 60193

3 1257 01680 2505

THOMSON

━━━━━★━━━━━ ™

GALE

Copyright © 2007 by Diane Fanning.

Thomson Gale is part of The Thomson Corporation.

Thomson and Star Logo and Five Star are trademarks and Gale is a registered trademark used herein under license.

ALL RIGHTS RESERVED

This novel is a work of fiction. Names, characters, places, and incidents are either the product of the author's imagination, or, if real, used fictitiously.

No part of this book may be reproduced or transmitted in any form or by any electronic or mechanical means, including photocopying, recording or by any information storage and retrieval system, without the express written permission of the publisher, except where permitted by law.

Set in 11 pt. Plantin.

LIBRARY OF CONGRESS CATALOGING-IN-PUBLICATION DATA

Fanning, Diane.
    Bite the moon : a Molly Mullet mystery / Diane Fanning. — 1st ed.
        p. cm.
    ISBN-13: 978-1-59414-549-0 (hardcover : alk. paper)
    ISBN-10: 1-59414-549-0 (hardcover : alk. paper)
    1. Policewomen—Fiction. 2. Widows—Fiction. 3. Texas Hill Country (Tex.)—Fiction. 4. Serial murderers—Fiction. I. Title.
PS3606.A55B58 2007
813'.6—dc22   2007005545

First Edition. First Printing: July 2007.

Published in 2007 in conjunction with Tekno Books and Ed Gorman.

Printed in the United States of America on permanent paper
10 9 8 7 6 5 4 3 2 1

This book is dedicated to Pete—just because

ACKNOWLEDGMENTS

Thanks to Agent Duane Deaver of the North Carolina State Bureau of Investigation, Brian Duckworth, and Judy Hubbard for invaluable background information. To Helen Ginger for her assistance and friendship.

To Miriam Goderich and Jane Dystel for their unwavering support.

And to Wayne, whose encouragement keeps my dreams alive.

CHAPTER ONE

Moonlighting a security gig at Solms Halle was as good as it gets for a uniformed cop. I relished every opportunity. There were few fights—even fewer drunks who maintained belligerence once you hustled them out into the open air. It was fun any night, but tonight was plum. Trenton Wolfe was the top bill.

When the management booked Wolfe, he had just finished recording his latest CD, Wolfe Pack, and had not yet released the chart-topping single, "Bite the Moon." Now that he had, he was riding a meteor into the stratosphere as the hottest new act in country music. The boisterous bodies packed into the old dance hall and stringing out into the street were proof that a legend was being born. The band honored the engagement in this obscure venue in gratitude for all the stage time Solms Halle gave them before anyone knew their name.

Although there was a chill in the air tonight, and all the wooden shutters were raised to let the fresh night breeze drift in through the screens, Solms Halle was hot and sweaty from the overflow crowd. The nightspot was nearly as old as Texas. Its unpainted, rough-hewn plank walls testified to its small-town dance-hall history.

The narrow picnic tables—worn smooth from the sliding of cold, wet bottles of beer—and the bench seats—shined to a high gloss by the rubbing of innumerable backsides—stretched out in tight rows perpendicular to the stage. The sitting-in-an-old-barn atmosphere was guarded with zealous neglect. Any at-

9

tempt to fancy-up Solms Halle was likely to cause its death as a Hill Country institution.

The driving country beat of Wolfe's music vibrated in the walls and floorboards, slid out the open windows and down the street where it danced on the rushing waters of the Guadalupe River. For half an hour, the band played old favorites for their longtime fans. When they started into a track off the new CD, I was enjoying myself too much to call it work.

Then, I heard the first scream. It echoed with the faintness of an off-mike back-up singer. Curious but not yet concerned, I headed up a crowded side aisle, pushing through the milling, bouncing, dancing gaggle of customers that blocked the way.

I was halfway up the length of the hall when the shriek of multiple female voices rose to a crescendo that overpowered the throbbing of the speakers pouring out a tale of lost love. One by one, the musicians stopped playing. The last to remain oblivious to the nearby panic was the drummer, who pounded out a mindless, manic solo—lost in the rhythm of his own world. I got a few steps forward while everyone else sat frozen in place listening to the eerie harmony of screams blending with the relentless drums like a ghoulish punk concerto. At last the silence of the other musicians disrupted the depths of the drummer's intense concentration. He lost his rhythm and his drumsticks clattered to the stage floor.

As if that sound were a secret signal, the stillness of the audience broke and they rose to their feet as one. My shouts for order dissolved in the cacophony the moment they passed my lips. Between the women fleeing from the restroom toward me, and the curiosity seekers pushing against my back, an impenetrable bottleneck grew.

I stepped up on a bench and from there to a tabletop. I jumped across from table to table, hoping to reach the stage, commandeer a microphone and calm the crowd. On the way, I flipped out my radio and called for assistance. I needed backup—bad.

I kicked over abandoned beer bottles, spraying foam on my pants legs and shoes, as I sprang across the room. When I reached the midpoint, I had a clear view of Trenton Wolfe. He stood on the stage and glared into the once captivated crowd that had transformed into an unruly mob.

Even in his state of apparent annoyance, the appealing good looks that had graced dozens of magazine covers were still intact. His perfectly sculpted six foot three frame had fueled my fantasies and those of most every other woman I knew. His chestnut brown hair, just long enough to brush the collar of his shirt, appeared as if it had never been fussed over and yet it was always in a perfect state of dishevelment—as if he just rose from a pleasurable encounter in bed. His face had a proportioned symmetry with a chin you could rely on. It was friendly, yet menacing. He had the bad-boy look that drove a lot of us crazy. His full, sensuous lips could part in a smile warm enough to melt a javalina's heart but, at the moment, they were pursed in disgust.

By his side was his bass player, Stan Crockett. He was a bit taller than Wolfe and leaner than Ichabod Crane. Skin wrapped around his bones like Saran Wrap clinging to a turkey carcass. His deep-set eyes and sunken cheeks perched on a scrawny neck with a prominent Adam's apple. That apparatus was balanced on a body so lanky, it appeared as if it might suddenly splinter at the waist. At the end of toothpick arms were hands with skeletal fingers that somehow created magic every time he touched a bass guitar.

Word was that despite his cadaverous appearance, Crockett was a laid-back, happy man who smiled easily and often. Unfortunately, on a face like his, a grin looked like a grimace and a full smile like the mocking of a ghoul. At the moment, he was not smiling. His compressed lips were in constant motion as he whispered to the mute star of the show.

I ran up the length of picnic tables toward the two. I jumped to the floor, battled my way through the dense crowd in the small space between the table and the stage and vaulted up onto the platform.

I grabbed the microphone and ordered the crowd back into their seats. My shouts were as effective as the whispered rebuke of a chaplain during a prison riot. By now, many of the intoxicated in the crowd were taking offense at the pushing and shoving and were throwing punches in response. Oh, man, oh man, where was my backup? I strained my ears but could not hear the sounds of approaching sirens, nor did a look through the windows reveal any flashing lights racing to the scene.

Mike Elliot, manager of Solms Halle, clambered onto the stage and shot me a glance of desperation. I didn't think it would do much good but I shouted into the microphone again. Mike tried to hustle Trenton Wolfe and his group out of the hall. Trenton was not making his job any easier. I could not hear a word he was saying, but he was yelling at Mike and his arms flailed the air like a windmill run amok.

Unlike more modern facilities, there was no backstage entrance at Solms Halle—no easy exit for performers. Mike and a few beefy volunteers formed an arrowhead that struggled to maintain its unity and pierce through the noisy crowd.

I slid off the stage and sidled along the wall to the ladies' restroom where all the brouhaha had begun. Light slipping through the crack at the bottom of the door illuminated a mishmash of bloody footprints on the floor.

I slammed my back against the wall by the doorframe and drew my gun. The churning chaos around me parted like the Red Sea. I took a deep breath and kicked open the door. I moved into the doorway with my gun extended in a shooter's stance. "New Braunfels Police Department. Throw down your weapons." I scanned the barrel of my revolver from one corner of the small bathroom to another. Nothing moved. But there were four stalls. Any one of them could conceal a perpetrator.

If someone in one of those stalls shot at me right now, I doubt the plywood doors would even slow down the bullet. I exhaled a guttural shout and kicked open the first stall door and drew a bead on the vacant toilet. I moved to the next one. I could taste the fear in my mouth. It coated my tongue with a green slime that made my stomach lurch. I kicked open the next door and the sick sensation grew.

What was behind the next door? The lady? Or the tiger? Again, I kicked. No victim. No bad guy. Nothing but porcelain.

Now all that was left was the last stall, I could smell my sweat and feel it form a clammy pool on the nape of my neck. I kicked that last door open. Nothing.

I breathed again. But it was ragged. What had started as a small spot of tightness in my chest had expanded to embrace my whole upper body in its painful grip. I turned back to the doorway to the hall where the tops of a few foolish heads leaned in to see what was up. When they saw my gaze turn on them, the heads pulled back like turtles retreating into their shells.

With flashlight in hand, I shone the light in the narrow hallway outside the restroom door. I followed the trail of blood to where it led in the other direction. It ended at another door. Through the crack at the bottom, blood still seeped—as thick as glue, as dark as dirty oil—but still it moved.

I grabbed a paper towel from the bathroom dispenser and crossed the hall. In my right hand, my gun was at the ready. With my left hand, I laid the towel on the knob. I tried to turn it. It was locked. From the hinges, I saw that the door opened out. A kick would not do the trick. I needed the key. I reached on top of the doorsill. No luck. I shone the flashlight around looking for a nail that held a key. Nothing there. I needed Mike. Whoever was bleeding in there might still be alive. From the consistency of the blood, I doubted it, but it was possible. I was torn. Guard the door? Go find a key?

Before I could decide my problem was solved—Mike Elliot was by my side, a chunky key ring in his hand. He slid the key in the knob and backed away from the door. I stepped up, turned the key and released the lock. I pulled the door open a crack then slid to the side where I would be shielded as I eased the door open with my foot.

I led with the barrel of the gun, then jerked into position—knees bent, gun pointed straight ahead. One glance and I returned the gun to my holster and traded it for my flashlight—whoever had transformed this ordinary utility closet into an abattoir was no longer there.

Sticky blood pooled like a major coke-syrup spill on the floor. Up the wall and across the cleansers lined up on the shelves, runny dime-sized droplets of blood formed a distinctive pattern—a line of streaky spatter rose up in a peak, descended and rose to a second peak—the classic formation of arterial gush, just like the pictures I saw at the seminar. It looked like the chart for an electrocardiogram—very bad news for the body sprawled at my feet in a lake of blood.

A small cardboard box nestled in the small of the victim's back, arching his body upward. Tossed across the upper half of his torso was an orange plastic rain poncho—the disposable kind Wal-Mart sells for a couple of bucks. It seemed odd that there were smears of blood all over the side of the poncho facing toward me, but I didn't have time to ponder that puzzle now.

I pushed the poncho aside with the butt of my flashlight to check for a pulse. His neck was sliced through to the spine, throwing his head back into a bucket where his hair floated on the blood that accumulated in the bottom.

I crouched down to check for vital signs. The spot where I should press to check for a pulse was no longer there. I knew it was futile, but still I lifted his limp wrist and held my breath as my fingertips sought any glimmer of life. No throb. No beat. No life.

Embedded in the shredded tissue of his throat, I saw a metallic glint. I focused the beam of the flashlight and discovered the source to be a guitar string. I followed its length and noticed the ends pulled through a block of wood and twisted tight. Death by guitar string—that had to be a first. And Solms Halle was the perfect setting for it. My moment of levity gave way to a sudden and severe bout of nausea—the bile rising at the back of my throat, its acid searing my tongue. I threw a hand to my mouth and squeezed my eyes tight, willing the upsurge to back down. If I lost it here, I would contaminate the crime scene and never hear the end of it.

As soon as I had my internal distress under control, I inched my way up to a standing position. I thought the movement was making my head ring but then realized the sound I heard was the distant, shrill wail of a siren. The posse was coming. In seconds, the spinning, flashing lights outside the windows lit up Solms like Las Vegas. I stood my ground by the door, shooing away a morbid looky-loo or two as I waited for my partners-in-arms.

CHAPTER TWO

A sea of blue flooded the hall and parted the mob into manageable groups. Quicker than a cap could fly off a longneck, the crowd was seated at the tables or in neat lines on the floor. Some nursed busted lips, others struggled to steady their bobbing heads, many rubbed mindlessly on the blue ink stamps on the backs of their hands.

When the first detective stepped into the hall, he made a beeline for my position. He flashed his badge with an air of condescension and commandeered my flashlight. When he pointed the beam into the closet, his air of superiority dissolved. He doubled over, covered his mouth and lurched toward the restroom. A newbie. Oh, joy. When he recovered, the look on his face encouraged me to bite my tongue and not speak a single word I was thinking. He took charge of the closet and I stepped in to assist with the drudgery in the hall.

I went table-to-table asking for drivers' licenses and jotting down names and contact information. While those of us in uniform released the crowd one small table at a time, detectives questioned staff by the vendor table at the entrance to the hall.

Outside an engine roared and a horn blasted the night air again and again in quick succession. A whiff of diesel fumes drifted through the windows and penetrated our noses with that thick nausea-inducing smell. Had to be Trenton Wolfe's tour bus making a heralded departure.

Moments later, Detective Tim Hawkins plowed into the hall

with all the grace of a bulldozer. His red face, clenched fists and quivering paunch were sure indications that someone on that bus did not accord him the respect he thought was his right. I've known Tim since I was a kid. And I liked him. But sometimes, his pompous manner opened him up for a full roundhouse punch to his sensibilities.

I turned back to the task at hand. I had to concentrate to keep from transposing digits in phone numbers and butchering the spelling of names as I carried out the mind-numbing chore. At last, the final group of stunned spectators drifted out of the hall and into the night. By morning, many of them would be relating tales of a near brush with death to envious friends who rued their decision not to attend the show. In no time, the town would be buried in an avalanche of half-truths and generous exaggerations.

Yellow crime scene tape encircled the bloodied area next to the stage. It seemed the local posse had called in the cavalry. A white cowboy hat announced the presence of a Texas Ranger. And judging by the stenciling on the back of the Tyvec suits, a herd of Texas Department of Safety Crime Scene Techs was on hand, too.

I was curious and apprehensive about who was lying in the pool of blood on the other side of the tape. I didn't think I knew the victim but I wasn't sure—I was too focused on the gore to notice his facial features. I hovered in the background snatching bits of conversation out of the air.

Relief washed over me when I learned the dead body belonged to a stranger. Then I felt ashamed. No one's death should ever be a relief.

The stranger was Rodney Faver, the general manger of Trenton Wolfe's band. That made me wonder why the tour bus wasn't still parked outside. I thought someone on board should be a suspect.

I didn't think I knew any of the personnel from DPS in Austin, but then I saw a familiar face dart under the crime scene tape and scurry outside. Jim Mendoza was a student from the days before I was a cop when I taught chemistry up at the high school. Now, it seemed, he was a DPS tech. I followed him and found him digging through the trunk of his car.

"What have you got in there, Jim?" I tilted my head toward the hall.

"Ms. Mullet?" Jim squinted eyes at me, not trusting the vision of his former teacher dressed in a blue uniform.

"Yeah. Only it's Officer Mullet, now."

"Jeez, this is weird." His eyes darted around in his uncertainty. "Keep this to yourself, Ms. Mullet, but Ranger Allen is having a fit. We got a dead guy connected to the band stuffed in the closet with a guitar string wrapped around his neck and that stupid cop let the band bus go."

He grabbed a hard plastic case from the trunk, slammed the lid and, with a nod of his head, disappeared back into the hall. Now I really wanted to know why Hawkins didn't hold that tour bus at the scene.

I wandered back into the hall where I was told I would need to file a report in the next couple of days but was now free to go home. Across the hall, I spotted Bobby Wiggins, the hall's janitor. His bowed head swung back and forth as he listened to Mike Elliot. I grew up on the same street as Bobby. He was ten years older than me, but when I was in elementary school, he acted my age. When I moved on to middle school, I realized that Bobby had not grown up at all. He was still a kid. A lot of my peers teased and tricked Bobby, but I usually heard the voice of my mother rat-a-tatting too loud in my head to join in their cruel fun.

I pitied Bobby back then. But as I became an adult, I grew to appreciate the simple dignity he possessed in the face of ridicule and the gentle nature he displayed under pressure. With every passing minute, he fidgeted more and more at the words that flew from Mike's mouth. I moved a step or two in their direction but decided it would not be wise to interfere in their discussion. Not here. Not now. I'd catch up with Bobby later.

I was off-duty the next day and putzed around the house, cleaning up little pockets of debris. I had a horrible habit of forming little nesting areas whenever I sat anywhere for more than a minute. Scraps of paper, pencils, magazines, newspapers piled up by every chair. I put things away and dusted tabletops. Leaving the house was not going to be an option for me today.

It seemed everyone had heard I was at Solms Halle the night before and everyone wanted a firsthand account.

I allowed my answering machine to serve as my gatekeeper as one whispered message after another spooled on to the tape.

"Molly, Molly, call me right away."

"Molly, I heard you were working at Solms Halle last night, call me."

"Molly, how many people were killed in the shootout last night?"

"Molly, is it true Trenton Wolfe is under arrest?"

The truth was weaving into a web of deceit faster than a spider could wrap a fly.

CHAPTER THREE

Monday, I went in early to file my report and snoop around for the latest news about the investigation before my shift started. I sat down at a desk, pulled out a form and got busy.

Lisa Garcia, a nineteen-year-old administrative aide, sidled up beside me and peered over my shoulder without saying a word. "Yes, Lisa?" I said without looking up from my work.

"Did you hear about the arrest?"

"Arrest?" Now I was interested.

"Yes, arrest for murder." The last word stretched out of her mouth as if it were a hundred letters long.

"Rodney Faver's murder?"

"Yes." Her brown eyes twinkled as she held on to her moment of superior knowledge. She leaned her small rump against the desk, using one brown arm to keep her balance. With the other hand, she covered her mouth. She was the most enthusiastic—yet most coy—gossip in the whole department.

She wanted me to beg. So I obliged. "Come on, Lisa. Tell me. Who was arrested?"

"You will not believe this."

"Tell me."

"Bobby Wiggins."

"Bobby Wiggins?" I said as I dropped my pen and jumped to my feet. I looked at Lisa's bobbing head and stared into her dark, twinkling eyes. Was she excited that she got to break the news? Or was she just jerking my chain? "Lisa, if this is your idea of a joke, I am not amused."

A wide-eyed look of indignation swept across her face like fire over a dry prairie. She popped off my desk and stood as straight and tall as her five-foot-two frame would allow. She pivoted on her heel, and I laid my hand on her forearm before she could escape. She shrugged it off, tossed her head and blurped out a sound of disgust.

I hate these girly games but I had no choice. "I'm sorry, Lisa. Of course I believe you. I was just shocked. Please forgive me."

My pleading paid off. She spun back around, beaming. Leaning forward she confided, "Mama says it's ridiculous—grade-A ridiculous."

"Your mama is right."

"Oh, I don't know about Mama." She shook her head slowly. "She's had this thing about the police department ever since they picked up Uncle Jesus and questioned him about that bank robbery . . ."

I tuned her out and put my head in automatic-nod mode. I'd heard the story about Uncle Jesus at least a dozen times this year already. I'd have to wait until she finished before I could get any more information about Bobby's arrest. It made no sense. Every member of the band had more potential motive than Bobby. Did the investigators back off because of their celebrity? There had to be a lot of other possible suspects, too. Trenton Wolfe's meteoric rise had to have spawned some enemies. Someone had to hate Faver more than Bobby was capable of hating anyone.

I zoned back in as Lisa wrapped up her soliloquy. "So, I'm not so sure about Mama. I told her that in my experience with the police, I've learned that almost anybody can do almost anything for almost no reason at all."

"What makes them think it's Bobby, Lisa?"

"He confessed."

"Confessed?"

"Yep. Lieutenant Hawkins says he's got him dead to rights—dead to rights is exactly what he said—he got him dead to rights and it's all on tape, too."

"He taped it?" Damn, a written statement would have been better. It would be so easy to argue that Bobby didn't understand what he was reading. Whoa. Alien thought. Where did that come from? I'm a cop, not a defense attorney.

My mental darting must have danced across my face like a crazed tango. Lisa gave a sideways glare through slitted eyes as if she feared my head might make a full circuit and spew pea soup at any second.

"Lieutenant Hawkins, you said?"

"Yep. Yep. Lieutenant Hawkins. You okay, Officer Mullet?"

"Yeah, I'm fine." I patted Lisa's shoulder, hoping to reassure her as I walked out of the room. I felt her eyes on my back as I left and wondered if she was going to call Hawkins and warn him that a lunatic was on the way.

I peered around a cubicle wall and spotted Hawkins at his desk. His short bristle cut made his incipient baldness difficult to detect at first glance. His jowls and gut seemed to sag a little more every time I saw him. The smell of fast food wrapper and discarded banana peel wafting from his overfull trash can filled the air with a greasy sweetness that churned my stomach. "Lieutenant Hawkins?"

"Hey, Mullet!" He grinned. "You heard the word? Go ahead," he said, thrusting a shoulder in my direction. "Pat me on the back."

I kept my distance and wiped any emotion from my face. "I heard that you think you solved the Faver homicide."

"Think? Think, my ass, Mullet. I solved it and bagged the perp before the blood was dry. With a little luck, the DA will throw away the key."

"Bobby Wiggins, Lieutenant?" It was taking a lot of effort not to raise my voice or clench my teeth.

"Yeah. Ain't human nature a kick in the butt? You think you know somebody and, bam, they go do something you never expected."

"Maybe you didn't expect it because he didn't do it?"

"Mullet, Mullet, Mullet," he said, shaking his head in broad swings. "How long you been on the force?"

Oh, I hate this. Someone was always reminding me that they had more seniority—and more experience—than I did. "I've known Bobby Wiggins all my life, sir."

"Oh, cut the 'sir' crap, Mullet. You've known me most of your life, too." He looked down at his watch. "You got some time before shift. C'mon, have a seat."

He hooked his foot under the rung of the metal chair and dragged it around to the business side of his desk in front of the VCR-TV combo perched on the makeshift credenza by the wall. "C'mon. I'll show you the tape. Sit. Sit. I've got it cued up a couple hours into the good part."

I wanted to see the tape. But I didn't want to see Bobby say he did it. I was afraid I would believe him and I didn't want to. I slumped into the chair.

"Wipe off that long face, girl. Here's your chance to learn something about being a cop—a real cop."

The video camera shot down from an angle above, giving a perspective that made the room look a bit larger than it really was. It was a plain, ugly room with scarred beige walls and stained, white-speckled floor tile. No one went all out for furniture either. There was one of those old metal tables with that strange spongy gray surface composed of a substance no one still living could identify. The metal chairs had thin built-in back and seat cushions of cheap green vinyl—the kind you can repair with a piece of color-coordinated electrical tape.

Bobby's head hung over the table. His shaggy hair blocked his eyes. The fingers of each hand worried each other—picking, scraping, rubbing. Tim Hawkins' back was to the camera as he leaned toward Bobby. Both his palms rested flat on the desktop and supported the weight of his upper body.

The wall cuff hung loose on the wall. At least Hawkins hadn't restrained him. But Bobby's body language spoke of such a pervasive misery, I wasn't sure it even mattered.

"Hey, Bobby," Hawkins said on the tape, "didn't your mama ever tell you that she can forgive you for anything s'long as you don't lie to her?"

Bobby raised his head, his eyes wide. There was a look of wonder on his face as Bobby tried to figure out how Hawkins knew that. He nodded his head.

"All right, then, Bobby. It's the same with me. Why don't you just tell me what you did, Bobby, so as I can forgive you?"

"I didn't . . ."

"And then, Bobby," Hawkins continued, "we can let you see your mama. Wouldn't you like that?"

Bobby's head fell forward. A large wet tear plopped on the desktop. Hawkins leaned forward further. His lips were nearly on Bobby's ear. He whispered, "You do want to see your mama, dontcha?"

Bobby raised his wet eyes to the officer. His lower lip quivered. He nodded his head.

"Then tell me what happened in that closet, Bobby."

"I don't . . ."

"What did that bad man do to make you so mad?"

"He didn't . . ."

"C'mon, Bobby. Your mama's worrying about you now. What did the man in the closet do to make you so mad?"

"He, he, he . . ."

"Yeah, Bobby?"

"He, he was messin' in my closet. I don't like nobody messin' in my closet. I keep it all neat. There's a place for everything and a thing for every place and I keep everything in its place." Bobby looked up begging for approval.

"You do a good job, Bobby. What happened in the closet?"

"I keep everything in its place then I can find what I need when I need it."

"That's right, Bobby. Then what happened?"

"Um, I asked him iffen I could help him. On accounta if there was a mess to clean up, that was my job."

"What did he say, Bobby?"

"He, he, he . . . He didn't say nothin'. Nothin'. He acted like I wasn't there."

"Did that make you mad, Bobby?"

"Mad?" Bobby's head tilted sideways and a frown furrowed his brow.

"Yes, Bobby, he ignored you. Didn't that make you mad?"

Bobby's eyes darted back and forth as he sought the right answer. "Mad? Yeah. Yeah. That made me mad all right."

I sat and watched without comment. I tried not to telegraph my thoughts by folding my arms across my chest, but they kept going there of their own accord. Next to me, Tim Hawkins fought a smug grin that sought to conquer his face. Tim liked to say he was in homicide but this small town did not have enough murder in a year to keep him busy for a week. In fact, Tim's position was major crimes and even that was not enough to keep him from the occasional drunk and disorderly arrest or juvenile bike theft.

On the tape, the manipulation continued. "After you wrapped the guitar string around his neck, what did you do, Bobby?"

"Held on?" Bobby looked at the Lieutenant whose head gave a slight nod. "Yeah. I held on."

"And what did he do, Bobby? What did he look like?" Hawkins pushed.

Bobby's eyes had a faraway look as if an old Bugs Bunny–Elmer Fudd cartoon rolled scenes of comic violence through his head. "His eyes—his eyes bugged out. And his feet danced. Yes. His feet danced."

"Then what did you do, Bobby?"

"Uh, I closed and locked the door and went back to work." Bobby's eyebrows raised and he nodded his head. The look of a puppy desperate to please romped across his simple face.

Hawkins turned and faced the camera. He was all smug satisfaction as he drew an index finger across his neck. The screen went black.

A big sigh hissed unbidden through my clenched teeth as Hawkins rose and turned off the VCR.

"What?" Tim's arms, sleeves rolled to his elbows, folded across his chest so tight that they forced his oversized paunch a little further over his belt buckle.

I stood, shook my head and took a step away from his desk.

"What, Mullet? No comment?"

I knew I should just keep on walking away and not say a word. But keeping my mouth shut was never one of my strong points. I spun around. "You call that a confession?"

"Yeah. And a damned good one at that."

I headed back for the door. I had to get out of there before I said anything else.

"Hey, Mullet, what's your problem?"

"You are my problem, Lieutenant." I needed to shut up.

"You coppin' a 'tude with me, Mullet?"

Oh, yeah, that made this scene complete: a middle-aged, balding, overweight white guy spouting ghetto slang at me. Heaven save me from that midlife urge to be hipper than my age allowed. "You could say that, sir. I do not like coerced confessions. I do not like the crass manipulation of someone with limited mental capabilities. I do not like how you're railroading Bobby Wiggins when there are so many other real suspects out there."

"You'll never be a real cop, girl. You just don't think like one. You sound like a defense attorney looking for any lame question you can use to create reasonable doubt. What are you doing in that uniform?"

I turned and left then. I had nothing more to say. Quite frankly, I was no longer sure I knew the answer to his question.

CHAPTER FOUR

The shift that evening was routine and dull—a few drunk and disorderlies and a couple of domestic violence calls. Fortunately for all concerned, the domestic complaints were tame—heavy on broken crockery and light on physical assault.

My finesse was at an all-time low. There were too many questions squealing their tires through my head tonight. Questions about Bobby Wiggins. Questions about Tim Hawkins. Questions about myself.

I didn't realize my mind had strayed from the job until I noticed my left hand rubbing on the outside of my right arm. Seeing that, my mind jogged down a rabbit trail of regret.

It was the summer of my junior year in high school. The college girls were back home for their annual break. A small pack of them adopted me as their pet nerd. I was in awe of their worldliness and sophistication.

One muggy night in July, they invited me to tag along with them to explore the excitement on Sixth Street in Austin. I felt honored. I lied to my mother and joined the merry band of revelers.

The seven blocks running from Interstate 35 to Congress Avenue were a lively blend of bars and other live entertainment venues along with a diverse offering of restaurants, art galleries, tattoo parlors and funky shops.

On weekend nights, Sixth Street throbbed to the beat of every rhythm from hip-hop to country. The people walking the streets were just as eclectic—crowds bobbed with cowboy hats, corners flashed with transvestites and purple hair was so common only the tourists bothered to stare.

We bounced from club to club up and down the street. Waiters always brought a soft drink to the table for me but the more potent beverages ordered by the older girls were within easy reach.

The conversation turned to tattoos. By the glow of a tiny keychain flashlight, they displayed their body decorations to one another in a dark corner of the club. A heart on the swell of a breast. A dragon in the small of one back. A ring of ivy encircling an upper arm. But the one that most intrigued me was on the basketball star. On her arm, just below her shoulder, a basketball swished through a hoop.

I wanted a tat, too. I wanted a unique one that spoke of my passion. I wanted a lab beaker of bubbling liquid emitting chemical fumes. The vision was so clear in my mind. And so cool.

At first they tried to discourage me. Then one girl mentioned a friend who had an older brother doing tattoos just a few blocks from here. By the time we arrived at his seedy unlicensed studio, we were too intoxicated to care when she added that he learned his craft in prison. By the time he got to work, none of us was sober enough to focus on his work.

It wasn't until the next morning that I realized my frothing fluid-filled beaker looked more like a fresh, steaming cow-pie than anything ever seen in a chemistry lab. I should have had it removed long ago but I feared it would hurt more coming off than it did going on. Instead, I never wore a sleeveless blouse again.

Every time I tried to force my mind off of that unfortunate memory, my thoughts traveled the circuit again. Bobby, Tim. My life. My tattoo. It was hopeless. If I encountered a serious situation, I would not have been much help to anyone.

The next morning I left home early again. This time, however, I didn't go straight to the station. I paid a visit to Thelma Wiggins. I turned into the street where I grew up and memories rolled in like fog. I never knew Mr. Wiggins, but I did remember what the older kids said about him. Their graphic descriptions of his demise were designed to gross me out as well as keep their own demons at bay.

Mr. Wiggins, it was said, went into the shed in the backyard with a revolver and blew his brains out all over the lawnmower. More than once, I was goaded into peering through the fence looking for pieces of Mr. Wiggins on the mower while Bobby pushed it around the yard. Looking back, it was, in all likelihood, not the same mower, but when kids were in a ghoulish frame of mind, there was no room for logic.

All my life, I knew a dour Mrs. Wiggins who never smiled. She was never mean or ugly to me—often gave me cookies and milk and other treats. But she looked and acted as if she'd escaped from the *American Gothic* canvas and wanted nothing more than to return to that unchangeable two-dimensional world.

My mom told me that she was different years ago. Before Bobby was born. Before Mr. Wiggins died. Before living beat the life out of her. At one time, Thelma Wiggins was a lively, vivacious young woman with a ready smile and a bellowing laugh. All that was left was the shell of that woman—a shadow who seldom peered over the wall she built around her heart.

When I lost my husband, I tried to reach out to her. We had something in common after my Charlie's death, but my efforts were wasted; it never brought us any closer.

I parked in front of my old house out of habit and walked cater-corner across the street to the Wigginses' home. I thought I was being paranoid when I felt eyes crawling on my skin as I

he sides of their heads were so close together that the
ds of Bobby's blond hair entwined with the deep chestnut
n of Molly's. Their eyes gazed upward, their faces
ixed with awe—they were so still Thelma wondered if they
olding their breaths. What in heaven's name could have
ted them so?

ma found out a few minutes later when Bobby burst
kitchen, trembling with excitement. He was so full of
y he wanted to tell, he struggled to form the words.
y, the tiny. Black legs. Dangle. Oh. M-m-m-m-molly-
"

wanted to help him—but she knew he had to do this
. She waited with patience—love and sorrow steeping
brew of emotions in her chest.

obby found his words. "Molly showed me the hum-
he showed me their legs as they sipped on the flow-
ack legs. Little bitty bodies. Molly said they is
gle—dangling legs. There, I said it. Dangling. Molly
iny black legs dangling from little bitty bodies.
Molly say. Molly has good words. And the hum-
ey talk to us. Talk, talk, talk. They talk a lot,
ays, Bobby tried to imitate the hummingbird
amed through the house and the yard. The more
deeper grew Thelma's gratitude.

day of the dead mouse that endeared Molly to
Bobby caught Thelma red-handed on her way
ith the limp rodent hanging from the trap.
. You killed him," Bobby wailed, tears raining
puddling in the corners of his mouth. Bobby
roked the gray, bloodied fur. "Poor mousy.

g is filthy. Don't touch it."

Mama? How could you?"

---

traversed the sidewalk and climbed the three steps to the porch.
But the second I raised my hand to rap on the wooden screen,
the inside door flew open and there stood Thelma Wiggins.

Anxiety dug into her face like a putty knife gouging deep furrows of sorrow and worry. Her watery blue eyes looked vacant
as we stared at each other through the mesh screen. I waited for
an invitation to come inside. When one didn't come, I swallowed hard and spoke. "Mrs. Wiggins? You remember me, right?
From across the street?"

Her mouth compressed tighter than a new rosebud and a
spark of anger resurrected the life in her eyes. "What do you
want now?"

"Mrs. Wiggins, I came by to see if I could be of any help."

"Haven't you people done enough? I've told you everything I
know. I told you Bobby did not, could not, would not do this.
What more do you want from me?"

I realized too late that it was a mistake to come here on my
way to work. In my uniform, I'd been transformed into the
enemy. "Mrs. Wiggins, I am not here in an official capacity. I'm
here as a family friend. I don't believe Bobby did this. I want to
help."

Her shoulders sagged and the anger fled her eyes. "Molly,
you're one of them. You can't be of any help to me. I can't trust
you, and my lawyer says I can't talk to anybody connected to
law enforcement or the district attorney's office. Why, he even
told me to do my grocery shopping at odd hours to avoid running into any of you all. I can't talk to you anymore, Molly."
She pushed on the door as she said my name.

Before she could close it all the way, I blurted out, "Wait,
Mrs. Wiggins."

She peered around the edge of the door, shaking her head.
"I'm sorry, Molly."

"Lawyer? Did you say you've got a lawyer?"

"Yes. Dale Travis."

I couldn't have heard her right. "Dale Travis of Foster, Travis and Crum over in Houston?"

"Yes, Molly. Goodbye." The door clicked shut.

Dale Travis? One of the most high-powered—and high-priced—criminal attorneys in Texas. How did Thelma Wiggins pull that off? How could she even dream of raising the retainer? Nothing about this case was making any sense.

I went down the steps and sidewalk and swung open the gate. I turned back to look at the house. A curtain was pulled back in the window to the left of the door. As soon as I zeroed in on it, it twitched, then fell closed.

CHAPTER FIVE

Thelma hated turning away from M rare real friends Bobby'd ever had. B years old, she had become a regula house. By then, Bobby was eighteer measure of maturity, Molly was ra

Before Molly came along, ther to play, but they all had a hidde laugh at Bobby's expense. Son and guffawed along with the r unsettling for them to handle meanness elsewhere. Other Bobby cried. His distress pointed fingers and laugh drove them away.

Molly was no parag Sometimes she would Bobby with the rest shared her vision of generosity of spirit

Her lips formed back a couple of first times she was on a breezy window and s orange and re

"Bobby, it's just an old, nasty field mouse."

"That's what you think. What if it's a special mouse? What if it's Mighty Mouse?"

"Honey, Mighty Mouse is too strong to get caught in a trap."

"Not if he was ordinary. Not if the trap caught him so fast he didn't have time to put on his cape and stuff. What if you killed Mighty Mouse? Who's gonna save the day?" Bobby broke into blubbering sobs.

Thelma was lost in her own pain. Her twenty-year-old son with the heart and mind of a four-year-old. She felt his sorrow and she felt her own. She hung her head and wanted to die. She ached to turn back in time. To change the past. The present—the future—it was all more than she could bear.

"Bobby, it's okay," Molly said as she crossed the yard. Thelma lifted her bowed head and looked into a face filled with the empathy of a saint. Her deep, dark brown eyes were framed by a short brown cap of pixie cut hair and a smile so beguiling it could make a mad dog sit up and beg.

Molly approached Bobby and patted his arm. "I just saw Mighty Mouse, Bobby. On my TV. Let's go see if he's on your TV."

Bobby wiped his wet eyes and runny nose on his shirtsleeve and took Molly's offered hand. She spent the whole day with him driving every trace of the morning's sorrow from his mind.

And, now, that little girl was a thirty-two-year-old grown woman, but the sweetness never left her face. Her chestnut brown hair was longer now, sweeping across her shoulders when she moved. Her brown eyes were so dark, it was difficult to tell where the pupils began and her irises ended. In their depths, Thelma saw deep wells of honesty and empathy. *And yet I slammed the door in her face,* Thelma thought. She shuffled away from the front door and into the kitchen and looked out the window to the shed—the shed where her husband Stuart took his own life nearly thirty years ago.

There were days when Thelma thought the shed looked like a good place to die. Today was one of those days. Thelma drew her arms tight around her body as she embraced the idea of death. *Good thing Dale Travis got rid of Stuart's revolver,* Thelma mused. *Good thing I never bought one of my own.*

She poured another cup of black coffee and slumped in the kitchen chair. She sipped. The bitterness of her life scalded her tongue.

CHAPTER SIX

Weary before my day had begun, I climbed into my car and drove into work. I saw Detective Hawkins pacing by the back door as I pulled into the parking lot. I hoped he wasn't waiting for me. My hopes were dashed as soon as I opened my car door and I heard him shout, "Mullet. There you are."

"Hi, Detective. I've gotta get in to roll call."

"You've got a few minutes, Mullet. Come on. I've got to show you something."

"I don't have much time."

"Don't need much time, girlfriend. C'mon. C'mon."

Hawkins walked off faster than I thought he was capable of moving. I trudged behind him with the same enthusiasm I exhibited on my way to a root canal. When we reached his cubicle, he flourished a piece of paper. "Look," he said. "Look at this. You know what this is, Mullet? Vindication, that's what. Vindication, Mullet."

"Hawkins, if you'd stop wiggling it around, I'd look at it."

He laid the paper on his desk and although it didn't need it, he smoothed it flat with both his hands. I scanned the document. It was a laboratory report. Item tested: a key. Results: positive for blood. Blood Type: A positive. The item was sent to the state forensics lab in Austin for DNA testing.

I looked at Hawkins and shrugged. Whatever it meant, I'd bet it did not bode well for Bobby. The detective was grinning from ear to ear.

"See. See," he said pointing to the blood type.

"See what?" I asked.

"The blood is A positive. Rodney Faver's blood is A positive."

"Yeah. Well, the man bled a lot, Hawkins, you should find his blood at the scene."

"Bobby Wiggins' blood is O positive."

"Yes. And?" I made little circles with my hands hoping to encourage him to get to the point.

The smile slid off of his face. His eyes turned as cold and hard as a polished chunk of onyx. "The key is the closet key."

He paused. I held my breath.

"I found the key in Bobby Wiggins' pocket."

For a moment, I was stunned into silence. My left hand jumped to my right arm and rubbed with frantic strokes. Faver's blood on a key in Bobby's pocket? There's something wrong with this picture. The report is wrong or information is missing. Something. "No," I spat out at last.

"No? Whadya mean 'no'?" He grabbed the sheet of paper off his desk and waggled it in my face again. "No, Mullet? I don't think so. It's right here in black and white. Ten years ago, it was all we'd need to walk in court. And win. Now, we'll wait and get the DNA test results. When they come back, it'll be a slam dunk for the DA. Slam dunk, Mullet. Slam dunk."

I tried to bite my tongue but I started talking before I could bear down. "I don't think Dale Travis will think it's a slam dunk, Detective."

His eyes squinted up like those of a suspicious child. "Dale Travis? What's he got to do with anything?"

"Dale Travis is representing Bobby Wiggins."

His face paled. His lips moved without making a sound. Then he slapped his desktop and burst into a belly laugh. "Good one, Mullet. Where'd you pick up that idle gossip? From the old-

timers browsing down at Henne Hardware or from the farmers'
wives down at the feed store?"

Damn his arrogance. "From Thelma Wiggins, sir."

"When did you see Thelma?"

"This morning. I dropped by to offer my help with Bobby's
case." I spun around and walked away. No sense telling him she
shut the door in my face.

"You did what? What are you—what did she—what do you
think—you're a disgrace, Mullet. A freakin' disgrace."

His words still rang in my ears when I reported to roll call.
They would not leave my head. They were stuck there because I
suspected he was right. I shouldn't be wearing a badge. I
shouldn't be in uniform. One unremarkable morning nearly six
years ago, a horrid event unfolded before my eyes. It was that
dark day that sent me careening down this path. For all the
right reasons, I had made a very wrong decision.

CHAPTER SEVEN

I can't believe how silly I felt that morning. Married three years and I still got excited over a respectable rendezvous with my husband. But the night before was such a lonely night. The nights were always lonely when Charlie worked the overnight shift. I didn't think there was enough time in our lives for me to get used to sleeping without him.

So there I was, pulling into a parking space at McDonald's, feeling like a teenager on her first date. "All you're doing, Molly, old girl, is meeting your husband for breakfast," I chastised myself. After the romance in our own fast food heaven, I'd head to work and Charlie would slide into our lonely bed seeking traces of the warmth I'd left behind. While he dreamed, I'd spend a day at the high school trying to teach chemistry to a few kids who gulped down the knowledge like a drunk on a binge and a whole lot more kids who viewed any science class as the high school equivalent of doing hard time.

Behind the counter was one of the latter group from my fifth-period class. Joey's cap was askew and his eyes were glazed from the too early hours of the pre-school breakfast shift. "Good mornin', Ms. Mullet. Whaddaya want this morning?"

"Two Egg McMuffins and a pair of coffees, Joey, thank you."

"Comin' right up, Ms. Mullet."

Damn, how do any of us survive our teenage years? Awkward limbs, protruding ears, acne arcades setting up shop on our foreheads. Even if you didn't have any of these problems, you thought you did or you knew you surely would by the next sunrise.

I trundled to a table for two that had a clear view of the door so I could signal to Charlie when he came in. The yeasty, eggy aroma wafting out of the bag tested my self-control. Patiently, I just sipped my coffee and tugged on my sleeve to make sure my tat was undercover. All the while, I searched my mind for any untended worries or neglected chores while I waited for my favorite guy.

A whimper drew my eyes toward the restaurant counter. Before I identified the source of that pathetic sound, the air was torn with a voice screaming, "Now!"

Time froze as my eyes focused in on the unfolding tableau. On my side of the counter, a male in a gray sweatshirt with its hood pulled tight around his face, pointed a shotgun at Joey. Joey's eyes caught mine and pounded waves of terror across the room.

I rose to my feet, my synapses firing in rapid time seeking a solution, a strategy, an answer. Before I could formulate anything more than fear, the blast blew through my eardrums and red blossomed in full bloom on Joey's shirt.

Instinctively, I moved towards him and as I did the shotgun swung towards me. Sensual acuity rocked me. The smoky scent of gunpowder, the stink of sweat, and the stench of fresh blood overwhelmed the everyday smells of grilling burgers, frying potatoes and sizzling sausage. I felt a sticky spot beneath my foot where the mop had missed. The air was crisper, edges sharper and colors brighter. And everywhere I looked I saw the brilliant red of Joey's blood pulsing to a salsa beat.

The barrel shook as he pointed it at me. One of my students? I couldn't tell. The sweatshirt hood concealed everything but two glazed eyes peering above the drawstring.

A tiny click drew my eyes to the door to the outside. It was opening. Oh my God, no. I saw a uniformed sleeve pulling the door open. The armed man saw it, too. He swung his weapon towards the sound. I screamed, *"Noooo!"* just as Charlie stepped through the door.

Too little. Too late. Charlie turned in the direction of my voice and the gun fired. I ran for Charlie. The shooter ran for the opposite door. The blast struck Charlie between his chin and his chest. A geyser of blood shot into the air. I pushed down on the wound, trying to stop its flow. It squirted through my fingers, spattered in my face. I had to stop the bleeding. With the shooter gone, other patrons crawled out from cover and handed me stacks of napkins. They soaked through as fast as I could apply them.

For a brief, jubilant moment, I thought it was working. But my efforts had not slowed his rapid loss of blood, Charlie was losing blood pressure. He was bleeding out.

"Charlie, don't you do this to me. You promised, Charlie. You promised we would grow old together. Damn it, Charles Mullet, stop bleeding. Stop it!"

I knew it was hopeless. I knew he was gone, but still I raged on. My anger built as his life faded, as if the fires of my ire could raise him like a phoenix from the ashes left in its wake. "Breathe, Charlie. Damn it, breathe!"

When the police arrived, I sat, arms hanging limp, eyes reflecting no light, all of me covered in blood and surrounded by mountains of bloody napkins embossed with the McDonald's arch. Gentle hands slid under my arms and lifted my limp body off the floor. Someone else slipped their fingers beneath my legs and laid me on a stretcher.

As they carried me away, I saw Charlie lying there waiting for the ID techs before he left for the morgue. I, on the other hand, was bound for the hospital—probably the psycho ward. "Charlie, Charlie, take me with you, please."

Charlie did not answer. He didn't even utter a mumble or grunt the way he did when he wasn't really paying attention. Charlie was gone.

I was numb. I heard words, I saw lips move, but all I heard was gibberish. The world did not look right. It all blurred and tilted like a mean nightmare ride at a maniacal carnival. And all I could smell was the desperate scent of fresh-spilled blood even after I was miles away.

Chapter Eight

I attended the funeral loaded with Xanax. I was numbed, tearful and surrounded by blue uniforms. Each blue chest bore a badge with a stripe of black electrical tape. Black tape for Charlie. The same black tape that wrapped around my heart, holding the pieces together. All was black and blue.

I yearned to crawl into the coffin and snuggle up next to my Charlie. I wanted to hear the lid shut over my head, the latches lock in place, binding us together for eternity.

On the drive home from the cemetery, I stopped at HEB. My cupboard was bare, my refrigerator an empty shell. I roamed up and down one aisle after the other like an automaton. I grabbed what appealed to me: bags of potato chips, half gallons of ice cream, chocolate chip cookies, four bright red bags of dark roast Community Coffee. I thought I was ready for checkout until I looked into my basket. I had to buy real food.

I rolled through produce and picked up nothing. I pushed my cart through the meat department but the sight of the bloody packages invoked a swell of nausea. I ended up in the frozen foods aisle where I grabbed a few TV dinners. I picked the same ones that Charlie stocked in the freezer at his apartment before we were married. I teased him about those dinners once. Now, I piled them in with my junk food.

The checker had to have thought my assortment of groceries was odd. But if she said a word, I did not hear it. She even had to ask me twice for payment before it registered that she had spoken.

I unloaded my car and withdrew into my home. I did nothing but eat and sleep. I tried to read but every time I reached the end of a page, I realized my mind had only seen a clutter of words and had not formulated them into a sentence or a thought. I might as well have picked up a book filled with the Cyrillic alphabet or Japanese characters.

I ignored the telephone when it rang and never checked my messages. Soon it was full and no more could be recorded. I did not respond to the ringing of the doorbell. Mail piled up in my mailbox.

About four days into my hermit state, the front bell rang and rang and rang. I peered through the bathroom window and saw the mail delivery truck parked in front of my house. When it pulled away, I eased open the front door and snatched up rubber-banded bundles of mail. I dropped them on the dining-room table, grabbed a bag of potato chips and climbed back in bed.

I wanted to be dead. Gone. Deceased. With Charlie. I wasn't suicidal in the active sense. I didn't dwell on the means I could use to dispose of myself. I'm not sure why I didn't travel down that road. There were means all over the house. A gun in the bedroom closet. Pills in the medicine cabinet. Knives in the kitchen. I did not go there. But I did wish I were dead and prayed for release as if I could will my heart to stop its beat.

A few days later, another persistent visitor arrived. First the bell rang—again and again. Then, a fist pounded on the front door. I slid down in the bed until my head was covered. I heard a mumbled voice but I had no desire to investigate. Silence. Yes. Another well-wisher foiled. I lowered the blankets off my face.

Two seconds later, I exploded out of my bed. It was just rapping on the glass of my bedroom window but it might as well have been machine gun fire the way adrenaline was now coursing through my bloodstream. I sat on the bed wanting to hold my breath but panting instead.

"Molly. Molly Mullet. I know you're in there. Molly. Let me in this house now."

It was Franny. Francine Albert—the woman I normally considered my best friend. Right now, she was the bane of my existence.

"Molly. I am not leaving until I see you."

I knew she wouldn't. I pulled back the curtain and gave her a flash of my face.

"Molly, don't be a smart-ass. Open the front door."

I did not move. I did not speak.

"Molly. If you do not open that door in the next thirty seconds, I am calling the police. And don't tell me they won't come. I'll tell them you attempted suicide. I swear I will."

I recognized the futility of my resistance, rose to my feet and plodded to the front door. I swung it open and retreated to my bed before Franny could get up on the porch.

"Molly Mullet," she exclaimed as she walked into my room and ripped the covers off my body. She grabbed both my hands and pulled me to my feet. "Look at you. Charlie would be ashamed."

"Not fair," I hissed at her.

I stood there in my unwashed hair, one of Charlie's ratty old T-shirts and his pair of jalapeno-pepper-adorned flannel pants. I looked down. There were chocolate stains on the shirt. I forced myself to stand in the shower every day but I never had the energy to open the bottle of shampoo or pull fresh clothes out of the closet.

"Life's not fair, Molly Mullet," she said as she dragged me into the bathroom. There she grabbed the shampoo and a towel and pulled me into the kitchen. She turned on the water, got the right temperature and dunked my head under the faucet. The whole time, she tsked at me.

I took no independent action, but I cooperated—mostly out of surprise. On a typical day, Franny is a disorganized, unfocused airhead whose conversations hopped from one pad of thought to another like a frog on speed. In the classroom, she was an inspired and inspiring art teacher. Her flakiness branded her as a real artist—an eccentric—to her students. But here was a new Franny—the woman in charge.

She cleaned me up and dressed me down and planned my future. "Molly, I'll be by at 7:20 Monday morning to pick you up. It's time for you to get back to your students."

I acquiesced. What else could I do? As soon as her car pulled away, I grabbed a bowl of chocolate chunk ice cream and went back to bed.

I reported to school that Monday morning, but I still wallowed in my slough of despond. My dull outlook on life drowned any sparks I may have lit with my students earlier in the year. I continued to drug myself with food, and my clothes became formless as I packed on the pounds.

A small pod of girls surrounded me after my honors chemistry class a few weeks after my return to school. Alison Knieper with her perfect straight blond hair, no-nonsense blue eyes and flawless complexion was the leader of the pack. She always would be. She was centered and focused beyond her years. Her straightforward face and squared shoulders underlined her agility with language and her natural knack for communication.

She gave me the dead-on look that Clint Eastwood perfected. Her girlfriends shuffled their feet and stared at the floor as intently as if the meaning of life was embedded in the tiles. "Are you pregnant?" she asked.

Tact was not one of Alison's virtues. I stared back at her and willed my slack jaw to return to closed position. I stroked my right upper arm. I had expected most anything from Alison, but that never crossed my mind.

"I know this is blunt, Ms. Mullet. And quite personal. We are well aware of your personal loss and have great empathy for your situation. We've stood by and watched you disintegrate. You had warm brown eyes that always seemed to be laughing at the world. Now they look like dead, charred holes to an empty soul. What used to be bouncy brown curls framing an optimistic face are now dirty limp rags bracketing an expression of total despair. If you are the only individual involved in this miasma of misery, then that is your prerogative. However, if you are pregnant you have a responsibility to pull yourself together. And we have a moral obligation to conduct an intervention."

I wanted to say, "Leave me alone," and flee to the teachers' lounge, where not even Alison would follow. But I could not deny the girls before me. In the timid, eye-darting, creased-brow faces gathered around their leader, I saw genuine concern. And I remembered with clarity my concern for them that I had buried beneath my avalanche of self-pity.

"Ms. Mullet?" Patience was not one of Alison's virtues either.

I pulled in a deep, stalling breath and returned Alison's intense stare. "Thank you, Alison, girls. You are right to be worried about me. I've been wrapped in my misery. I've been self-indulgent. But, no, I am not pregnant."

A chorus of sighs and a flash of weak smiles punctuated my statement. "Thank you, Ms. Mullet," Alison said. "Please let us know if there is anything we can do to help." She turned on her heel and led her gaggle out of the classroom.

I stepped into the doorway and watched them disappear down the hall. I shook my head and smiled. It had been so long since the corners of my mouth turned upward, I could hear my cheeks creak with the effort.

When I got home that afternoon, I took the first step to regaining my life. Grabbing a cardboard box from the garage, I marched to the pantry. I filled the bottom with packages of cookies and bags of chips. Then I hit my squirrel drawer, pulling out seven candy bars, four packs of cheese crackers and a monster bag of Hershey's kisses. The refrigerator was next. I relieved it of a gallon of ice cream and a box of chocolate-chocolate ice cream sandwiches.

I delivered it all to my next-door neighbor. With four active boys and a constant parade of other neighborhood kids in and out of her house, the snacks would disappear in dissipated energy without leaving an added ounce in its tracks.

That night, I took a power walk around the neighborhood. Well, at least it started as a power walk. I returned home panting as if I'd run a marathon. The next day, I signed up at Curves and forced myself to make the circuit of machines three times. I knew if I focused on the physical, my thought process would clear and sharpen. I needed that. I had a lot of thinking to do.

I loved teaching chemistry. Now, though, it just didn't seem to be enough. A T-shirt I saw on one of my students summed up my feelings best: "If you're not living on the edge, you are taking up too much space." I wanted to find my edge.

I followed that siren call and did not sign a contract for the coming school year. Instead, I filled out an application for the police department. I passed the tests, went to the academy and joined the force.

Here I stood, five years older than I was the day Charlie died. Three years older than when I joined the force. Was I any wiser? I hoped so. I thought I had found my life's path when I embarked on this journey. But now I realized it was just a side trip—a blind stumbling after Charlie. I had lost my way in a blur of misplaced grief and good intentions. It was time to alter course.

CHAPTER NINE

Commander Ed Schultze had an open-door policy but that didn't make it any easier to cross his threshold. Pity for all the students I'd ever sent to the principal's office washed over me. Now I knew how it felt.

I took a timid half step into the room where Schultze sat facing the computer instead of the door. I saw the back of his salt-and-pepper brush cut and watched him pound keys that looked far too small for his broad fingertips. My watery knees caused me to sway as I stood in place. I was thinking about backing out of the doorway when Schultze spun around and spotted me.

"Mullet! Come on in. Have a seat. I'm armed but I'm not dangerous," he said with a small chuckle. He'd been using that line for more years than I'd been on the force. You'd think by now it would have ceased to amuse him.

An involuntary swallowing spasm racked my throat as I took wooden steps across the floor to the chair. I sat down with all the grace of a tumbling two-by-four.

"Mullet," he continued. "I'm glad you stopped by my office. If you hadn't, I would have had to send word."

That was not a good sign. Schultze never sent for you to tell you that you did a good job. It always meant trouble.

"I had a concern expressed to me this morning . . ." he began.

"Lieutenant Hawkins," I interrupted. There was a full sentence formed in my head, but only his name could escape my lips.

"As a matter of fact, yes. It was Lieutenant Hawkins. I imagine it was all just a misunderstanding. Why don't you explain the situation to me from your point of view?"

That statement pretty much summed up why Schultze was a commander—diplomatic, savvy, a constant projection of fairness. But would he peddle it this softly if I were a male officer? Maybe. Maybe not. Rumors had it that he had aspirations to be Chief of Police, either here or in a jurisdiction nearby. A reputation for having a good rapport with women and minorities improved his chance for success.

Schultze donned his fatherly mask that exuded an air of infinite patience. But I could tell his patience was running thin. A tiny tic just below the corner of his right eye gave him away.

I jumped to my feet and pulled out my badge and my gun. The fear that skittered in his darting eyes told me old Schultze had been out of the field a little too long for comfort. When I laid the badge and the weapon on the desk in front of him, he tried to hide his sigh of relief, but it slipped through under his faked cough.

"You don't need an explanation from me, Commander. I'm sure Lieutenant Hawkins gave you an honest appraisal of the situation. What you need from me is a resignation, and you've got it."

"Thank you, Mullet," Schultze said. And that was it.

I spun around and left the room, hot patches burning like coals on my cheeks. I went to his office to quit. And I quit. Not much fuss. Not much bother. It was done. So why did I feel so humiliated? Why did I want him to make at least a lame attempt to change my mind? Stupid pride. Now, damaged pride. Fine, Molly, take that sting and use its energy to do something constructive for Bobby Wiggins.

When I reached home, I clicked on the Internet and found the phone number for Dale Travis, Bobby's hotshot Houston attorney. I was not put through to the great man, of course. Instead I left a message with a snotty-voiced woman. I kept it simple, asking him to call me about the Bobby Wiggins case and leaving my home phone number.

I called Thelma Wiggins next. "Hello, Mrs. Wiggins. This is Molly Mullet." I heard a clunk. "Mrs. Wiggins? Mrs. Wiggins?" Damn. She hung up on me. I disconnected and hit the redial button. "Please don't hang up, Mrs. Wiggins. I've resigned . . ." Clunk.

Call me tenacious. Or call me pig-headed. Either one will fit. I pressed redial again. This time, the phone rang and rang—ten times, eleven times, twelve. I hung up.

I clattered around the house like a lone rusty nut in an old coffee tin. I tried to read a book, a magazine article, Dear Abby in the newspaper. But it was no use. I could not concentrate. I attempted to take care of a few household chores. But the desire to do something concrete for Bobby distracted me. I left a dozen projects in a half-started state scattered around the house. I rubbed the skin red around that ugly little cow-pie on my arm. All day I stared at the phone willing Dale Travis to call until I saw double. I fantasized that a cheerful Thelma Wiggins would ring me up and apologize for being rude.

The phone did ring twice. The first time it was a vinyl-siding salesperson. I was not polite. The next time it rang, I heard, "I'm not trying to sell you anything today . . ." before I hung up. I went to bed that night tired but too agitated to sleep well.

When I woke the next morning, my mood was as foul as my breath. If I still had a dog, I might have kicked it. That made my train of thought even darker. I had still not gotten over losing Chase so soon after I lost my husband. I should have moved on by now. I should have gotten a new dog. But the pain of losing yet another companion was still stronger than my willingness to risk the joy of it.

I downed three cups of coffee in quick succession. Then I brushed my teeth. I began to feel human again. I placed another call to the offices of Dale Travis. Once again, I spoke to the snotty-sounding woman and left my cell phone number.

I called Thelma. "Mrs. Wiggins?" Clunk. Sigh.

CHAPTER TEN

At the other end of the line, Thelma Wiggins sighed, too. She could no longer remember the days when life was a carefree adventure. The dust of old memories sometimes stirred but never coalesced into a solid enough form to offer solace.

The day that altered her existence rolled over her like thunder. She and Stuart drove up to Austin and met Dale Travis and his wife, Cici, at a second floor bar off of Sixth Street. The original itinerary called for a drink there, followed by dinner at a new restaurant that was all the buzz and then finished up with some barhopping up and down the street.

Somehow, they never managed to leave that first stop. They spent the night nibbling on bar food, dancing to the jukebox and laughing hard at easy jokes. Pregnancy had made Thelma fatigued for the last few weeks but tonight was an exception and she took advantage of her unexpected energy—dancing with the carefree abandon of a cheerleader in the wake of victory on the football field.

She sipped nothing stronger than 7-Up all night, but she felt as giddy as if she had—a contact high from the high spirits of her mildly intoxicated companions. When last call reverberated across the room, the two couples grabbed purses, paid the bar tab and headed out the door.

At the top of the stairs, Thelma tripped on something—or on nothing—she never knew what. Her arm flew toward Stuart but was too short to even brush his shirt. Her body lurched forward.

There was only one person below her on the stairs—Dale Travis. If he had moved in her path to break her fall, her life journey would have taken another course. But he did not. Instinct made him flinch away when he heard the noise. Thelma tumbled past him in a flurry of arms and legs.

She hit bottom on her face—bits of grit embedding into her cheeks as they rested on the unforgiving concrete. She was afraid to move. The others raced to the bottom of the steps. She heard Stuart call her name again and again. She heard Stuart race back up the stairs to call for an ambulance. And that was all she heard, all she knew, for hours.

At the hospital, Stuart hovered over her like an angel of mercy bringing sips of water, little pecks on the forehead, little murmurs of love. Cici sat as still as death and held Thelma's hand. Dale paced back and forth, kneading his hands, muttering apologies and regrets.

It was touch and go for days, but, at last, Thelma's condition stabilized—she would not lose the baby. Her doctor, a nurse and Stuart gathered at the side of her bed with the bad news. He was concerned that the fetus was damaged. The baby would survive to full term, he said, but it would not be normal. He wanted to know if she wanted to continue her pregnancy.

Thelma felt her face distort in a kaleidoscope of expressions— from confusion to anger. She focused on her husband. "Stuart, what is he saying? Does he want me to have an abortion?"

"That is one option . . ." the doctor began.

"Hush," Thelma ordered. "Stuart, talk to me."

"Yes, Thelma. That is what he suggested," Stuart whispered.

"After days of struggling not to lose the baby and now they want me to dispose of it? After all of this?"

"Yes, Thelma."

"Do you think they're right? Do you think that's what I should do?"

"This is not my decision, Thelma."

"Not your decision. But Stuart, this is your baby, too."

Stuart took her hand between both of his. He closed his eyes and inhaled a deep breath. He blew it out and looked into Thelma's eyes. "You are the one carrying this child. This is happening inside your body. I have only a glimmer of what that means. I can only imagine how that feels. I promise you, Thelma, I will support you one hundred percent, no matter what you decide. Every day. I will never waver. But I am not a woman. I am not carrying this baby. I have no right to impose my opinion on you."

Thelma did not want to think. She did not want to decide. But Stuart was right. If he told her what he thought she should do, she would feel an unintended but powerful coercion to do what he wished—and this disempowerment would haunt her forever. "I want to go home, Stuart. I want to go home now."

Bobby was born in a moment of joy tinged with fear. Soon, that fear was justified. As an infant, Bobby's eyes did not track a moving object well. He hardly ever cried, prompting friends to say she was lucky—and then quickly turn away. Bobby's physical skills developed at a slow pace, his verbal skills even more slowly.

But Stuart kept his promise to Thelma. No matter how slow Bobby's progress, no matter how much it pained him, Stuart offered words of encouragement every day. Until the final day when he went to the shed and never returned.

CHAPTER ELEVEN

My next move was a visit to Bobby. As I pulled into the parking lot of the Comal County Jail, it hit me—I'm not a police office anymore. Seeing Bobby today was not going to be that easy.

I walked inside and hope was reborn. Monica Salazar was behind the front desk. She had never been in any of my classes but I saw her often. Three days a week, she stood outside my classroom waiting for her boyfriend, Ronnie White, to emerge. Every day, her tummy got a little larger and the bald yearning in her eyes got a bit more forlorn. Over the semester, we developed a smiling relationship. Then one day, she was gone.

I'd seen her around since she joined the Sheriff's Department a few months back, but we had never spoken. She looked less vulnerable with her uniform, badge and gun than she had standing alone in the hall in her oversized shirt. But I still saw the naked yearning in her eyes.

"Officer Mullet?"

"Yes." I should have corrected her. I could have claimed I responded out of habit. But I knew better. I knew what I was doing. I was impersonating an officer. I was breaking the law. "Monica. Or should I say Deputy Salazar? How have you been?"

"For you, it's still Monica. You were so kind to me," she said.

"I only smiled."

"That's more than . . . more than . . ." she looked down at her desk and fiddled with her files. She looked up composed. "What can I do for you today, Officer Mullet?"

"I'm here to see an inmate. Bobby Wiggins."

"Wait right here. I need to check and see if you need an escort."

Before I could stall her, she was gone. Maybe I should be gone, too. Then again, maybe I'd get lucky.

Brow furrowed, mouth pursed, she came back into view. "You are no longer a police officer." The blackness in her eyes accused me of every wrong ever done from the Lindberg kidnapping to the hanging chads in Florida. She leaned toward me over the counter, her voice barely above a whisper. "You try this again, Ms. Mullet, and I'll have to report you." A cloud of indecision passed across her face. "But I could get in trouble if I don't report you now."

"Monica, how is your baby?"

To my great relief, her face lit up like a tree at Christmas. "Oh, Cesar is not a baby anymore. He is in preschool. He is so handsome. He will break many hearts one day. Ah, let me show you." She pulled a frame off the top of her desk and pressed it into my hand.

A darling dark-haired boy beamed up at me. The photographer had captured that twinkle in his eye that foretold of much adolescent angst for the girls in his future. "Oh, Monica, if I was thirty years younger, I'd be falling in love right now."

She bent her head down and, in a whisper I had to strain to hear, said, "You know, I never married Ronnie."

"No, Monica. I didn't know."

"His family." She shrugged as if the flexing of her shoulders explained and excused the shadow racism had cast across her life.

Not exactly an upbeat morning. I'd failed in my mission. I'd tiptoed on someone's heartache. And I still had done nothing to help Bobby.

★ ★ ★ ★ ★

Back at home, I rattled around in the tin can again. Somebody had to listen to me. If I couldn't tell anyone what I wanted to do, I couldn't do it. I pulled out a piece of paper and wrote a letter to Bobby. If he put me on his visitors' list, then I could visit him just like any friend. I slapped a stamp on the envelope and slipped it into the mailbox just as the mail truck turned onto my street.

Now what? Bobby might be able to convince his mother to talk to me, but I doubted he could sway Dale Travis. The telephone wasn't the answer either. It was too easy for Travis to avoid my calls. Tomorrow, I'd drive down to Houston. I'd sit in the lobby of his office all day if need be. I wouldn't leave until he talked to me.

Chapter Twelve

With a plan in place, I slept well that night and woke up on my own before the sun raised its head. As soon as my eyes opened, I was charged up and ready to go. But if I left now, I'd hit Houston in the middle of rush-hour traffic, and driving in the Bayou City is difficult enough without complicating it more.

The morning sun was awake and glowing by the time I brewed up a pot of coffee. I grabbed a cup and a yellow pad and pencil on my way to the backyard. It was late February, but in South Texas that meant spring had sprung. The temperature had dipped into the upper forties overnight, but the first rays of the sun had already warmed the air up to sixty degrees.

I settled into a green Adirondack chair and reveled in the peaceful moment. The air filled with bird song. Green shoots of perennials and weeds pushed up from the ground. Bud stalks thrust up from the evergreen bed of columbine. Soon that patch would be a riot of yellow and red with hummingbirds swooping in to squabble over the nectar.

I pulled my eyes back to my blank pad of paper and started a suspect list. Of course, the first culprits on my list were the members of the band. At the top was Trenton Wolfe. Did I put him there because he was the most likely perpetrator or because he was the least likeable person? I'd think about my motivations later. Now I needed to figure out his motive. He struck me as an angry young man. Buried rage echoed from many of his lyrics. Did he write those words or just deliver them? As leader of the group, he'd be in a strong position to clash with the manager. Over money? Over scheduling? Over marketing? Or was it personal? I made a note to check on any possible overlap between spouses and girlfriends of Faver and the boys in the band. For that matter, I'd better look for boyfriends, too—a threat of revealed secrets often invited violent reactions.

Next on my list was Stan Crockett. Of all the people on the stage, he had the most influence over Wolfe. Was that a source of conflict with Faver? But he's so skinny, so pale, so low-key, he looks half dead himself. It stretched my imagination to believe he possessed enough passion to wrap a guitar string around anyone's neck with sufficient force to kill.

That thought brought up the image of the pools of blood in Solms Halle the night of Rodney Faver's murder. In a flash, the vision morphed into the ocean of red surrounding my Charlie. The memory was so vivid I could still smell the distinct odor of fast food mingling with the scent of spilled blood. A dull ache shot out from my heart to the tip of every limb and swathed my mind like cotton batting.

Oh, Charlie. If only we had met somewhere else. If only we had not met at all. I squeezed my eyes tight and forced the image to fade. I drained my coffee cup and turned my attention back to my list.

Happy Parker—the guy on the drums. A name like that would make me homicidal. Was it his real name? I could only hope it wasn't, but the tags some women hang on their children made me believe childbirth was the leading cause of temporary insanity.

The keyboard guy was next. What was his name? You never heard a thing about him. That in itself could be a reason for him to be hostile toward Rodney Faver.

Who else could've clashed with the band manager? Mike Elliot, the manager of Solms Halle was a good prospect. I couldn't imagine Mike doing something that violent, but then, that's what all the neighbors say when the police haul away the serial killer living next door. Mike was a more probable suspect than Bobby. He had access to the keys. He was smarter than Bobby—smart enough to do the deed unseen and slip the bloodstained key into Bobby's pocket. But would he let Bobby take the rap?

Who else? That question took me back to thinking about the spouses and girlfriends again and brought to mind Faver's other clients, the road crew and the inevitable groupies. Who in that herd of humanity could be angry or desperate enough to kill? I needed to get lists of names and look at each one.

I couldn't think of anyone else right now. But I was sure more names would crop up as soon as I started digging. But no one had authorized me to dig yet. Time to get dressed and down to Houston.

I pulled open my closet door. The contents were depressing. I'd been wearing uniforms to work for too long. The only new clothes I'd bought in years were jeans. My teaching wardrobe still hung on the rod, but it was all so dated and schoolmarmish. I settled on a black and tan jacket dress that looked like it might have a life outside the classroom. I checked to make sure the short sleeves were long enough to conceal the botched indiscretion on my arm. I pulled out a pair of black pumps from the bowels of the closet. I hadn't worn them for such a long time, I had to wipe off the dust. I thought about polishing them, but then decided the humid Houston air would strip the shine off in two seconds flat.

I hopped into my red Beetle and hit the road. I drove down Route 46 past scenic vistas, trashy trailer parks and rickety emu pens. Then I whipped onto the most boring stretch of pavement ever created by man, Interstate Highway 10—more than 200 of the ugliest miles on the planet stretching down to Houston. I popped in a Susan Tedeschi CD to mute the pain.

"No, I would not. But thank you just the same. I'll just wait here until he has a free moment."

"As you wish," she said, slamming the planner shut.

I took a seat as far from the officious woman as I could. I laid my portfolio on the coffee table, damaged side down and slid out a paperback, *Jolie Blon's Bounce,* by James Lee Burke. I suppose I should have selected a book with a more dignified title, but I knew I could depend on Burke to make the wait seem much shorter.

I was three-quarters of the way into the novel when I realized Ms. Frosty was standing in front of me. "Yes?" I asked.

She stared down at me with a look of distaste distorting her mouth. Her eyes were focused on my upper arm where the bottom of my cow-pie beaker winked below the sleeve. I tugged the arm on the jacket down and smiled.

She switched her gaze to my face. "I am going to lunch now. I would prefer that you would go, too. In fact, it would be best if you did not come back. You are wasting your time here and disrupting our office."

"Lunch sounds great. Where should we go?" I asked, beaming a high-intensity ray of artificial innocence in her direction.

Her eyes flared wide. She pivoted on the ball of one foot and returned to the fortress of her desk where she stared straight ahead, her peripheral vision keeping me in view.

I surrendered and went to find something to eat. *But never fear, Ms. Arbuthnot, I shall return.*

At long last, I arrived in the thriving metropolis itself. I didn't know if it was real or just an illusion, but the lanes of the highways in Houston felt narrower than those on any other major thoroughfare in the country. I clenched my teeth as I navigated through the tight terrain.

I arrived downtown and pulled into the parking garage for the high-rise office tower that Foster, Travis and Crum called home. The cost of getting my car out of that inner sanctum sounded more like a ransom than a parking fee.

Inside the office tower, I stepped into the elevator and pressed twenty-seven. There was a twenty-eighth floor, but access to it required the insertion of a membership card. There was no indication of what kind of membership card, but I guess if you had one, you knew it.

The doors opened into the lobby of the esteemed legal giants. Straight ahead, across a football field of deep gold carpet, were the glass walls of a conference room. Looking through it, you got a megalomaniac's view of the cityscape beyond. To my right was a cluster of three seating areas. The chairs and love seats in each grouping were upholstered in rich burgundies and golds.

To my left was an extravagant curve of walnut topped with a custom cut slab of glass with rounded edges—the desk of Ms. Arbuthnot, according to the bronze nameplate on its surface. I now had a name for the snotty-voiced woman. The fact that she did not disclose her first name on that plate confirmed all my worst suspicions about her.

"May I help you?" she asked in a tone that rattled my teeth. Her gray suit was buttoned up top to bottom. Her black hair pulled back so tight it stretched the skin on her face and revealed a pair of crafted ears adorned with small gold hoops. Her lips did not curve in welcome but slashed two fine parallel lines of radish red across her face. She had an elegant but razor-sharp nose designed to look down and disapprove. At the moment, it was pointed at me.

A woman like this summoned up two polar opposite sensations in me. One was the urge to flee. The other was the perverse desire to stick out my tongue or give rude gestures with my hands. I controlled both reactions and plastered a pleasant smile on my face as I approached. "Good morning," I chirped. She arched one plucked eyebrow in response. "I'd like to see Mr. Dale Travis, please?"

"Do you have an appointment?" she asked but I didn't know how. I'd swear her lips did not move.

"No ma'am, I don't. But I drove up from New Braunfels regarding the Bobby Wiggins case." Up went that eyebrow again.

"I'm terribly sorry you drove all that way, Miz—Miz?"

"Mullet."

"Miz Mullet. Yes, I am sorry you drove all that way, but Mr. Travis is far too busy today to accommodate you."

"That's fine, Ms. Arbuthnot. I'll just have a seat and be ready when a small window of opportunity opens in his schedule."

Her mouth opened and closed.

"I'm in no hurry," I added.

"As you wish," she said and swiveled away to rustle a stack of papers.

I passed a ponderous afternoon in the august presence of the ice queen. Entertainment was very limited. A few clouds scudded by, breaking the monotony of the pale blue sky. Men and women in suits darted past on their way from the offices on the left to the offices on the right and back again. Few spared the time to give me even a cursory glance. Ms. Snotty Arbuthnot turned her back to me whenever she talked on the phone to ensure that I could not eavesdrop. Drats.

A few hours into my vigil, I yearned for a trip to the restroom but dared not ask my hostess for the location of the facilities. I

rose to walk off the urge. My movement provoked a frosty that drove me back to my seat. I tried not to squirm.

As if a hidden mechanism ejaculated her from her sea Arbuthnot popped up like a jack-in-the-box behind her She stared at me until she was certain she had my full atte "The offices are closed now."

"Is there any possibility . . . ?" I began.

"You must vacate the premises immediately," she insist

I concentrated on my posture as I walked with mea steps to the elevator door and pressed the button. On th down, I decided I had to give it one more day. I'd hole Houston for the night. After ransoming my car, I stoppe picked up a toothbrush and other necessities, a hand paperback books and a leather portfolio from the distr merchandise rack. It had a stain of indeterminate origin o side but if I held it right, no one else would know.

The next morning, I flashed a fresh smile at the refrige visage of Ms. Arbuthnot. She looked much like she did th before but unlike me, she had a change of clothes. She w navy blue suit, its cut as severe as its predecessor, but th was buffered a bit by the gleam of blue topaz on each earl

Her eyes narrowed. She recognized me, but she was not to acknowledge it. "May I help you?"

"Certainly, Ms. Arbuthnot," I smiled. "I need a mome Mr. Travis' time."

"Do you have an appointment?"

"Alas, no," I said. *Rein it in, Molly.* "But I am certain Mr vis would like to hear what I have to say."

The eyebrow cocked up again. "I am sorry but Mr. T calendar is far too full today to accommodate you." She fl the pages of a day planner. "He does, however, have a opening available two weeks from Thursday at eleven Would you care to make an appointment for that time?"

CHAPTER THIRTEEN

I returned from lunch before the dragon at the gate. I was tempted to slip past her fortress in her absence and sniff out the lair of the elusive Mr. Travis. Before I could act on that impulse, Ms. Arbuthnot returned to her desk. She glared in my direction. I pulled out my book and began to read. Before I reached the bottom of the page, she was looming over me again.

"I asked that you not return, Miz Mullet."

I inserted my bookmark, closed the book and lifted my eyes to hers. But I did not utter a word.

"Miz Mullet, I said that you are no longer welcome at Foster, Travis and Crum."

"That's a shame, Ms. Arbuthnot. But if I can't have your hospitality, I'll just have to accept your hostility. I cannot leave until I have seen Mr. Travis."

Her nostrils flared so wide I expected to see flames issue forth and singe my eyebrows. "As I have told you before, that is not possible without an appointment. You will have to leave now."

I held her gaze for a moment and then leaned back and reopened my book.

Ms. Arbuthnot did not respond well to being ignored. "Fine. You leave me no other recourse. I will have to call the police." She spun around and just missed collision with the figure that materialized behind her.

"That will not be necessary, Ms. Arbuthnot. I will handle the matter from here."

Without another word, the ice queen glided to her desk and the interloper turned toward me and stuck out his hand. "Ms. Mullet? Dale Travis."

I lurched to my feet, and *Jolie Blon* bounced from my lap to the floor. I took his hand. "It's a pleasure, Mr. Travis."

Pleasure? It was a mouth-drying, palm-sweating moment of panic. There he stood. Each dark brown hair on his head rested in tailored repose; even the wisps of gray at his temples were aligned in perfect symmetry on either side of his face, as if he controlled which ones could change color and when. His eyebrows, thick as wooly caterpillars, hung like a cliff over deep-set, anthracite eyes. His expensive suit appeared to be carved on the broad shoulders of his six-foot, three-inch frame. In my tired, two-day outfit, I felt like a vagrant lost in the piney woods.

"Follow me, Ms. Mullet," he said as he turned and headed for the hall.

Under the frosty gaze of Ms. Arbuthnot, I gathered up my fallen book and portfolio with all the dignity of a demented squirrel stashing nuts. When I stepped through the doorway of Travis' corner office, my jaw dropped. The view from the lobby was magnificent but this was enough to make an eagle drool. Two walls of glass met at right angles in the corner revealing 180 degrees of sweeping cityscape. At Travis' request, I slipped into a leather armchair in front of his paperless desk.

He leaned back in his chair and rested his right ankle on his left knee, revealing the luxury of an ostrich quill boot—hand-tooled, hand-fitted and hand-sewn, no doubt. He steepled his fingers before his face. "Bobby Wiggins?" he asked.

"Yes, sir."

"What about Bobby Wiggins, Ms. Mullet?"

"He's innocent."

"I know that."

"He did not kill Rodney Faver."

"I know that."

"And I am here to help."

"Do you know something I should know?" Travis asked.

"The police are not investigating any other suspects."

"I didn't think they were. They do have a confession."

"It's bogus. Bobby was manipulated into that confession."

He uncrossed his legs and leaned forward on his desk resting his weight on his forearms. "You were there?"

"No. I saw the tape. Well, the part where he confessed, anyway."

"Really," he said with a soft smile. "Tell me about it."

I related every word and detail with as much accuracy as I could. At times in my narrative, I doubled back to clarify. When I finished, Travis stood. "Thank you very much, Ms. Mullet. This gives me a lot of insight into how to proceed."

I remained seated beneath his look of impatience. "That's not all."

"Yes?"

"They found the bloody key in Bobby's pocket."

"Excuse me?"

"The closet key," I explained. "There was blood on it. The same type as Faver's blood. They've sent it off for DNA analysis. It was in Bobby's pocket."

His brow furrowed, sending ripples through the caterpillars above his eyes. His focus turned inward then snapped back to me. "Thank you, Ms. Mullet."

I remained seated, refusing to acknowledge his body language that insisted the meeting was over. "I didn't just come here to tell you what I know, Mr. Travis. I want to help you find out more. I want to investigate the suspects the police are ignoring."

"I'm sorry, Ms. Mullet, but . . ."

"I've started already," I interrupted. "I've made a list of

suspects and their possible motives." I whipped the pad of paper out of my portfolio and slapped it on his gleaming desk.

Finally, he sat back down. He slid a pair of half-frame reading glasses from the interior pocket of his suit jacket, making noncommittal noises as he read my notes. "I can see you've given this a lot of thought, but I'm afraid I do not have the funds to expend on an investigator. I'm providing my services and that of my staff *pro bono*. Still, it will be a stretch for Thelma Wiggins to find a way to pay for the associated expenses. She doesn't have the budget for investigative services," he said, sliding my note pad back across his desk.

I did not make a move to pick it up. "I'm not looking for a job, Mr. Travis. I'm volunteering my services." At the sign of a raised eyebrow on the other side of the desk, I continued. "I have not touched a penny of my husband's life insurance payout. It's just been sitting there getting a little bigger each year. I can live on that while I work on this case. I can worry about what I'll live on later after Bobby is home where he belongs."

"Your husband Charlie died before your eyes, the victim of a homicide. And here you are, wanting to help an accused murderer?"

A vision of Charlie and his blood flashed behind my eyes and made me flinch. I refused to lose myself there. I pulled my attention back to Travis. "How did you know that?"

"Ms. Mullet, you've been sitting in my offices for two days— that's plenty of time for a detailed background check."

For a few ticks of the clock I was silent. How naïve of me. It never crossed my mind that while I was dancing with the dragon, he was digging up dirt. "You had no right," I said.

"Yes, I did. In fact, I had a right *and* an obligation. I have a client with diminished capacity sitting in a jail cell for a crime he did not commit. And an ex-cop—or a woman posing as an ex-cop—waltzes into my lobby and takes up residency. DAs

have pulled sleazier tricks than that to get the upper hand."

I launched to my feet. Red-hot anger sent flames across my face. I came here to help and I was accused of playing games. I slapped the palms of my hands on his desk and leaned into his space. "This is *not* a trick."

"I know that."

If he said that one more time, I might explode. Do they have a special class in law school called Effective Irritation? "I've known Bobby Wiggins all my life. I know he is not capable of this. I know he does not understand what is going on. I know that there were times in the past when I should have stuck up for him and I didn't. I owe Bobby, and I want to even the score. And, Mr. Travis, I just want to make a difference. I want to do something that matters." I felt a growing quiver just below my solar plexus. It flared and burbled like a magical Fourth of July sparkler that kept burning even after a thorough dousing in a bucket of water.

"Please sit," Travis murmured. He closed his eyes and leaned back in his chair. His fingers steepled together once again.

I leaned back and slid into the chair. The silence tickled my nervous urge to start talking. I clenched my jaw to keep my mouth shut.

His eyes popped open. "You have a bachelor's degree, right?"

"A BS in Chemistry. Yes."

"And how long were you on the police force?"

"Three years."

"Fine," he said as he lifted the receiver on his telephone and punched in a speed dial number. "Hi, Kristi, this is Dale Travis. Get me Arnie, please," he said to the person at the other end.

"Arnie, this is Dale," he said and paused. "Yes, yes, Arnie, I won't forget, but right now I'm calling about the Bobby Wiggins case." A scowl crossed the attorney's face. "No, Arnie. I am not calling to ask for something for nothing again. I've already got someone who will work for nothing." He rolled his eyes upward as he listened. "Oh, shut up, Arnie. She has all the legal qualifications. I just need her to work under your license." He shook his head and sighed. "Cut the chauvinistic crap, Arnie. You don't believe a word you are saying. You've told me a thousand times that the best investigators you ever encountered were women." He put his hand to his forehead. "Yes, Arnie, of course. The best investigators *after* you." After another pause, he said, "No, Arnie. She's here now. I'll send her right over." He formed an O with his index finger and thumb and shot it in my direction. "Thank you, Arnie."

Hanging up the phone, he turned to me and said, "Okay, we're all set. Used to be easier. I could just send you out with my authorization. Now I have to have you work under a licensed investigator." He pulled a business card out of the top left-hand drawer of his desk. "The Agency. I know it sounds so ominous it's corny but that's Arnie. I begged him not to use a name that sounded like the CIA, but he was young then and now The Agency is established. So . . ." he shrugged.

"Did he do the background check on me?" I asked.

"Of course. I trust him completely. For years, he has saved me from unpleasant surprises in the courtroom. You'd be amazed at the things people think they can hide from their attorney and the court. Secrets never are really secrets."

The taciturn Mr. Travis transformed in to Chatty Cathy right before my eyes. He rattled off his list of expectations for reports. Gave me directions to Arnie's office—just a five-minute walk, he said. *And* Travis gave me the number for his direct line. Hallelujah! An Arbuthnot bypass.

He escorted me back to the reception area, talking the whole way. In front of the ice queen's desk, he thanked me again and gave me a pat on the back before retreating to his office. I gave Ms. Arbuthnot one of my sweetest smiles. She looked as if she was fighting off the urge to spit on my shoes. I wiggled my fingers in her direction and headed down to street level.

I wound my way down one block, then another, past buildings that blocked the sun but did nothing to suppress the omnipresent, suffocating humidity of Houston. I approached the far shorter, less imposing, building that housed The Agency—less imposing by big-city standards, that is. Picked up and stuck in my downtown, and it would be the most impressive thing for miles.

The third-floor offices did not provide much of a view—just the exteriors of other buildings and a glimpse of the street below. Unlike the loftier office of Dale Travis, this one was close enough to earth for the honks and screeches of the traffic below to seep through the walls.

The furniture in the lobby was nondescript Naugahyde—a couple of rips repaired with discreet color-coordinated tape—built to use, not to impress. Behind a desk plate that read "Kristi Nichols," the woman who greeted me bore no resemblance to Ms. Arbuthnot. She had a wholesome blond-haired, blue-eyed look and exhibited as much enthusiasm and good cheer as a Girl Scout peddling Thin Mints. Her smile beamed even broader as I approached. "You must be Ms. Mullet," she said.

"Molly," I said, returning her smile.

Her eyes just about disappeared as her smile expanded to an even greater width than I thought possible. "Okay, Molly. Arnie is expecting you." She wiggled her index finger and added, "Follow me." I walked behind her, wondering if I had ever in my entire life had that much bounce in my step. I half-expected her to break into a skip or turn a cartwheel as we made our way down the hall.

Kristi led me to an office with one clear surface—the seat of the visitor's chair. The L-shaped desk had a computer station

on each end. In between, tilting towers of files, loose papers, au-
diotapes and videotapes fought to maintain their personal space.
Behind the desk, Arnie's broad form overflowed a red secretary's
chair. His eyes riveted to one of the monitors, his pudgy fingers
pounded on the keyboard.

His fingers remained in motion as he glanced at me for a
nanosecond. "Got a driver's license?"

"Yes," I answered.

"Give it to Kristi. Got a conceal-carry permit?"

"Yes."

"Give it to Kristi. Kristi, make copies and bring them back."

Arnie swiveled to face me, plunged a hand into one of the
stacks on his desk and slipped out an unused file folder with the
dexterity of an accomplished sleight-of-hand artist. He thrust it
in my direction. "Here. Write your name on the tab. And make
it legible."

I followed instructions and handed back the folder. Kristi
bopped back into the room, handed my documents to me and
the copies to Arnie. He slid them into the newly labeled folder.

"Kristi's got a digital camera. Before you leave, she'll snap
your photo. Have you got any distinguishing body features?"

I glowed deep red.

"What?" he asked. "A scar? A piercing? A tattoo?"

My face burned hotter.

"Show it to me," he ordered.

With great reluctance, I slipped my arm out of the jacket and
turned my bicep toward Arnie.

"What the hell is that supposed to be?"

"It's a chemistry thing—a beaker filled with toxic liquid."

"Looks more like a pile of crap to me," Kristi said, then
blushed and muttered, "Sorry."

"Please put your jacket back on," Arnie said. "You know you
can have those things removed with lasers now, don't you?"

"Yes."

"Well, at least nobody will have any trouble identifying your body at the morgue." He laughed as he swiveled in his chair.

Kristi tittered behind the hand that covered her mouth. I sat stiff and red-faced in the chair.

Arnie cleared his throat and turned to Krisiti. "Set up user IDs and passwords for all our data source accounts for . . . for . . ." He glanced at the folder in his hand. "For Molly here. Make sure you give her the URLs, too, or it won't do much good." Arnie punctuated his remark with a deep laugh that bumped his belly against the edge of a keyboard and rattled it in place.

Kristi giggled in response. Obviously, someone, at some time, did not get the Internet addresses. From the twinkles in their eyes, I guessed that the mistake was not accidental.

As Kristi departed, Arnie folded his arms across his upper chest and rested them on the shelf formed by his massive mid-section. "Okay, Molly. Here's the deal. Technically, you work for me as an independent contractor. But you don't really work for me, you work for Travis. Actually, since nobody is paying you, 'work' might be the wrong term. For some reason, you're busting your butt for free."

My mouth opened to respond but Arnie waved me off. "None of my business, girl. That's between you and Travis. I do not want to get involved. Anyway, to keep the bureaucrats happy up in Moscow on the Colorado . . ." he stopped mid-sentence, his eagle eyes catching the confusion on my face. "Austin, girl. You telling me you haven't heard that before?"

I shook my head.

"Don't you get it?"

Again, I shook my head.

"Oh, Jeez. You know, Moscow—the former capital of the evil empire? The USSR? You know, pinky, commie, weird Austin, the state capital? On the banks of the Colorado River? You know, the river that the locals for some demented reason call Town Lake?"

The puzzled look stayed firmly planted on my face. Oh, I knew what he meant. I just did not want to admit it. His exasperation was entertaining. He rolled his eyes and shook his head. Ah, sweet surrender.

After a big sigh, he continued. "Anyway, you need to send in a report every week—send it to Kristi's e-mail. I don't want any details—that's for Travis. Just sketch it out. I talked to four suspects. Staked out the house of another. Bribed a public official. Whatever. Things get more formal if we develop a more permanent long-term relationship. Like if I actually pay you for doing something. But that's it for now. Any questions?"

He paused long enough to finger brush his comb-over off his forehead and back over his bald spot, but not long enough for me to fashion the first word of a question before he was off again.

"Kristi's setting up access for you to the most comprehensive privacy-invading tools we have at our disposal. Addresses. Phone numbers. Social Security numbers. Credit reports. Criminal records. You name it, you get it. Don't share the passwords with anyone.

"Before you leave, Kristi will give you a disk with a template of the business card. Get your cards right away. Our twenty-four hour number is on there and you'll need to add your own. If you don't have a cell phone, get one. I'm always available if you need any professional advice." He extracted a business card from another monumental mountain of files and flipped it toward me.

"About that bribing an official remark I made: that was a joke. You do anything illegal, I don't want to know about it. Any questions?" Without pause he swiveled back to his monitor and the commotion of fingers in motion began anew.

Kristi tapped a finger on my shoulder and I started with enough violence to jar my teeth. I hate when I do that. She wiggled her index finger and I followed her again.

She handed me a typed sheet of paper with all the necessary access information, including technical support numbers. Then she went through the instructions for using the programs with all the simplistic detail required for someone who had never booted up a computer in her life. I'm not kidding—she actually told me that if the little lights did not come on, I needed to make sure the computer was plugged in. I was tempted to interrupt, but she seemed to have her spiel memorized, making me fear if I intruded, she'd have to take it again from the top. She wrapped up with a huge synapses jump: "I really did like chemistry class."

I shook my head to reorient my thoughts.

"Well, I did have this really dreamy chemistry teacher so I'm sure that helped," she said with a languid smile and a deep sigh as the memory flickered the old flame in her heart. "I'll bet the boys in your class felt the same way."

"How did you know I was a chemistry teacher?" I wondered if there was a scarlet C emblazoned on my forehead.

"Oh, I helped Arnie do the background research on you for Mr. Travis."

Welcome to the twenty-first century, where privacy is just an illusion. Soon even our genetic make-up will be an open book.

Kristi's features puckered into a look of pain. "Oh, Molly, I am so sorry about your husband." She shook her head, patted my arm and the furrows faded even quicker than they had formed. "But I know you're going to get that poor boy out of jail. I just know it. Now that Bobby's fate is in your hands, everything will turn out just right."

I looked at her eager, glowing face and longed to share her

faith in my abilities. I smiled back at her but inside I grimaced. The weight of the burden I'd sought and acquired now fell on my shoulders with a thud. I had a job to do, and I hoped to God I was up to it.

CHAPTER FOURTEEN

By the time I escaped from downtown, Interstate 10 in Houston had transformed from a highway into long stretches of rush-hour parking lots. I oozed through town, crawled through the suburb of Katy and finally broke loose. I-10 was still crowded, but at least movement was perceptible. A few exits west, I was up and over the seventy-mile-per-hour speed limit. To break up the monotony of the miles home, I slid in a Tracy Nelson CD recorded live at a women's prison. By the time she hit the cut with her old classic about Mother Earth, I was singing along and oblivious to the ugly scenery that flew past my windshield.

At the house, I slapped together a sandwich and plopped down in front of my computer with my passwords to the magical world of Internet privacy invasion. I ran reams of reports on each of the members of the band. I was disappointed to discover no criminal records, except for a few traffic violations and a couple of bounced checks. Of course, there was no telling what could be contained in sealed juvenile records. I'd ask Arnie if there were any legal—or not so legal—way to get into those.

Next, I ran Mike Elliot, manager of Solms Halle, through the databases. Mike was a local boy and I thought I knew all I needed to know about him. We were never close, but I had known him most of my life. Surprise! Surprise! Mike showed up with a criminal record. While out in Lubbock attending Texas Tech, Mike was busted for attempted robbery. My, my, my. I'll have to have a talk with Mike about that. He was found guilty but served no time, except for the few days he spent in jail until he could post bond. He paid a fine and court costs and did community service. Obviously, the authorities did not deem him to have a lifelong inclination to commit acts with felonious intent. Sure would be easier if they had. On the other hand, I would just as soon find out that someone I did not know killed Rodney Faver and framed Bobby Wiggins.

The sudden onset of small stabs of pain in my shoulder blades reminded me of the toll of the last couple of days. I signed off the Internet and climbed into bed.

I hadn't set my alarm the night before and woke up a little later than usual. I clambered out of bed about ten past eight, feeling a little guilty but quite rested. After downing a dose of hot, liquid caffeine, I called Thelma Wiggins.

"Good morning, Mrs. Wiggins. This is Molly Mullet . . ." Slam. *Damn,* I sighed. Travis must not have informed her about the latest developments.

I scooted by the printer's office and dropped off the disk for my business cards and then drove to Thelma's house. In the car, I scratched out a short note to Thelma explaining that Dale Travis could confirm that I quit the police force and was now working on Bobby's case. I went up to the front door and knocked. The curtain in the window twitched but, as I expected, the door did not swing open in welcome. I knocked again and heard only the sounds of silence. I did catch a whiff of baking bread sliding around the edges of the front door, causing my mouth to water and my ire at Thelma to reach a new high. I stuck my note between the wooden screen door and the jamb and went home.

I ran a few more possible suspect names and found nothing of interest. Then I ran Rodney Faver. Here was a colorful background. Faver had a long list of traffic violations, including driving while intoxicated charges in a number of states. He had also been charged with misappropriation of funds, fraud and assault and battery. The charges never mounted to more than a speed bump in Faver's life, though. A few convictions were settled with a small fine; the rest were dismissed.

In another database, I found a long list of civil cases. Some were charges brought against Faver, but a much longer list was of suits he initiated. He was a litigious little guy. He must have accumulated a lot of enemies with that practice.

I made a round of phone calls to the numbers for the band I had uncovered on the databases. Most numbers dialed reached an answering machine promising a prompt response. I suspected that all were hollow promises, but I left a brief message about the reason for my call. When I called Happy Parker, though, someone answered the phone. It was a woman who sounded half asleep, under the influence or both. She mumbled, dropped the phone with a thud and went off hollering "Happy" in a long-suffering whine.

" 'o," Happy said after fumbling with the phone.

"Happy Parker?"

"Yep. Who's this?"

"Happy, I'm Molly Mullet. I am working for Dale Travis on Bobby Wiggins' case."

"Bobby who?"

"Wiggins. The boy who has been accused of killing Rodney Faver," I explained.

"No. No comment. Nothing to say. Bye."

Once again, someone hung up on me. It was getting more than a little annoying. I called back. The phone rang and rang. After twelve times, I gave up. I hoped he was hungover and each signal drove a spike through his brain.

I needed to expand my list of people I could use as suspects or sources of information. Research of media coverage of the band would provide a wealth of that kind of information. That required a trip to the main public library in San Antonio. We had a public library in New Braunfels but for in-depth access to periodicals, San Antonio was the place to go. If I had a San Antonio library card, I could look at a lot of that material on-line at home. But I always balked at paying the huge annual fee required for a non-resident card. Besides, I loved visiting the library downtown.

A half-hour drive down Interstate 35 and I was there. The second I spotted the library building, a grin of appreciation stretched, as always, across my face. I loved its massive enchilada-red structure at first sight. When the stuffy Anglos of the town shrieked and sniveled at the ostentatious color and design, I was delighted. Those elitists stayed worked up over the library until writer Sandra Cisneros was kind enough to distract them with a powerful purple paint job on her house in the historic King William district.

I paused outside to absorb the power of the colors and the emotions they evoked. The structure rose up from its bland institutional urban surroundings, making a statement that could not be denied. The brilliant cream-of-tomato-soup hue had dramatic accents of Aztec gold. Around the grounds huge geometric sculptures were tossed in the grass as if they were the abandoned toys of the children of a race of giants. The library and its grounds shouted: "Here I am. Come inside. I am an exciting place to be."

The interior reflected the same demand to be noticed and an in-your-face defiance of subdued Anglo tradition. Everywhere I looked, my eyes captured splotches of sunny yellow and royal purple with highlights of Aztec gold. The vaulted ceilings created a sense of grandeur that said here was a place where the exploration of human knowledge was as vast and limitless as the human imagination itself.

I made my way up the stairs to the periodical section and camped out at a computer catalogue. By working in the computer files, I was limited to the past ten years. The band had not been around quite that long, so I probably wouldn't need to dig farther back in the paper indices.

I was making a list of names and jotting down any pertinent information I could harvest from the feature articles I found when I felt an odd and startling sensation on my leg that catapulted me out of my chair. My heart was pounding and my breathing disintegrated into gasps before I recognized the source of the odd feeling. I had forgotten I had set my cell phone on vibrate and slipped it into my pocket.

By the time I extracted the phone, the caller was gone. I swung my gaze around the space hoping no one had noticed my startled gyrations—either no one did or no one cared. Grateful, I went outside to return the call. When the phone answered, I recognized Thelma Wiggins' voice right away.

"Hi, Mrs. Wiggins. This is Molly Mullet. Sorry I didn't get the phone out in time to catch your call."

"Well, I'm sorry I hung up on you this morning and didn't answer the door when you came calling. I talked to Mr. Travis, and I'll talk to you now if you want to come on by. I was fixing to brew up some fresh iced tea and I got some banana nut bread just baked this morning."

The memory of that escaping aroma caressed my nose again and induced another round of excessive salivation. "I'm down here in San Antonio just now but I'd be glad to stop by this evening after supper."

"You know you can't do that, Molly Mullet," she snapped. "It's Wednesday night."

Oh, yes. Wednesday night. Prayer meeting night at the Baptist church. Thelma was as devout in her attendance there as the average Texan was with Friday night football games at the high school. "I'm sorry, Mrs. Wiggins. I forgot it was Wednesday."

She sniffed, but she was mollified and continued the conversation in a more pleasant tone of voice. "Come on by in the morning, Molly—say about 7:30. I'll fix you up some breakfast and we'll talk a spell."

"That would be real nice, Mrs. Wiggins. I'll see you in the morning."

"Don't be late, now. I'd rather eat cardboard than cold eggs," she warned.

"Yes, ma'am. I'll be on time."

At last, one person was willing to talk to me. On my way back, I'd stop in and see if Mike Elliot would give me the time of day. First, though, let's see what the archives here reveal about his unsavory misadventures out in West Texas.

CHAPTER FIFTEEN

On the way into town, I picked up my business card order and then headed out to the historic community of Solms. I parked in the big lot across the street from the gray, weathered boards of the building that housed Solms Halle. I found Mike inside talking to the driver of a beer delivery truck. I flipped one of my new cards in his direction and said, "Hi, Mike."

"Well, well, well. This is very interesting. How are you, Molly? And just what are you up to with The Agency?"

"I'm doing fine, Mike. And my job right now is to find the information necessary to get Bobby Wiggins out of jail."

"More power to ya, Molly. Bobby doesn't belong behind bars."

"I'd like to talk to you for a few minutes about that night."

"Not a good time," Mike objected. "I've got a lot to do."

"C'mon, Mike. It's Wednesday night. It's not like I dropped by on a weekend."

"C'mon yourself, Molly. You were here that night. You saw everything I did—maybe more. I don't have anything new to offer. And I've answered the questions of cops and nosy neighbors till I'm sick of it."

"I really need to scratch you off my list, Mike."

"List? List of what? Suspects?" He gave me that you-lost-it-now-Molly-Mullet look. I'd recognize it anywhere. I just nodded.

"Oh, give me a break. I'm about as suspicious as a piece of

road kill. I was so busy that night, I didn't have time for a threat, let alone follow through. You know that. You were there. See you around, Molly." He laughed and turned away.

"Your criminal record automatically qualifies you as a suspect," I snapped at his retreating back.

He swung around and faced me. "Damn it, Molly." He prodded my shoulder with the knuckles of one hand. "Take it outside."

On the sidewalk, he continued his harangue. "That was uncalled for, Molly. What did I ever do to you?"

"You turned your back on me, Mike. You didn't leave me a lot of options. I, for one, care about what happens to Bobby Wiggins. I thought you would, too."

"I do care about Bobby. I'm sick about it. But I don't know anything. My stupidity in the past has nothing to do with Bobby. My staff is unaware of my record and I want to keep it that way."

"I'm not trying to cause problems, Mike. I'm trying to find answers. I suppose you haven't told your employer about Lubbock, either."

"Well, you supposed wrong," he spat back. "I was totally up front with him."

"Really? Then why would he give a thief a position of such responsibility and authority? Explain that, Mike."

"Because the whole thing was just so stupid."

"Felony charges go beyond 'stupid' in my book, Mike."

He blew his exasperation through his lips like a horse. "It was all reduced to a misdemeanor in the end. I'm not proud of it. But it happened. And it's over."

"What happened?" I asked.

He shook his head as if in refusal but then he began. "Me and a couple of buddies were screwing around one night. Too much to drink. Too little to do in that dusty outback we called home for four years. Somehow, we thought it would be funny to pull off a gag robbery. I tied a bandana around the bottom of my face while the others waited outside peering through the windows.

"I pulled out a water gun, struggled to keep a straight face and an upright position and drawled, 'This here's a stick-up.'

"The guy behind the counter was not amused. He pulled out a real shotgun and said, 'Yeah. And I'll blow a hole in your empty head big enough for a dozen dust devils to dance.'

"I dropped my plastic pistol and put my hands on top of my head. I focused my eyes on the barrel of the gun and concentrated on not wetting my pants until the police arrived. My buddies were so shit-faced, they were still doubled over giggling in the parking lot when the flashing lights pinned them in place."

"You're right, Mike. 'Stupid' is an apt description. What were you all thinking?"

"We weren't, Molly," he said with a sigh. Tugging on the right sleeve of my T-shirt, he added, "We all did stupid things when we were younger."

"Okay, Mike," I said brushing his hand from my arm. "Let's just say, for the sake of argument, that you concealed this stupid incident from your employer . . ."

"But, I didn't, Molly."

"Yeah, but just for the moment, let's say that you did." He started to object again but I waved him quiet. "So your employer doesn't know. But, somehow, Rodney Faver finds out and he blackmails you."

"Aw, c'mon, Molly."

"That would be a good motive for murder." I looked him straight in the eye and watched the color drain from his face. Then bright red patches appeared on his cheeks and anger flashed in his eyes.

"Yeah, it would be a good motive. But it didn't happen. I just can't believe you, Molly Mullet. How could you possibly think I'd do such a thing? Now, don't get me wrong. I can see how you would think I could kill some lowlife blackmailer. But, damn it, Molly, how could you possibly believe I'd sit around twiddling my thumbs while they hauled off poor old Bobby Wiggins and slammed him into jail." In his agitation, Mike's voice rose in volume and pitch. He fidgeted in place. He was drawing stares from passersby.

I moved closer and placed a hand on his arm as I spoke. "You really do care about Bobby?"

The nervous energy lifted from his shoulders and his arms slumped by his sides. "Bobby is a bit older than me, but in a way he's like a little brother. I fought to get him this job—not many people want to hire somebody like him. But he's a hard worker, he follows instructions and he never misses a day of work. He even put waders on and trudged in here after the last flood. He's a simple but good man. There's no way he killed that weasel Faver."

"You didn't like Faver, I take it?"

"He was scum. Good riddance. I guess that's not a smart thing for me to say under the circumstances. But I never liked him. I can't believe Wolfe did not dump that garbage a long time ago. Faver was probably blackmailing somebody—it wasn't me—and maybe it was more than one person. Figure out which chicken he was plucking and you've figured out who killed him. And it sure wasn't Bobby Wiggins."

"Thanks, Mike. I'll have to check and make sure your employer is aware of your background. But as long as that pans out, I'll be moving you to the bottom of my list."

"Let me make it easier for you." He whipped out one of his business cards and jotted the name and phone number of the owner of Solms Halle. "Just do me a favor. Don't ask for any passes in the same conversation."

We turned away from each other and a question popped into my head; I spun back around. "Say, Mike, one more question."

His shoulders slumped but he turned back to face me. "What, Molly?" he sighed.

"There was an orange rain poncho lying over the body when I opened the closet. Could it have belonged to anyone who worked for you?"

"Yeah," he laughed. "Any one of them. We buy those things in bulk and keep a stack in the closet for rainy days."

"That's interesting."

"Interesting. Yes. But it also points the finger right back at Bobby. Besides me, he is the only employee with a key to the closet."

When I got home, I made notes about my talk with Mike and cruised the Internet for contact and background information for the names I uncovered at the library. I came up empty on some of them and would have to turn to the databases. But that could wait till tomorrow.

I climbed into bed to finish *Jolie Blon* before I slept. I didn't quite make it. The last sound I heard was the thunk of the book spine hitting the floor beside my bed. I slipped deeper into oblivion, expecting a good night of sleep.

CHAPTER SIXTEEN

Noise. Loud noise. Obnoxious noise. My hand slid out from under the covers and slammed down on the snooze button on my alarm. The noise did not stop. I bashed my clock again. A little too hard. It hurt. But the pain woke me up enough to recognize the sound of the telephone. I flipped on the lamp and squinted at the clock face. Little hand on three, big hand on two—3:10 in the morning—time to panic.

Adrenaline surged. Mind raced. Dad in the hospital? Dad dying? I grabbed the phone. "Yes," I rasped into the receiver.

"Molly Mullet?" the voice asked. It was not a family member. Was it a doctor? A nurse? A cop? A minister?

"This is she." My voice trembled.

"Back off, girl."

"Excuse me?"

"You heard me. Back off." There was something wrong with the sound of that voice. It was as if the caller was trying to talk though chipmunk cheeks packed with Milk Duds. It was a muffled, slurpy sound.

"Who is this?" I asked.

"Just let it go, Molly Mullet. You're asking for more trouble than you want. More than you imagined."

"What are you talking about?" I knew the answer, of course, but I hoped if I kept him talking the who or the why might start making sense.

"You know what I'm talking about. Just leave it alone. And

don't worry about idiot boy. He doesn't have enough sense to appreciate the difference 'tween a bedroom and a cell. With him behind bars, his mama will get a well-deserved break. So back off and let justice run its course."

"Lieutenant Hawkins, is that you? Is this some kind of joke?"

The caller laughed and then segued into a choke as if one of those Milk Duds got lodged in his throat. "That's a good one, Molly Mullet. But I'm not making jokes or playing games. There are a lot of guitar strings floating around Texas. You'd be wise to keep that in mind."

A charge surged through my body, making my fingers and toes tingle. I was not talking to a prankster. I was talking to Rodney Faver's killer. The guitar string was a holdback—it was not released to the media. And it had not been leaked.

"You still there, Molly Mullet?"

"Yes."

"You might want to check your mailbox for a special delivery."

I heard a click but just sat there on the edge of the bed gripping the phone. I didn't hang up until that annoying recording intoned, "If you'd like to make a call, please hang up and dial again."

What do I do now? Common sense made it simple: Don't go outside until daylight. But sun-up was hours away. I wanted to know what was in my box. I lifted a slat on my bedroom blinds and peered into the darkness. There, at the end of my driveway, sat my mailbox looking innocent and ordinary in the glow of the street lamp.

I should go back to sleep. Yeah. Right. Like I could sleep. I had enough adrenaline flowing through my bloodstream to alarm a dozen people. I pulled on a pair of jeans and padded barefoot out to the living room. I stood back from the window and surveyed my street. Was he out there watching me?

Everything looked normal for the middle of the night. Darkness consumed the interiors of some homes. The faint aura of a nightlight wavered in others. Three doors up, a cat skulked across the street, belly low to the ground, feet moving fast. I closed my eyes and listened. The only menacing sound was the hoot of a predator owl.

I wanted to go out to the mailbox. Now. But what if it was a trap? He could be hiding anywhere. I scanned the cars parked along the street and in the driveways looking for any sign of movement, any flashing gleam from the reflection of the street-light. Nothing.

He could be anywhere. He could be beyond the truncated backyards of the houses across the street—crouched in Panther Canyon with the deer, the opossums and the skunks. Peering at me through a pair of binoculars. Laughing at my panic.

Or he could be closer. In this old neighborhood, the established trees provided a lot of cover for the stealthy. He could be behind that tree. Or that one. Or the one down the street.

Or he could be even closer. He could be hiding beside my steps, the long stems of the bridal wreath bush forming a canopy over his head. Waiting. Just waiting for me to open that door.

Or he could be long gone, believing he left me as a prisoner in my own home. Amused at my discomfort. Tantalized by my fear.

That did it. I slipped feet into a pair of sandals and ap-proached the front door. My hand grabbed the bronze knob and I paused. I rested my forehead on the cool wood of the door. Fumes from decades of polish tickled my nostrils with a faraway hint of lemon.

I steadied my breath and jerked open the door. Nothing moved. No one jumped out. My confidence edged up one tiny notch. I stepped out on the porch. I heard my heart pounding a desperate staccato in my ears. I pulled the door shut. But not tight enough to engage the latch.

I walked down the steps—one at a time. With each descent, a dozen more beads of sweat popped out on my forehead. The clammy wetness on my neck spread another inch. The itching in my palms intensified.

I headed in a diagonal line across the lawn. I heard the blades of grass crush down and bounce back beneath my feet. I felt the moistness of the dew on my toes. I heard nothing but the continued pounding in my ears. If someone didn't kill me, I might keel over dead just the same.

I stood before my round-topped rectangle of red-flagged aluminum and prayed it was not a Pandora's Box or stuffed with the latest in Unabomber-like technology. Would it blow up? Would a rattlesnake spring out and kiss my neck? Or would it be as empty as an unused tomb?

I swallowed and pulled. No explosion. No strike. Just a circular coil of guitar string. I reached in and pulled back. I shouldn't touch it. Crap. I shouldn't have touched the mailbox either. I could have obliterated good prints. I won't get any prints off of the string. But maybe some DNA from the sweat of Milk Duds man. Anything's possible.

I looked around on the ground till I found a short, broken piece of branch from the tree above. I slid its tip inside the loop of wire and eased it out. I stopped myself before I touched the mailbox latch again.

Balancing the guitar string on one stick, I searched for another. When I found it, I poked shut the hinged lid of the box. At that moment, I remembered my gun. It was still by my bed on the nightstand, cozied up to a box of ammo. I wanted to make a mad dash to the house. Instead, I took measured steps balancing my newly found treasure with all the grace my shaky hands could muster.

I nudged open the door like a surgeon going into an operating room and pushed it shut with my foot. I wanted to stop, lock it, slide to the floor and cry. But I couldn't—not yet.

I pulled a paper lunch sack out of the cupboard and with the flick of a wrist popped it open. I stuck the tip of the stick inside and watched the loop of string slide down and plop on the bottom of the bag. I folded the top down with three creased folds and went searching for tape to seal it. Before I could find the tape the phone rang. My stomach lurched. I picked up the receiver without a word.

"See what I told you about guitar strings?" Milk Duds mouth said. "They show up everywhere."

He paused, waiting for my response. I did not oblige.

"You know," he continued. "Next time a guitar string could sneak up on you from behind. Next time, it could slip over your head and cut into your neck. All in the split second you spent breathing out one solitary, final breath."

He paused again. Tears formed in the corners of my eyes. My lower lip quivered. I wanted to scream in outrage. Sob in fear. But I gave him nothing but silence.

"Think about that, Molly Mullet. Think about it next time you go to open your door. Think about it real hard. And back off, Molly Mullet. Let it go."

The phone clicked again. I pried my petrified fingers off the receiver and cradled it on the wall. I stood rooted in place until my negligence hit me like a punch in the gut. The front door. I stumbled toward it. I slid the dead bolt home. I spun around and threw my back against the wooden surface. I slid inch by inch down to the floor. And I rubbed my right arm and sobbed until no more tears could form.

s my own. I felt her agony shred through my skin and cut
wn to the bone. Tears welled up in my eyes and spilled over.
Oh, please, it's okay. You're only human."

She shook her head in violent swings. "No. What I said—
hat I thought—is unforgivable. It is an unpardonable sin."

"No. No. No," I begged.

"Yes. It is. I will never forgive myself. I'm sorry, Molly. I'm
sorry. Please let yourself out? Please. I need to be alone."

I stumbled through the house, out the door, down the steps.

In my car, I dropped my forehead down on the steering
wheel. *Pull yourself together, Molly. You've got work to do. You've got
to dust your mailbox for prints. It's time to catch the bastard who created this whole mess.*

*So what do I do now? I can't stop at Henne Hardware and pick
up fingerprint powder. If I make a career of this, I'll have to talk to
them about that. I'm sure there's room to squeeze it in between the
ten-penny nails and the wrought-iron drawer pulls.*

*I bet Arnie could get what I need. But I don't have the time to run
down to Houston to pick it up. I need to dust that mailbox before the
mailman handles the box again. Lieutenant Hawkins would have
what I need—can't exactly see him being cooperative. Lisa. Lisa
Garcia. She's in and out of every office at the Police Department.
She could get what I need. But would she do it?*

I whipped out my cell and called her direct line while I drove
in the direction of the police department.

"Good morning. New Braunfels Police Department. Garcia
speaking."

"Hi, Lisa. This is Molly Mullet. How are you . . ."

A sharp intake of breath was followed by a rapid expulsion of
words. "How could you? How could you just walk away? You
didn't even tell me. You didn't say 'goodbye.' What am I supposed to think of that? I had to dig and dig to find out what
happened. You should have stuck it out. I would have helped

Chapter Seventeen

At 7:28 the next morning, I pushed the doorbell at Thelma
Wiggins' house. She opened the door and held open the screen.
"C'mon in, Molly. You're right on time."

As if I dared be late.

"I thought we'd eat in the kitchen," Thelma said leading me
through the house.

I hadn't been inside for years, but everything looked pretty
much the same. The colors were a bit more faded with the pas-
sage of time. The sofa slumped a bit lower to the floor. The
sheen on the hardwood floor was dulled by years of footsteps.
But everything was as clean and free of dust as ever. In a fifty-
year-old house that was a feat that required eternal vigilance.

Thelma was as faded as her home. Her dull gray hair was
pulled pack tight to her neck where it was fastened with a red
rubber band. Her brow looked like harrowed rows in a barren
field. The blue of her eyes reflected nothing but the sorrow on
the other side.

Beneath her red-and-white-check apron, her simple shirtwaist
dress was a soft blur of color. Once it held a vibrant small
flowered print on its surface. Now the definition of its design
had disappeared after years of laundering.

I slid on to an old Windsor chair, its finish darkened nearly
black with age, and rested my elbows on the kitchen table—in
places its thick coat of white paint was chipped, revealing a peek
at the green paint beneath. The aroma of fresh-brewed coffee,

sizzling bacon and fresh-baked biscuits swirled around my head making my stomach growl. I hoped she hadn't heard.

"Won't be long now, Molly." She did hear it.

"Coffee?" Thelma asked.

"Yes, ma'am. Thank you."

She slid a thick white mug in front of me and plopped down a small glass pitcher. "That's real cream. I still go out to Schultz's farm and pick some up every week—just like your mama used to do. The eggs are from out at Schultz's, too."

I poured the white liquid, thick as honey, and watched it swirl downward through the black in my cup. I sipped. Strong coffee. Real cream. Heaven by the cup.

"There you go, Molly. Eat up," Thelma said as she slid a plate in front of me—a little mountain of tender crisp bacon on the left, two perfect white ovals surrounding farm fresh orange yolks and flanked by two steaming biscuits on the right. Right in the middle was a generous red and green mound of *pico de gallo* pungent with the scent of fresh-cut cilantro.

"I made that *pico* hot, just like you like it, Molly."

I was surprised she remembered. We ate in silence for a few minutes until Thelma dropped her fork and stared down at her plate.

"I don't know what to do. Oh, I know to trust Dale. If anybody can get us out of this mess, he can. But I want to do something. Not just sit here counting the minutes away." She looked up at me, her eyes searching my face. "Can you understand that? I just want to do something. Anything. But Dale just says to rest up for the trial. How can I rest when my Bobby's in jail? He looks okay when I visit him, but you hear all sorts of stories about what goes on in jail. I'm so scared for him." Her head fell into her hands.

"Mrs. Wiggins, I know some folks at the jail. I'll talk to them. I'll see what I can do. And I'll visit Bobby as soon as I can."

She looked up again and said, "Yesterday wh[...] told him to put you on his visitors' list. He said [...] check and make sure he did when I go visit tomor[...]

"Thank you, Mrs. Wiggins," I said. We fell int[...] silence. I took another bite of biscuit and chewed slo[...]

"Molly, you know Bobby. You've known him for a l[...] Do you think he could do this? Do you think he co[...] someone? Do you think he could ever hurt anybody?"

"I doubt Bobby could hurt anyone," I told her. "I su[...] it's possible. But this murder? No way. This is a brutal cr[...] and I do not for one minute think that Bobby is capable of [...] level of violence."

"Then, why, oh why, did he confess?" Thelma asked.

"He wanted to see you. He thought if he told them what they [...] wanted to hear, he could go home."

"Damn it. How could he be so stupid?" As soon as those words formed sound waves, Thelma's hand flew at the speed of light to cover her mouth. Above her fingers, her eyes grew large and seemed to pale even more as I watched. She gulped for air and trembled so intensely, the table shook. "How could I say that? How could I think that?" A keening wail rose in her throat.

A wet, suffocating blanket of misery fell down upon us both. Instinct brought me to my feet, ready to hug, to hold, to comfort. But I stopped myself. Thelma was not a toucher, and she shrank from those who were. I sat down—uncomfortable, uneasy, helpless.

I stretched my hands out across the table—close to her but not touching her. "I understand. It's okay."

"No it's not. You don't understand. Oh, Dear God, forgive me. I didn't mean it. Oh yes, I did. For that moment, I really, I truly meant it. But oh, dear God, I love him. Please don't take him from me. Please bring him home."

No pain has ever been more vivid, more visceral, unless it

you. You should have spat in their eyes. Spat on their shoes. I went to that squealer Lieutenant Hawkins and just looked at him. I did not need to say a word. He knew I was not pleased. He knew that the next time he needed a favor, the next time he needed a report typed I would not be there to save his sorry butt. And you, Molly? What am I to do with you? What am I to think of you?"

"Well, I was kind of hoping you might be able to help me, Lisa," I interrupted, and winced as I awaited another torrent of words.

"What?" she snapped with more petulance packed in that one word than most people could stuff into a five-minute soliloquy. "You want me to help you? You turn your back on me, and now you come looking for my help?"

"Lisa. I need your help. Please."

All I got in response was a snort that led to silence.

"I'm sorry. Really, Lisa. I am sorry. I wasn't thinking too clearly."

"You should have come to me first," she insisted.

"Yes, Lisa. You're right. Will you help me? Please."

"I shouldn't," Lisa said, "but what do you need, *Mija?*"

Mija? Oooh. Nice. Whenever she called me that, she would do anything I asked. I explained what I needed and she promised to call back. I pulled into the parking lot of the police station and slipped my car into an unobtrusive slot. In a few minutes, my cell rang.

"I'll meet you here. Park in front of the station," Lisa said. "Don't get out of your car. I'll find you." She hung up before I could let her know I was already there.

After my secret mission was accomplished, I returned home with my pilfered and smuggled goods—or borrowed supplies, as Lisa insisted on calling them. And my cohort in crime had not missed a thing. Fingerprint powder, application brush, lifting tape, mounting cards, even a couple of pairs of disposable gloves.

Beside my mailbox, I opened the folding wooden table Dad had built and set out my equipment. I hoped none of my neighbors were peering out their windows. First I dusted the front of the flap door. I couldn't find a print, not even where I was sure I had touched it myself when I removed the guitar string. Odd. I dropped the flap and dusted the inside. Nothing. The box had been wiped clean? No. It couldn't have been. I ran the brush across the outside surface, up and down the little red flag, even on the back on the box. Not one print.

He wiped the box clean. When? While I was at Thelma's or the police station? No. Not in broad daylight. He put the string in there under the cover of darkness. He would do the same when he wiped it down.

He had to have done it after I took the guitar string into the house. Probably after he called. Probably while I leaned against the front door and sobbed. Did he hear me? Did he sneak up the steps and listen to me cry? Did he smile?

A shiver raised goose bumps on my arms. *Is he watching me now?* My prayer that no neighbors were watching changed into the devout desire that all of them were—that their nosy curiosity would shield me from harm. I scanned the windows of the nearest houses. No twitching blinds. No shadowy forms behind the windows. I was alone. I was vulnerable.

A car door slammed at least a block away. I jumped as if the sound was right beside my ear. As quick as my quivering hands could manage, I packed up my supplies, folded up the table and tucked it under my arm. I moved as fast as I could to the front door. I dropped everything in the hall and headed straight for my bedroom. I fastened on my holster. And slid my gun in place. I wouldn't go anywhere without it anymore.

CHAPTER EIGHTEEN

The urge to go to the firing range was strong, but without my police I.D., I wouldn't get past the front door. I really needed to shoot at something to regain my confidence in my ability to protect myself.

That's when I thought about Eddie Beacham. I've known Eddie since middle school and even knew at that early age that he was a threat to my self-control.

Eddie didn't need to work. He'd inherited enough money to support himself and a busload of buddies in style for the rest of his life. But Eddie did work—sort of. He was an attorney who kept banking hours. No burning the midnight oil for Eddie.

In the courtroom, he didn't really convince the jury of reasonable doubt or persuade them of his client's innocence. He just charmed the female jurors into believing every word that fell from his lips.

It was more than charisma. Eddie was one fine male specimen. He projected the image that women fantasize about: strong but vulnerable, aggressive but gentle, chivalrous but not condescending. And Eddie had the looks to go with it: dark hair, blue eyes, broad shoulders and a smile fit to melt any woman, virgin to harlot, coed to dowager. He almost got to me once, but I had the sense to pull back before he moved in for the kill. I'd seen Eddie around town a lot over the years. I always made sure it was never just the two of us alone in any room.

As dangerous as he was in social circles, he was even more

deadly in the courtroom. In one case where he represented a teacher accused of killing a drug dealer who sold illegal substances to his students, there were four trials. Each time, the District Attorney tried to get all of the women off of the jury, but never quite made it.

The state came close the last time. The only woman on the panel was a seventy-eight-year-old great-grandmother. I imagine the prosecutor thought he was safe with her. I guess he didn't know that Eddie was at his masterful best with women in their dotage. That sweet little old lady fell for Eddie the first time he smiled in her direction. There were four hung juries before the state finally gave up.

Eddie was careful never to defend any really nasty killers. No capital cases for this guy; it was just too much work. And he never took on more than one case at a time. As a result, Eddie's defeats were rare, his victories occasional, but his list of mistrials went on forever.

But believe it or not, Eddie's ability to make sensible women, in and out of the courtroom, transform into mindless worshippers was not the skill in which he took the most pride. It was his talent, as he put it, to shoot a fly off the rump of a skittish colt while it chewed its oats without causing the critter to even blink an eye.

I'd received invitations to use Eddie's private shooting range out at his place near Canyon Lake a few times, but I always demurred. I had an alternative then. Now I was desperate.

I called his under-worked secretary Sara and asked if he was available. Of course, he was. He was always available. But Sara took my name as if she didn't know me and put me on hold while she checked.

"Hello, Officer Mullet," Eddie oozed into the phone, somehow making that official title sound sexy.

"Hey, Eddie. How are you? I was calling to see if that invite to your firing range was still open."

"Of course. I'm always willing to cooperate with an officer of the law."

"Well, you see, I'm not one anymore."

"You're not on the force?"

"No."

"Why not?"

"It's complicated, Eddie."

"Okay. Let me guess. You were fired for not sharing your charms with your commanding officer. And now instead of relying on an attorney to file a sexual harassment suit on your behalf, you are taking matters into your own hands and planning to gun down your supervisor but you want to hone your skills a bit before going in for the kill. Now, Molly, as an officer of the court, I cannot condone this behavior or enable you in any way. But I'll be glad to defend you when you're charged."

Maybe calling Eddie wasn't such a good idea. I felt the heat of red flaming my face. "C'mon, Eddie. Give me a break. Let me use your range and I'll tell you the whole story."

"You promise you're not going to set me up as an accessory before the fact."

"Eddie, I have no intention of committing any crime."

"Oh, maybe not, Molly. But I know you've got it in you. There is a fiery passion smoldering beneath your all-together surface that I think is capable of almost anything."

"Cut the crap, Eddie. Can I come out and shoot at your place or not?"

He laughed. He knew he'd won this round of our perpetual head game. "Sure, sure, Molly. Today?"

"That would be great."

"See you at two?"

"Two? Won't that disrupt your busy attorney-at-law schedule?"

"Tsk, tsk, Miss Molly. Sarcasm is no way to show your appreciation. We'll find some better ways this afternoon."

Before I could spit out a snappy comeback, he was gone.

CHAPTER NINETEEN

I turned down River Road and followed the course of the Guadalupe River. The water shifted from one side to the other at each crossing—slim two-lane concrete slabs without guardrails where the road dipped down and forded the river. Along the way, the many campsites were populated with a few intrepid visitors. In a few weeks, this peaceful road would be bumper to bumper with the warm weather deluge of river rafters, RVers and tent campers.

At Sattler, the road diverged from the Guadalupe, and I pushed on to the lake and its huge wall of dam built by the Army Corps of Engineers. I drove past the pull-off and spotted four people walking across the top of the dam, a perilous precipice at their backs, a glorious view of the lake sprawled at their feet.

A short distance later, I turned onto a private road and wended my way up the hill. At the top was Eddie's aerie of glass and stone perched with a God's-eye view of the glistening body of water below.

I stepped out of the car and Eddie hurried to my side. He looked ready to embrace me so I took a step back. He stuck out his hand instead. When I took it, he wrapped his other hand around too. His eyes stared deep into mine as if I were the only woman in the world—ever. My stomach flipped. My knees quivered. I had not received a look like that since the day I shook hands with Bill Clinton at one of his stops on his Texas bus trip the first time he ran for President. I held Clinton's gaze then. Now, I averted my eyes and pulled out my gun.

Eddie raised both hands in the air. "I'll lie face down in the dirt if you promise to frisk me."

"Cut me some slack, Eddie. I am not pointing the gun at you. Put your hands down. I'm here to shoot bullets, not to play mouse to your cat. Let's get to it."

He executed a mock salute and pivoted on his heel. "This way, sir."

He proceeded ahead of me in a comic march and skip he probably stole from a grainy black and white movie from the thirties. I did not want to be amused but I was.

We went to a large commercial steel building tucked out of sight in the folds of the hills. He pulled open the door and placed his hand on the small of my back as if escorting me to a table in a restaurant.

Charlie danced through my mind as the warmth of Eddie's hand seeped into my back. I felt a swelling in my lips and a tingling in my fingers. I faked a coughing fit to prevent Eddie from seeing the naked longing in my eyes.

I imagine somewhere some law enforcement agency had a range as sophisticated as Eddie's facility. I'd never encountered one except in the movies. Electronically controlled pulleys moved targets forward and back. LCD read-outs displayed the distance for the target in each lane. Quite impressive.

I popped on my ear protectors, loaded my gun and fired. Not at all impressive. I reloaded. On the fifth time, I felt in control of my emotions and of my weapon. On the sixth load, the gun and I were one. Eddie hit the button and rolled the target forward. Six shots. One hole. All straight through the heart.

"You're good, girl."

"What?" I said as I pulled the protectors off of my ears.

"You are good," he said in a whisper as his face closed in on mine and his lips pressed into my lips.

I closed my eyes and saw Charlie. I yielded to the memory and to the moment. Then, Eddie's hand slid up under the back of my shirt. His skin touched mine and the spell was broken. It was not Charlie's touch. It was not Charlie's kiss.

I pulled my arms up between us, placed my palms on his chest and pushed. "No."

"No?" he said as his fingers caressed my right cheek.

I batted his hand away. "No."

"I thought you might still be embracing Charlie's memory, girl. But memories are cold in bed. It's time to move on." His voice was heavy with pity.

Damn him. Damn his lips. Damn his hands. He was right. I was not over Charlie yet. Maybe I never would be. But I sure wasn't going to admit it to him. "Oh, please, Eddie, give me a break." I pulled up my ear guards and loaded my gun. "Just because a woman does not crumble at your feet does not mean she's weighted down with emotional trauma. You're not that good, Eddie."

I stepped over to another target and unloaded my gun. My performance made a lie of my words. Eddie didn't press the button to reel it in. Even from a distance, we could see that not one shot touched the outline of the man. I packed up.

Eddie did not speak and did not move until I pulled open the door. "Hey!" he shouted.

I looked back over my shoulder. "What?"

"I thought you were going to tell me about why you're not a cop anymore."

"Later, Eddie," I said, pulling the door shut behind me. I drove off, telling myself I was angry with him. But I knew I was really mad at me.

CHAPTER TWENTY

Happy Parker was the only band member who engaged in even the most cursory conversation with me. The others didn't return my calls, making them suspicious, rude or out of town. But Happy hung up on me. Odds were that meant Happy knew something or feared someone. It seemed like a good place to start.

Happy lived out near Wimberley, a community filled with artisans, artists and oddballs. As a rule, I took highway 35 to San Marcos then cut across the town of San Marcos as I headed west to Wimberley. In early spring, it was not your typical monotonous interstate trek; a riot of color erupted each year. Thanks to God's handiwork and Lady Bird Johnson's hard work, the sides of the roadways and the median strips were alive with wildflowers. The main feature in the beginning of the blooming season was wave after wave of the pride and joy of the Hill Country, the beautiful Texas bluebonnet. Its vibrant blue is accented by the striking red of Indian paintbrush, the pale, delicate pink of mallow and the sunny yellow of coreopsis. It was a bit early in the year for the fullness of this flamboyant display, so I took the back way via Purgatory Road and the Devil's Backbone. A few wildflowers were open, cast like jewels among the cactus. The cactus itself was still a couple of months away from its annual moment of glory when the buds swelled and burst into gaudy and captivating yellow and red blooms.

There was no shortage of another harbinger of spring:

armadillo road kill. Although I saw copious corpses basking in
the sun in the middle of the road around here, it took a trip to
Aransas Wildlife Refuge for me to see a living, breathing
armadillo. It raised its funny armored body up on its hind legs
and twitched its nose as it checked me out. Apparently, I was of
little or no interest, because he settled back down to all fours in
less than a minute and waddled back into the brush.

I rolled past ranches with intriguing names like Eagle's Peak
and Eden's Rest, some filled with cattle, some with goats and
even one with emus. The emu ranch advertised the benefits of
its herd with a sign proudly proclaiming the virtues of emu oil
for treating arthritis.

Up high on hilltops were a smattering of majestic stone
homes looking out over picturesque rolling hills and weaving
roads and looking down on the tarpaper shacks, ramshackle
trailer homes and the junked cars and pick-up trucks that sprang
up sporadically like litter on the roadsides.

Before I hit the town square of quaint shops and studios,
where sturdy pastel painted buildings stood side by side with
teetering gray weathered wood structures, I spotted the small
farm-to-market road that led to Happy's place. This barely two-
lane byway curved back and forth for no discernable reason. I
spotted Happy's mailbox. It wasn't labeled with a name or address but it had to be his. A weathered bongo drum perched on
its side atop a metal pole. The flag was a drumstick painted red,
and hinges and a latch transformed the drumming surface into
a small door. I wondered what it looked like on the inside but
decided to pass. The federal offense of tampering with the mail
might extend to mailboxes, and it was a little too early in my
career to ask my employer to bail me out of jail.

The farm gate stood wide open and judging by the weeds
growing around it, no one had closed it for quite some time. I
eased my car across the bumps of the old cattle guard and

headed up the dirt drive. I traveled a few hundred yards before I turned the corner and a pristine new log cabin came into view.

I parked my Beetle next to a mud-splattered jeep, rolled down my window and listened. The only sound I heard was the gentle tinkling of the wood chimes hanging from the eaves of the broad front porch.

I opened the car door and a cacophony of barks shattered the peace. Bounding toward me were two large white Great Pyrenees, 120 pounds apiece, at least, and a small tan Corgi. The big dogs didn't worry me. Big dogs are big babies by nature, but the little one made me nervous.

I slid out of my car, shut the door and turned to greet the canine hospitality committee. Leaning forward, I slapped my hands on my knees. The two big dogs responded by hanging their heads, wagging their tails and sidling towards me. I rewarded both of them with a scratch behind the ears.

The little Corgi was not as easily mollified. He still seemed intent on extracting his pound of flesh. Every step I took forward, he made another lunge at my ankles. We were both distracted from our dance steps by the screeching of a screen door. A shrill voice whined, "Pete, Labia, Crapper, come here."

The two Pyrenees obeyed her command without hesitation and lumbered up on the porch. She was dressed like an old hippie with a long denim skirt that swept the floor, bare feet and a retro T-shirt proclaiming "Free Love." Her short, styled haircut and make-up contradicted her dress. The scowl on her face said she was not glad to see me.

The Corgi ignored her, stood his ground between the house and me and snarled. "Crapper. Cut it out and get up here. Now."

With one last growl, the Corgi swung around, gave me an evil backward glance and leaped onto the porch, where he faced me and bared his teeth. I walked up to the steps, taking care not to get too close to Crapper, the ankle-nipper. "Hi, I'm Molly Mullet. I'm looking into Rodney Faver's murder and would like to talk to Happy."

"Come on up on the porch. Don't worry about Crapper. He won't bite. I'll go see if Happy is here."

Crapper won't bite? Right. And bears don't crap in the woods. And "I'll go see if Happy is here"? Sure. I know this was a good-sized cabin, but it's not that big. He's here all right. But is he here for me? That was the question.

I stood on the porch waiting while the two Pyrenees bumped into me, begging for attention, and little Crapper circled around my ankles making menacing noises. After five minutes, the woman returned, held the door open and invited me in.

The two Pyrenees plopped down on the porch but the Corgi, unfortunately, followed me in—his eyes pinned on my ankles. The living room was rustic and sophisticated. High cathedral ceilings with rugged hand-hewn beams, a bold rock fireplace on the far wall and lots of windows for an exquisite view of the rugged countryside formed the backdrop for a United Nations of drums. Everywhere I looked, I saw drums from around the world: a djembe from the Ivory Coast, a pandero from Puerto Rico, a dondo drum from Nigeria, bodhrans from Ireland and ashikos from New Zealand.

"Happy's not here now, but I'll be glad to answer your questions," the woman said and stuck out her hand. "I'm Heather. Have a seat."

I settled into a dark brown, distressed leather sofa and asked, "Were you at Solms Halle that night?"

"What night?" Heather said as she twirled a ring in circles on her right ring finger.

Was she really that dumb? "The night that . . ." I began.

"Oh, oh, yes, of course. The night that Rodney died. Oh, yes."

"Yes? You were there?"

"Oh, no. No. I wasn't there. I . . ."

A small thud echoed in the back of the house. Heather's eyes darted side to side as she gasped and jumped to her feet. "You know," she said in a louder voice, "I don't really like country music all that much. I'm really more of a blues person. You know, why don't we listen to some blues while we talk?" She walked toward the CD player.

A muffled crash made her jump. "One of my favorites of all time is a duet with John Lee Hooker and Bonnie Raitt. It's called *In the Mood*. Have you heard it? I just love it. Here it goes. Listen to this."

She cranked the CD up just past the comfort level to cover up any other noises Happy—who was not here—might make. I'd heard this song. I liked this song. But I definitely preferred it at a few decibels lower, where it would not distort as it came out of the speakers.

Heather still prattled on in her attempt to distract me, but although I saw her lips moving, I could not hear a word over the loud music. Deep in the background I heard a rumble that was not part of the soundtrack. A rumble that turned into a throaty growl. I realized it was the telltale sound of a Harley just a moment before it flashed past the window.

I jumped up and ran to the door. Before I reached it, I was hit from behind. Heather was on my back like a rabid monkey. I staggered forward and fell on my face. I liked hardwood flooring, but not when it smacks me in the nose. I looked up and there was Crapper's nose just inches away from mine. He snarled. I rolled. Heather fell to the side.

I scrambled to my feet. I launched out the front door. Saw a flash of chrome turning out of sight down the drive. Then I tripped over a big white lump of dog and tumbled down the steps. The side of my face slid on the stone walkway before I came to a stop. The pain from that scrape barely had time to register in my neural pathways before Heather was on my back again.

I pushed up with both my arms. Hard and fast. Heather lost her balance and hit the ground with a thud. But Crapper was still attached to my leg. My jeans prevented him from digging into the skin but I could feel the sharp edges of his teeth scraping on the outside of my ankle. I yelled. He dropped his grip. Good. As much as Crapper was annoying me, I did not want to hurt the little dog.

Pete and Labia, peaceful and oblivious, were roused to their guardianship of the property by my yell. Now, barking and galloping, they pounded their big paws at me, drool flying in every direction. I slipped into my car. Slammed the door. I backed up as quickly as I could while taking care not to hit one of the dogs—not an easy feat, as they minced around my car liked crazed carnivores on speed.

Once I cleared the dogs, I tore down the drive, following the motorcycle dust. I reached the end, no motorcycle in sight. I rolled down the windows and listened. There. To the right. I heard the throb of an engine echoing in the hills. I whipped out onto the road following the sound.

I took curves faster than the law and my ability as a driver allowed. I pushed the car and myself trying to gain ground. Then the road ended in a T. Where now? I listened again but could not hear the faintest rumble. I'd lost him. Crap.

The burning sensation on the side of my face screamed for my attention. I flinched as my fingers traced the tracks of the tears in my skin. I lowered the visor and regretted it. Red, scraped, raw. It hurt twice as much now that I saw the damage. Wincing with each touch, I flicked tiny bits of dirt off the surface. My face throbbed with more intensity than one of Happy's drums.

I turned right and headed back to New Braunfels. What did Happy's flight mean? The first, most obvious, conclusion was that Happy killed Faver. Coming in a close second: Happy knew who killed Faver. Then there was the third, useless but practical theory: Happy was a paranoid freak.

Couldn't think of any more reasons now. I had to decide which one was right. Three possibilities. One suspect. It was like the Lady and the Tiger or the—wait, that's three choices. Damn, what a day. I couldn't even get my analogies to fit.

CHAPTER TWENTY-ONE

The next day, I made another weary round of phone calls. Every band member's number ended in an answering machine except for Happy's. There the phone rang and rang and rang. I imagined Heather standing beneath the cathedral ceiling with both hands covering her ears as she muttered, "I can't hear you. I can't hear you." All the while, little Crapper stood by the telephone, back hair bristled, teeth bared, throat throbbing with a suppressed growl, knowing it was me on the other end of the line.

I continued down the list of phone numbers of band associates, my mind tuning out a bit more with every digit I pressed. When someone answered a phone call at last, I was stunned and confused. I'd lost track of what numbers I dialed. "Hello, how are you?" I said, stalling for time to reconfigure my brain.

"Fine. Who is this?"

I rapidly scanned my list and decided most likely I'd just reached Faver's ex-wife. "This is Molly Mullet. Is this Teresa Faver?" I winced, hoping I'd guessed right.

"Tess. It's Tess. But not Faver anymore. I dropped that SOB's last name and went back to the one I was born with—Tess Holland. Who are you?"

"Molly Mullet."

"Well, I got your name first time 'round, sweetie. But your name don't tell me squat. Who are you?"

"I'm an investigator looking into Rodney Faver's murder for

Bobby Wiggins' attorney."

"You need money for that boy's defense fund? As soon as the estate settles, I'll be glad to make a contribution. In fact, I was fixing to have a statue of Bobby erected in the town square."

Red flags were flying up faster than gnats on a summer evening. "So you are not at all distressed by Rodney's passing?"

"Good riddance is all I have to say. Good riddance to bad garbage."

"You mentioned the estate?"

"Rodney Faver was a festering boil on the rump of life. I'm glad that kid lanced it."

As we talked, I looked down at a years-old photo I got off the Internet. A bunch of people in a typical stilted publicity shot. There on the far right was Tess, a big-haired blonde with a big-as-Texas bosom. Rodney was on her left and, no surprise, his eyes were not focused on her hair.

"Yeah, but about the estate? I thought you were Rodney's ex-wife."

"And praise the Lord for that."

"Then how would you get anything in an estate settlement?"

"Hank Schoch, that's how."

"Excuse me?"

"Hank is the leanest, meanest divorce lawyer this side of the Rio Grande. He got a settlement for me that made the angels sing. I got a big lump of cash up front and a lifetime of alimony checks that would make the angels blush. Even if you divide it by the twenty-three years I put up with his crap, I still came out good. But best of all is what Hank got me if Rodney died. The court ordered Rodney to maintain a million-dollar insurance policy with me as beneficiary. And that was just for starters."

"Oh, really? And what would you say Rodney is worth to you now that he's gone?"

"Shoot, I don't know. Probably more than I can count. Wait a minute, honey, are you implying something here? Well, just hold on a minute. The police done went down that road and it's a dead-end street. I was in Vegas with three girlfriends, happily investing Rodney's alimony check into slot machines one quarter at a time. You wanna pin this on somebody other than Bobby, don't be pointing at me. I got a lot from Rodney while he was still alive. There's other folks that were getting nothing but screwed."

"Like who?"

"Take a good look at Trenton Wolfe. He had a love–hate relationship with Rodney for years. One minute he loved him for the success. The next minute he hated him because he was sure Rodney was ripping him off—and he probably was. I never could figure why Trent didn't move on. He had other better-connected managers beating on his door but he stayed with Rodney. I wondered if Rodney had something on him."

"Like what? Like something he could use as blackmail?"

"That's what I been thinking. But shoot, how should I know? Rodney never talked to me much when we were married. He sure hasn't talked to me since. But I'll tell you what. There's something not right about that Wolfe boy. Like he's hiding something."

"But you don't know what?"

"Not a clue. I just sensed it."

"Okay. Trenton Wolfe. Who else do you see as a likely suspect?"

"There were always a bunch of ticked-off people under Rodney's feet. But there was one in particular who'd been foaming at the mouth the last couple of months."

"Who was that?"

"Jesse Kriewaldt."

I paused for more, but she did not oblige. "Who is Jesse and why was he so mad at Rodney?"

"Jesse is a so-called songwriter. He thinks his songs are a gift from God. He's been pitching one after another at Rodney for years. He's been pissed off at him for just as long 'cause Rodney never bought one single song for any bands he represented. Jesse seemed to think he was entitled. But now, the boy's gone over the deep end. He insists that he wrote 'Bite the Moon.' 'Course the credits say that Trent wrote the lyrics—and personally, I can hear his ego in every word—and Stan wrote the music. But Jesse said he wrote it all.

"He was supposed to meet up with Rodney that same day. As I hear it, Rodney was planning on giving him some pittance to make him shut up and go away. I thought that was a stupid idea. I know Jesse. And Jesse cares more about song credit than money."

"So what are you saying, Tess?"

"I'm saying that maybe they did meet. I'm saying that maybe Jesse was insulted by Rodney's offer. I'm saying that maybe things got real ugly."

"Do you know if they met?"

"Nope. Can't say that I do."

"Where can I find Jesse?"

She rattled off his phone number and address and I asked, "What about Happy Parker?"

"Happy? Happy is hopeless. You mean Happy as a suspect?"

"Yes."

"Oh, have mercy. Happy can't cope with anything that is not perfectly aligned with the stars. He's probably sitting up in his cabin in the hills with a quilt over his head pretending that none of this ever happened. Probably trying to convince himself that he never even knew anybody named Rodney Faver. He's pathetic."

"You don't think he had a reason to kill Rodney?"

"Happy doesn't have a reason to do anything but beat his

drums. But you know who I think did it?"

"No. Who?"

"That Bobby they arrested. I think he did him in."

I wanted to come to Bobby's defense, but knew this wasn't the time or place. I stripped my voice of emotion and asked, "Why?"

"Rodney was rude and insulting to anybody he thought was not as smart as him, and that included almost everybody. He'd be especially cruel to someone like Bobby. Rodney talked a lot about euthanasia for the hopelessly stupid. Rodney could've pushed the wrong button, and Pow! The kid went off. Not that I'd blame him."

I hoped the prosecution would not put her on the stand. "Who are the three friends who were with you in Vegas?"

"Oh, so we're back to me again. Back off, honey. I'm not having you annoy them. It's bad enough I had to sic the police on 'em. One of the girls isn't talking to me for that. I've tried to help you, and this is what I get. Well, go bark up another tree, honey, and leave me alone."

The slam of the receiver clapped in my ear. For now, Tess was still a suspect—not on the top of my list but still among the prospective candidates.

CHAPTER TWENTY-TWO

I got only a couple of steps from the phone before it rang. I grabbed and said, "Tess?"

"No, ma'am. 'Fraid not. I'm Stan Crockett, and is this Molly Mullet?"

"Yes, Mr. Crockett, so nice of you to return my call." About damned time, to be precise.

"I understand you've been trying to get hold of me, and I understand you're working for the attorney of this guy who killed Faver."

"I have been trying to get in touch with you, and I am working for the defense in the Faver murder case, but Bobby Wiggins is innocent until proven guilty, Mr. Crockett."

"Stan. Just Stan. Hold on to the Mr. Crockett stuff till I'm too old to know any better, okay? And you're right. Nobody's proven that boy is guilty yet. I suppose you don't think he is."

"No, I don't. That's why I want to talk to you."

"I'll tell you what—why don't we talk over lunch. If I spend too much time on the phone, I start getting itchy."

"Sounds good to me."

"Meet you in forty-five minutes at the Old Solms Mill?"

"Sure. Want to meet out front?"

"You got it. I'm kind of tall and skinny . . ."

"I know what you look like, Stan," I assured him.

"Good. See you then."

The Old Solms Mill? A coincidence or a meaningful choice? The restaurant was right next to Solms Halle. You'd think he wouldn't want to go near the place.

I climbed out of my pajamas and into a pair of jeans and headed for the door. Just in time I remembered that I hadn't brushed my hair yet that day and rushed into the bathroom. I wished I hadn't. My face looked more angry and inflamed today than it did yesterday. I gingerly grazed the side of my face with my fingertips and winced. From eye to chin, the left side of my face was scraped raw.

Half an hour after Stan's call, I pulled into a parking space in the lot across the street from the restaurant. Solms Halle hunkered on the side of the road as if it was getting ready to cross it. The Old Solms Mill, in contrast, was set back from the street, a long curvaceous path leading the way to its door. Full and half whiskey barrels of herbs and brightly colored annuals and perennials flanked the entrance. The fragrance of rosemary teased the air. I couldn't resist running my fingers across the closest one and breathing in a more intense rush of the intoxicating scent from my skin.

The silvery-gray weathered wood of the old mill loomed high at the end of the path. I took a seat on a wooden bench in front surrounded by more flower-filled barrels to wait for Stan.

I recognized him as he approached the other entrance to the path. Even in the bright sunshine, he still looked two days dead. He loped up the walkway with a loose, disjointed stride.

I stood up, called his name and introduced myself.

We followed the hostess through the dark, cavernous inside dining room with its rustic bare-beam ceilings—like most folks on a sunny day, we chose to eat outside on the multileveled dining deck. All along the way, people stopped eating or talking and turned to stare. I didn't know if they recognized that it was *the* Stan Crockett walking in their midst, or if they were just ogling one of the weirdest looking lanky bodies on the face of the earth. But it was a comfort to know they weren't eyeballing me.

The waitress led us to the lower level where, because of the sudden drop of land, we were perched more than seventy-five feet over the rushing waters of the Guadalupe River. After placing our lunch orders, we sat in comfortable silence contemplating the water.

After the waitress set down a pair of lime-crowned Coronas, Stan said, "Okay now, what do you want to know from me?"

"I'd like to know who you think had a reason to kill Rodney Faver."

He leaned back and laughed. "Who didn't is a better question. Faver seemed to enjoy aggravating people."

"I don't think Bobby Wiggins had a reason."

"Maybe. Maybe not. I doubt if he knew Faver well enough to cultivate a genuine dislike for the man."

"What about you, Stan?"

"Me?" A smile crinkled the corners of his eyes, making him look almost alive.

"Did you have a genuine dislike of Faver? Did you have a reason to kill him?"

He grinned and cast his gaze up to the sky. "Probably. I did dislike the bastard. Reason to kill him? Probably had three or four." He leaned forward on his elbows and looked into my eyes. "But you know what? I also had a lot of reason for gratitude. Yeah, maybe we could have made it without Faver— but maybe not. There's a lot of serendipity to any success in the music world. All these little pieces come together in a pattern of random magic and an unexpected synergy erupts and propels you to the top. Remove one little piece, take away one word said or one small action taken, and all you worked for could crumble at your feet."

"So, you're saying a live Faver was more in your self-interest?"

He shrugged and dropped his eyes. "Maybe. Maybe not. But when things were going as well as they were for us, what reason do you have for taking unnecessary risks?"

The waitress approached and slid our lunch orders on the table. Stan two-handed his burger, took a big bite and wiped his mouth. "So, besides me, who else have you got in your sights?"

"How about Tess?"

"Tess? Hmmm." He took a long swig of his beer, his Adam's apple bobbing like a large yo-yo in his scrawny neck. "It was all a little too messy for Tess. She talks like she's hard-core, but she's pretty prissy. She'd be worried she might break a fingernail or mess up her hair. But could she hire somebody to do it? All I can say is that there is no mess involved in a cash transaction."

"You think she did?"

"Maybe. Maybe not."

"How about Happy Parker?"

"You're just twisted over him because he scampered off on you the other night. Happy avoids confrontation like a rabbit—stays away from all kinds at all times."

"Then all he had to do was refuse to answer the door when I knocked."

"True. True."

"Made me wonder if he was guilty."

"Happy? Naw. Happy's pretty harmless. The only violence he's capable of committing is the pounding he gives his drums."

"Well, then, maybe he knows something. Maybe that's why he ran. Maybe he knows who did kill Faver."

"Happy? Happy's not smart enough to figure that out."

"Maybe he's smarter than you think."

"I doubt it. He might be worried that Wolfe did it and if he's caught, all we've accomplished will turn into a mirage—just a shadowy glimpse of success but nothing more. And once you've seen a little piece, you want it all. Even a laid-back guy like Happy."

"Why would he suspect Wolfe?"

"Wolfe was convinced Faver was ripping us off. He bitched about it all the time."

"But he'd been doing that for years. Why would Happy think that now it would turn to murder?"

"I imagine the T-shirt influenced his thinking a bit."

"T-shirt? What T-shirt?"

"The one Happy found stuffed in his kick drum the morning after the gig at Solms Halle."

"And . . ."

Stan leaned forward again, his eyes searching my face. "What happened to you, anyway?"

"Me?"

"Your face looks like a tank ran over it."

"Thanks. Thanks a lot."

"Sorry. Guess that was a bit insensitive. But what the heck happened?"

"I tripped over a dog. Now, about that T-shirt."

"Big dog?"

"The T-shirt. We're talking about the T-shirt, not my beauty mark."

"Okay. Around the neckline of the T-shirt, there was a lot of blood."

"Wolfe's T-shirt?"

"I thought so."

"What did Happy do with it?"

"I don't know."

"Did he turn it in to the police?"

"Oh, I'm sure he didn't do that."

"Why not?"

"He wasn't about to point a finger at Wolfe."

"What about you? Would you point a finger at Wolfe?"

He leaned back in his chair, rocking on two legs. "If I thought he did it?"

"Yeah, if you thought he was guilty."

"Maybe." He clunked back on all four legs. "Maybe not."

"Do you think he did it?"

"Don't know. I've thought about it a lot. Wolfe's known Faver longer than any of us. He's stuck with him for years now, even though he was certain Faver was skimming off the top."

"If he thought Faver was stealing, why did he stick with him?"

"You know, I've asked Wolfe that question more than a few times. But I've never gotten a satisfactory answer."

"Do you think Wolfe is capable of killing Faver?"

"I don't like to think so. But then again, how well do any of us really know anybody?" He pushed up from the table. "Listen, I've got to run. You have any more questions, you just give me a call."

He strode across the decking, and he was gone. I looked at his plate. I hadn't noticed him eating except for that first big bite, but not a crumb of his burger was left. His fries, however, were untouched. I plucked two off of his plate, bit into their saltiness and headed out to my car.

It was visiting hours at the county jail. Time to see if Bobby had any information I could use. Not likely, but I had to try.

CHAPTER TWENTY-THREE

Monica Salazar was at the front desk again when I walked into the county jail. Her lips pursed, her brow furrowed. She said "Miss Mullet" in that same tone of voice my mother used when she said "Molly Anita, what are you up to now?"

"Hi, Monica. How are you today?"

"Miss Mullet, please. I do not want to report you."

"Monica, everything's cool. I'm on Bobby's visitation list. I'm here like an ordinary citizen who wants to visit someone behind bars. There is not a problem."

Her eyes formed tight slits. Her mouth pursed even tighter. She turned to her computer and tapped on her keyboard. As she scrolled down a smile replaced her frown. "Oh, Miss Mullet. I am so sorry. You are on the list. I am sorry for doubting you."

"It's okay, Monica. I deserved it."

"I feel so bad, though. I thought you were gonna . . . well, you know."

"Yeah, I know."

She handed me a numbered pass. "Sorry."

"No problem, Monica. Honest." I turned from the front desk.

"Miss Mullet," she whispered.

"Yes?"

"Lisa Garcia told me what you're doing."

"You know Lisa?"

She nodded. "I'm glad you are doing this. Let me know if I

can help." She cast her eyes around as if searching for eavesdropping ears. Seeing none, she said, "I shouldn't be telling you this, but Bobby's not doing so good."

"He's not?"

"No. They've talked about ad seg because so many of the other guys are teasing him."

I slumped. Ad seg—administrative segregation—just a fancy word for solitary confinement. Poor Bobby.

"But that's not the worst. A couple of guards think he should be on suicide watch. He's been crying for days and he won't eat. See if you can get him to eat. At least a little."

"I'll do what I can, Monica." I knew jail would be hard on Bobby but I thought his laid-back attitude would see him through this, too.

I went into the waiting room and sat down in a sea of ravaged hearts. Some of the visitors to the prison were so defeated by life, they looked barely alive. Others still had enough spirit to don a false front for the loved one they would see today, an artificial cheeriness that insisted, despite evidence to the contrary, that all was well.

The backdrop for their suppressed misery enhanced the futility of it all. Dingy walls with a sad line of the small grimy handprints of children running the length of the one where we lined up to wait our turn. A collection of mismatched furniture rejected from former offices because of its shabbiness. Whatever side of the bars you were on, the county jail was a sad place to be.

Despite my dreary surroundings, a smile stole across my face as my mind drifted back to more pleasant memories of Bobby. No matter what I wanted to do, no matter how nerdy my proposed adventures, Bobby was always willing to join me.

We extracted water samples from the creek and, under the microscope, I thought we discovered new life forms. We drew pictures of them and named them hopajiggers and blobs. It turned out to be mosquito larvae and egg cases but, heck, for one brilliant summer afternoon, we thought we were scientific wonders.

We mixed up gunpowder, saltpeter and charcoal and built rockets out of empty toilet paper and paper towels rolls. Our rockets maxed out at two or three feet but we were thrilled.

Then there were the more quiet moments of discovery. The hours we sat still at the edge of the woods watching spotted fawns frolic. We held our breath with awe when they paused in play to nurse from their mothers.

Bobby had been a big part of my childhood. I had forgotten how much our lives were intertwined. Now they wove together again even more in the face of crisis.

A sergeant barked an order and we all lined up in numerical order, but not in strict sequence. The sergeant went down the line checking our slips of paper, grabbing upper arms and moving one person forward and another back. He sent one young woman home for a bare midriff, another for a plunging neckline that left little to the imagination.

When I saw Bobby behind the glass, my heart fell. His head hung down, his back slouched over the counter—he looked as soft and as small as if he were folding inside of himself. I forced a smile to my face and grabbed the receiver. In slow motion and with great effort, Bobby raised one arm and picked up the one on his side of the glass. He held it loosely to the side of his head. Still, he did not look up.

"Hey, Bobby! What's shakin'?"

Bobby shrugged.

"Bobby, you know I'm your friend, right?"

He shrugged and mumbled a puny, "Yes."

"Bobby, did I ever steer you wrong?"

"No."

"You know I'm out here trying to find the evidence to get you out of jail, don't you?"

"Yes."

"Bobby. I need your help."

"Can't."

"Yes you can, Bobby. You've always been there for me. Whenever I asked. You've got to help me now."

Bobby made no response at all. His head still hung down, obscuring his face.

"Bobby, I need you to be strong."

A big sigh echoed through the line. "Can't."

"Yes you can, Bobby."

Another sigh whispered like a zephyr through the branches of a dead tree.

"Bobby, look at me."

Not a movement. Not a sound.

"Bobby, I need you to listen carefully. Look at me."

He raised his head and red-rimmed, waterlogged eyes turned to mine. His face stretched long. His cheeks sank in like potholes on a neglected road.

"Bobby, they tell me you're not eating."

He dropped his head and mumbled.

"Bobby, is that true?"

He sighed out another, "Yes."

"Bobby, Bobby. Look at me."

He raised his head again.

"Bobby, you've got to promise me you'll eat something."

His shoulders quaked. Tears coursed down his face. Childlike sobs choked his breath. I wanted to wrap my arms around him and rock him to a more peaceful place.

"I wanna go home, Molly," Bobby wailed. "I wanna go home to Mama."

"I know, Bobby. I want you to come home, too. I'm doing all I can."

"They said I could go home if I tole the truth. I done tole the truth, Molly. They won't let me go home."

"I know, Bobby." The helplessness I felt churned my stomach and throbbed in my head.

"I tole 'em I was sorry."

"Sorry for what, Bobby?"

"Just sorry. Sorry for everything. But they won't let me go home."

"Bobby, I promise you I will do everything I can to get you home. But you've got to take care of yourself until I do."

He shook his head.

"Yes, Bobby. You have to—for me—for your mama. Please, promise me you'll eat something for dinner tonight."

He swung his head back and forth.

"Not fair, Bobby. I made you a promise. Now you've got to make one to me. Remember. That's our deal. That's always been our deal."

He pulled his head up and a tiny twinkle of life sparkled in his eyes as he remembered our childhood litany. "Like the two musketeers."

"Yes, Bobby. Like the two musketeers."

"S'posed to be three."

"Yep. I think we lost the other one."

"Aw, we don't need him."

"Nah. The two of us will do just fine."

A smile struggled to find purchase in Bobby's face.

A guard leaned over my shoulder and said, "Time's up."

"Promise me, Bobby. Promise me you'll eat tonight."

"Promise," he said, hung up his receiver and gave me a thumbs-up.

I raised my thumb in response and placed my phone on the

hook. A weight like a lead X-ray apron settled hard on my body. *I cannot fail.* Of all the things I had ever done, nothing was more important than this. Nothing.

CHAPTER TWENTY-FOUR

What a long, long day. A hostile ex-wife, a bass player who left me with more questions than answers and a devastated, deteriorating friend behind bars. I knew I'd be too tired to boil water when I got home. I stopped by McBee's and grabbed a sliced beef barbecue sandwich with pickle, onion and extra sauce.

I kicked off my shoes as I walked in the door and headed to the kitchen. I poured a glass of wine and looked at my answering machine. Blinking. Damn. Three blinks. Double damn. I sighed and pressed the button.

"Hi, Ms. Mullet, this is Monica. I just wanted to say I'm sorry again for giving you a hard time. Let me know if I can do anything, okay?"

The second message was from Lisa Garcia. "*Mija*. You did not tell me. Did you find any fingerprints? Call me."

The third message was just some heavy breathing—not very appealing—followed by a click. Oh, give me a break.

I plopped down with my sandwich, glass of wine and the remote. I zoned in on some mindless entertainment. At some point, I fell asleep in the chair. I woke around eleven and toddled back to bed.

I was half past dead at 3:00 the next morning when I was rudely resurrected by the ringing of the phone. I grabbed for the receiver, knocked over a two-day-old glass of water, cursed my fate and growled, "Hello." I really wanted to say, "Who the hell is this?" but I restrained myself—just another victim of Miss Manners' indoctrination in my formative years.

At the other end, I heard something resembling a human voice, but I wasn't sure if it was speaking English, Spanish or any other language I ever heard. It was a series of gasps, sniffs and high-pitched yips that sounded like a wounded hyena—not that I've actually ever heard one.

"I don't know who this is but if you want me to understand you, you'll need to take a couple of deep breaths and talk slowly."

One deep breath that sounded like a death rattle battered my eardrum. It was followed by a loud round of sobbing.

"Okay. Set down the phone. Go get a glass of water. Take a couple of sips and try again."

The phone clattered and a wailing noise drifted away from the phone and back again. I heard a couple of noisy slurps followed by a whimper.

"Are you back?"

"Happy."

I knew she was not relating her current state of mind, so she must mean Happy Parker. "Is this Heather?"

"Yes," she said but the word was seven syllables long and was punctuated by a blubbering whine.

"Heather, what's wrong?"

"Happy."

"Heather, what's wrong with Happy?"

"Dead. Dead. Dead."

"Heather, where are you?"

"Happy."

"Happy's place?"

Again she responded with a seven-syllable version of "yes."

"Heather, lock your door. I'll be there as soon as I can." I wasn't sure what was going on, but I figured I had a better chance of making sense of this disjointed conversation in person.

I pulled on a pair of jeans and a sweatshirt, grabbed my gun and flew out the door. I was making good time in the light traffic until I got within a few miles of Happy's cabin. A vehicle larger than mine came up on me in the darkness and rode my bumper. Actually, the new Beetle doesn't have a bumper, but that's another story.

I drove on the shoulder to let him pass. Instead, the driver backed off. I pulled back into the lane and he was tight on my tail again. This time high beams flooded my interior with light and made it difficult to see the road ahead. I slowed down and drove over on the shoulder. Once again, he lagged back a bit. Fine, I'll just stay on the shoulder.

And for a few hundred yards, I did. Then the vehicle behind me sped up and drove on the shoulder as close to my rear as he could be without making contact.

Ahead I saw a bridge—and no shoulder. I turned the wheel to get back in the lane, but my tailgater was quicker. A dark SUV pulled up beside me, blocking my path—and the guardrail was straight ahead. I slammed on my brakes. The metal rail grew closer. Larger. My right leg quivered with the intensity of the pressure I applied to the brake. I braced for a collision. I felt a bump. Waited for more. Nothing. My car stopped with only a small nudge to the metal ahead. The SUV shot off into the night. Asshole.

I threw my head back and drew a few ragged breaths, put my car in reverse, backed from the rail and turned onto the road. My arms shook as I held the steering wheel. Too close. Too close.

Now I had to contend with another pair of high beams— these in the other lane coming in my direction. It came closer and the boxy shape of an SUV took form. Was it another vehicle? Or was it the same one doubling back? It was moving fast. Too fast. *Calm down,* I told myself. *Don't get paranoid, Molly. There are millions of SUVs on the road. Hang in there.* The SUV flew past me without braking. Thank God.

Another mile down the road and out of the corner of my eye, I thought I saw something approaching me from the rear. I looked full into the rearview mirror but saw no lights. I kept rolling, then I caught the movement again. Still no lights. But there was something behind me. And it was gaining on me.

A dark shape loomed in my rear window. Suddenly the lights washed me in a blinding stream of white. The turn-off to Happy's place was just ahead. But I couldn't see. Where was it? *Come on, girl. You can do it.* I squinted as I peered ahead. There it was. I flipped on my turn signal and slowed for the turn. I felt a jolt as the bumper nudged into my car and caused me to lurch forward. I struggled to stay on the roadway.

I turned sharp into the dirt lane and careened over the cattle guard. Teeth rattled. Eyeballs bounced. Bones banged against the metal in the seat. I raced up the hill. But the SUV was not following. It had stopped on the other side of the cattle guard. Whoever was in it tapped on the gas pedal over and over, revving the engine but not moving in my direction.

I parked in front of the cabin and jerked out my gun. The sound of my ragged gasps filled my ears. The staccato pounding of my heart gave it a backbeat. I could hear nothing else.

I spun out of my car and into a crouched stance—barrel pointed down the hill. Nothing. No lights. No noise. Then the barking began inside the cabin.

I turned and scrambled up on the front porch. I banged on the door with my fist.

"Who is it?" Heather asked.

"Molly," I hissed.

"Who?"

"Molly. Molly Mullet. Open the door, Heather."

"Pete, Labia, Crapper—shut up! I can't hear a thing."

The door opened a crack. "Who?" she said again.

"Me," I said pushing my face in front of hers.

"Oh, Molly, come on in."

I slid in before the door was all the way open. "Shut it. Lock it. Pull the drapes."

"We don't have any drapes, Molly. What happened to you?"

I put my hand up to the side of my face. No surprise she never noticed the damage the other day when she was riding my back. "You know, when I fell over your dogs and down your steps."

"Oh my, you are a mess," she said.

"Thanks," I said. She was no prize either. Her eyes were as red as overripe strawberries and the tip of her nose looked like Rudolph's on a drunken binge. But now, the tables were turned. She was calm and I was the hysterical one.

"Why, Molly, you've got a gun."

I leaned my back against the front door. "Yeah, a gun. Molly's got a gun. Now, please, get Molly some water. A nice cool glass of water."

Heather headed to the kitchen, casting a leery eye in my direction as she progressed. "You're not scared of the dogs, are you?"

"No. No. Not the dogs," I said between greedy slurps from the glass.

"They won't bite you, you know."

"Sure. Sure," I said.

Pete and Labia had quieted down and were now sprawled on the floor impersonating bearskin rugs. Crapper, on the other hand, still circled my ankles growling.

"C'mon. Sit down," Heather said guiding me by the elbow to the sofa.

I collapsed and in a flash, Crapper jumped up on the back of the sofa and walked across it as agile as a cat. He plopped down his rump and bared his teeth at me.

I rolled my eyes and figured the best tactic was to ignore him. "So, Heather, you rang?" I bit my tongue before I made a rude comment about a fool's errand.

"Happy is . . ." Her lower lip quivered, the tears rolled and the wailing began anew.

Oh, Jeez. I got up and held out my arms. She fell into them, sobbing. I'm not unsympathetic to another bawling woman. Lord knows I've had my moments. But now in the middle of the night, my sleep disrupted, my car nearly run off the road, my patience was a limited commodity. I had the urge to shake her until she pulled out of it but, fortunately, she sniveled her fit to a close before I acted upon my impulse.

We sat side by side on the sofa and I held her two hands between both of mine. "Now, Heather, I need you to stay calm and slowly, carefully, explain the problem."

"Happy is dead." She choked back a threatened sob. "They killed him." Her lower lip quivered and pools puddled in her eyes.

I patted the back of one of her hands. "Who killed him, Heather?"

"The same people that killed Rodney."

"You said 'them.' Do you know it's more than one person? Do you know who they are?"

She wailed again and shook her head.

"Come on, Heather. You've got to calm down and tell me what happened."

"They said it was suicide."

"Who said it was suicide?"

"The sheriff's people and that constable man."

"Why did they say that?"

"There was a note."

"Where?"

"In his wallet." The last word squeaked out as a new wail commenced.

"Where did this happen? And what happened?"

Heather sucked in a deep, wet breath. "Down on 306. They said he deliberately ran off the road over a steep incline. They say he was thrown from his Harley, and about a hundred yards away, his hog was in flames. But I know it's not true. I know it." Her drenched tissue-filled fist pounded down on her knee.

"How do you know it, Heather?"

"Because the note they say he wrote was all wrong."

"Wrong? How?"

"It said he killed Rodney and couldn't live with it. But he didn't. I know he didn't."

I was torn between jubilation that Bobby's release from jail could be imminent and horror that Heather might be right. Whoever killed Rodney might have struck again. Were they—was he—after the whole band?

Heather shook herself like a wet dog and snuffled down her tears. "Happy just could not do that, Molly. Happy runs away from everything. I'm the only backbone Happy's got. Molly, are you listening?"

"Yeah, Heather."

"I know what you're thinking," Heather continued. "This is good for Bobby. Now you can pin it all on a dead guy and Bobby can walk free. But you can't let them do this, Molly. You can't let them pin it on Happy. Maybe Bobby did do it. What then? You want a killer walking the streets? Getting away with murder? Do you?"

"Heather, listen to me. Bobby's in jail. If it was not suicide . . ."

"It wasn't," she shouted. "Aren't you listening?"

"Hold on, Heather. Just a minute. Hear me out. If Happy's death is a homicide, doesn't it follow that whoever killed him killed Faver, too? That means it's not Bobby. Who else could it be? Think."

Heather responded with a new mindless wail.

"Come on, Heather, help me. Where did Happy go when he tore out of here yesterday?"

"I don't know," she shrilled.

"Think, Heather. Where do you think? Who does he turn to?"

"I don't know. I don't know. Maybe Stan. I don't know. Stan keeps the band together. He takes care of problems. But, usually, Happy turns to me."

"Stan Crockett?"

"Yeah."

"Do you think . . ."

"Stan? No. Not Stan."

"Heather, you are going to have to trust me. My first responsibility is to get Bobby out of jail."

"But, Happy . . ."

"I know. I know. I won't forget Happy," I vowed. "I won't let them pin this on Happy without proof. But right now, every hour—every minute—hurts Bobby. A little delay can't hurt Happy now."

Her wail soared up and echoed on the cathedral ceiling. Oh, good grief. I should have chosen my words with more care.

CHAPTER TWENTY-FIVE

He pulled his black Expedition into the garage and shut the door. At one time he wished there were windows in here to let in a little daylight. Now he was glad that there were none.

He turned on the overhead lights and picked up a utility light with a 200-watt bulb. He turned it on and inspected his vehicle.

Dead bugs splattered all over his windshield. That indicated he'd been out in the countryside late at night. He made a mental note to clean off the glass before he drove out of the garage. The front grill held more insect carcasses. Ditto on that.

He knelt down to inspect the chrome bumper. As he suspected, there was a gash of red paint and a small indentation. He sprayed industrial cleanser on the spot and rubbed until every trace of red was gone. He set the rag aside to dispose of later.

He grabbed a small rubber mallet and lay down on his back on the concrete slab. He pulled his head and shoulders under the front of the Expedition. He tap-tap-tapped on the back of the bumper, pounding with a light touch in tedious repetition on the convex metal. At last, it was smooth.

He pulled himself out from under the SUV and examined his handiwork from the outside. No visible sign of indentation remained. He ran a hand over the surface and felt a slight, lumpy irregularity, but not enough to be significant.

He went to his workbench and cobbled together four pieces of one-by-six board, forming a three-foot-long rectangle. Using his power saw, he cut a piece of plywood to the same dimensions. He flinched with the noise and wondered if it would have been wiser to do it the hard way with a hand saw.

When he finished, he laid the piece of wood on top of his rectangle and hammered it in place. He flipped it over and surveyed his box, then caulked the outside seams.

He opened a bag of Quikrete and dumped its contents into a shiny wheelbarrow. He turned out the lights in the garage, raised the door and stepped outside. The first hints of daylight streaked the sky, but brightened little else. He scanned the area for observers. Seeing none, he rolled the wheelbarrow out of the garage and squirted water into it with a garden hose.

Back inside the garage, he opened the passenger's side and pulled out an SSG .30 caliber rifle from the floor of the backseat and laid it on the workbench. Using a plastic bucket, he scooped the wet concrete out of the wheelbarrow and poured a layer of it in the bottom of his box. Then he laid the green gun on top of it and sighed with regret. It had performed as promised and done its job well. He poured more of the concrete mixture over the rifle until the weapon disappeared, and the sloppy gray mass rose to tickle the top edge of the board.

He rolled the wheelbarrow over to the far side of the garage and tossed the bucket in it. He would have to dispose of them, too. What a waste. He picked up the rag with its smears of red paint and dropped it in the wheelbarrow as well.

He pulled Happy Parker's cell phone out of his pocket, pressed in seven digits and hit the button with the symbol of a green telephone receiver. When his call was answered, he said, "Lieutenant Hawkins, please." He shifted his weight from one foot to another as he waited for the detective to come on the line. At the sound of Hawkins' voice, he continued. "Molly Mullet was at Happy Parker's place in the middle of the day yesterday. She returned to his cabin about 3:30 this morning."

He pressed down on the red receiver button without further comment. He pressed the cell phone into the concrete by the barrel of the rifle and pushed it down below the surface.

He cleaned the windshield and scrubbed the front grill of the Expedition. He spotted more insect remains on the back of his side mirrors and wiped them down well. He tossed the rags and brush he used to clean off the bug remains into the wheelbarrow.

He opened the tailgate, lowered the back seats and covered the whole rear area with a sheet of heavy-duty plastic. He hoisted the wheelbarrow and its contents into the back. He drove off to dispose of his cargo while the concrete in the box set and hardened.

Chapter Twenty-Six

I punched Dale Travis' home phone number on my cell with more than a bit of trepidation. If it were me, I'd want to head up to New Braunfels. I'd appreciate getting a head start on the morning rush hour. But I wasn't an attorney and didn't think like one. At the butt crack of dawn, he might not care about any of his clients.

On the third ring, his graveled voice barked, "This better be good."

"I think it is, Mr. Travis, or I would not have called you at this ungodly hour. This is Molly Mullet."

"What is it?"

"There's a suicide-note confession to the murder of Rodney Faver."

"Was the suicide successful?"

"Yes, sir."

"Oh my God. Not Bobby?"

"No, sir. Happy Parker." *Does he have doubts about Bobby's innocence after all?*

"The drummer?"

"Yes, sir. I'm at his house right now."

"Is he there? Are investigators there? You aren't involved in his death, are you?"

"No to all three questions, sir. His girlfriend called me after she got the news of Happy's death."

"I'm heading your way. I should be there by eight this morning—barring a traffic jam in Seguin."

"A traffic jam in Seguin?"

"Big city sarcasm, Molly. Meet me at the coffee shop across from the courthouse at eight. You can do that, right?"

"Yes, sir. But there is one complication. I'm not sure that the cops are right. I'm not sure it was a suicide."

"That's not our concern, Molly. Our job is to get the charges dismissed against our client or, at the very least, get him out on bail while the DA sorts out this new development. Understood?"

"Yes, sir. But what if someone killed Happy? What if it was the same person who killed Faver? What if he's out to take down the whole band?"

"A lot of what ifs, Molly. But here is a certainty: Bobby is not coping well in jail. Our responsibility is the welfare of our client. The devil take the rest. Your job is not, and never has been, to solve this crime. Your job is to dig up enough information to create enough reasonable doubt that no jury will convict our client. Is that clear?"

"Yes, sir."

"Okay. Keep your priorities straight. See you at eight."

Looked like I was headed for another day without end. When I got home, I lay down to take a quick nap, but was too jazzed to sleep. After wasting half an hour trying, I got up, took a shower and dredged through my closet looking for something to wear. I settled on a brown straight skirt, long-sleeved white blouse and a tapestry fabric vest. It screamed teacher to me, but it could be mistaken for paralegal fashion.

I had more than an hour to kill when it struck me that Thelma Wiggins might not know what was going on. I decided to pay her a visit before I went to the coffee shop.

I climbed up the steps of her front porch and pulled back my arm to knock. Before my knuckles hit wood, the door swung open. Thelma stood in the doorway with something close to a smile on her haggard face.

"Good morning, Molly. Come on in. I know why you're here. Dale called me from somewhere on Interstate 10 just a little bit ago."

I must admit I was surprised. I didn't think Dale Travis would consider Thelma Wiggins a priority this morning. But sometimes lawyers surprise me and force me to remember they're human, too. Not often, but occasionally.

I followed Thelma back to the kitchen, where the enticing aroma of sausage and toasting home-baked bread filled the air with a celebration of life. "I figured you'd be here soon after Dale called, so I fixed us both some breakfast. Have a seat at the table. It'll be ready in a minute."

She cracked eggs into a cast-iron skillet where they swam and crackled in a pool of melted butter. "I want to thank you for visiting Bobby yesterday. It did him good."

"You've seen him since then?"

"No. But he called me last night—first time he's called in days. Said something about the two musketeers that made no sense to me at all. Then he told me that he ate all of his supper."

"Fantastic."

"Yes, it is," Thelma said as she slid a plate in front of me. "And he gave you all the credit. I suppose you must be the other musketeer?"

"Yeah. Just some silly thing from when we were kids."

"Not so silly, Molly. It got Bobby eating again." Tears welled in Thelma's eyes, and we finished our meal in silence.

Thelma surprised me by opening her arms for a hug. She clung to me for a moment and then sent me on my way with a whole loaf of homemade bread to take home—if I ever got to go there. When I pulled up to the coffee shop, I was a few minutes early, but Travis was already there. He was sipping from a thick, white mug, looking as polished and prosperous as a diplomat.

Before I could even say hello, he was off and running. "I've already checked. Judge Krause's not in yet, but they expect her any minute. Now, here's the game plan. I'm going to roust the judge as soon as she arrives. I want you to go out to the sheriff's department and get copies of any documents you can on Happy's death. Anything. And I'll call you when we get a hearing set. Keep your cell with you at all times."

He threw back his head and drained his coffee cup. He slapped the mug on the wrought-iron table and picked up his briefcase. "While you're out there, see if you can find out where they sent Happy. He could be at the Bexar County Medical Examiner's Office in San Antonio, or Travis County could have taken him up in Austin." Without a goodbye, he was gone, power-walking across the street to the courthouse.

I drove out to the Sheriff's Office and danced with the bureaucracy. I was heading back to my car when my cell phone rang. Once again, I was not able to blurt out a greeting before Travis started talking. "What did you get?"

"Just the preliminary incident report and it doesn't say much. Just the time, the place and the name of the victim. I begged and pleaded, but they insisted nothing else was completed."

Travis grunted. "Where's the body?"

"I don't know. They pled total ignorance to that question."

"Liars. They just want to be difficult because they know they're wrong. The hearing is set for 3:00 this afternoon. I want you there at 2:45. And since we do not have full police reports, we'll need Happy's girlfriend here, too. Don't trust her to get here on her own power. Drive out there, pick her up and bring her in. And keep that cell with you at all times. Don't even go to the bathroom without it. I need a constant, reliable line of communication with you today. See you at 2:45."

The hearing was more than five hours away. Maybe now I could take a nap? Fat chance. I was too keyed up for sleep. I had to keep busy. I spent my leisure time vacuuming the house, dusting the furniture and rearranging a disaster area in one of my closets.

While I did these mindless chores, I tried to fill my head with positive thoughts. *This afternoon,* I told myself, *Bobby gets out of jail. Today is the day the judge will dismiss the case. This evening, Thelma is going to make dinner for her son, smiling and humming with the same cheerful abandon she knew before Stuart died.*

I tried all the positive reinforcement I could muster, but it was no use. A niggling premonition of doom chewed on every upbeat morsel I could produce and spat it back out at my feet.

Chapter Twenty-Seven

I needed less than two hours to drive out to Happy's, pick up Heather and get back to the courthouse. But I knew I couldn't be late and gave myself a cushion for the unexpected by leaving the house at noon. As I traveled down the road, the weather alternated between patches of light drizzle and stretches of sunshine, aping the yo-yoing of my thoughts.

Flashing colored lights approached me from the rear. I pulled over, expecting the sheriff's department vehicle to speed past me. To my surprise it pulled up behind me and came to a stop.

I couldn't have been speeding. Or was I? What was the speed limit here anyway—forty-five, fifty-five? It changed back and forth so much on these little country roads that I never knew for sure.

A uniformed Hays County deputy stepped out from behind the steering wheel. *Is he really unsnapping his holster? Oh jeez, he is and he's drawing his freaking gun, too.*

I rolled down the window as fast as I could. "Officer, what's wrong? What's the problem? Was I speeding?" I couldn't believe it. He was approaching me in the elbows-locked stance.

"Get out of the car, ma'am. Now. Right now. Keep your hands in my sight at all times. Push the door open slowly. Step out of the vehicle. Slowly. One foot at a time. Step up to the front of the car and put your hands on the hood."

I followed his instructions with impeccable care. I had too much respect for guns to do otherwise. I leaned on the sloping hood of the Beetle and hoped I wouldn't slip down. He approached from behind. He put a hand in the small of my back to hold me in place as he wedged one foot between mine and tapped on them.

"Feet apart. Feet apart."

I spread them as far as my skirt would allow. The steadiness of my position on the hood grew more precarious. The passenger side door of the cruiser opened and the head of Lieutenant Hawkins popped out. *Crap. What was he up to now? And what the heck was he doing with a Hays County deputy?*

He sauntered toward me with all the grace of an overfed duck. My anger grew with every step he took.

"Well, Mullet, looks like you're in a heap of trouble now."

I started to rise up to snap out a witty rejoinder but felt the deputy's hand pressing me back into position.

A car drove by, slowing down to let its passengers stare with open mouths and questioning eyes. Man, this was humiliating. "What do you want, Hawkins?" I snarled like a cheap gangster from an old black and white movie.

The deputy shoved me forward. I stiffened just in time to keep my face from striking the metal surface.

Hawkins put the tip of his index finger on my chin and turned my face toward his. "My, my, my, Mullet. Looks like you've been in a bit of a scuffle." He pushed up the sleeve of my blouse. "And looky here, more signs of a struggle on your arm. Cuff her, deputy. We're taking her in."

"Are you crazy, Hawkins?" I shouted.

The deputy grabbed my right wrist and jerked it back. As he twisted, fire burned in my shoulder, my elbow, my wrist. He slapped on the cuff and the pressure eased.

As the pain subsided, I spat out, "Hawkins, have you lost your mind?"

The deputy grabbed my left arm and put pressure on my

thumb. For a moment, all I could see was pure white with brilliant shooting sparks. I fell forward—face first—on my car. The deputy jerked me backward off the car. I clenched my teeth to suppress a scream.

Hawkins stepped into my space, his oversized belly bumping into my breasts. "You are a person of interest in the Happy Parker homicide, Mullet."

"Homicide?"

"You betcha. As I said, Mullet, you are in a heap of trouble. Stick her in the back, Deputy. I'll follow in her car."

Holding my cuffs, the deputy pushed me forward. When I stumbled over the loose gravel, he bumped my rump with his knee. As he pushed down on the top of my head to stuff me in the car, I hollered out, "Hawkins. Do you know how to work a shift?"

Hawkins laughed and climbed into my poor little car.

As we pulled out, I twisted my body around to peer out the back window. My car jerked a bit as it started out but he did not appear to be abusing my transmission too much. Hawkins' arm came out of the driver's side window. I saw the little daisy-filled vase that brightened my dashboard go flying out of the car and smash on the side of the road.

Chapter Twenty-Eight

Transporting me from the cruiser to inside the station did not bring out the deputy's chivalrous side. He manhandled me as if I were twice his size. Hawkins followed with my purse swinging from one of his beefy fingers. My cell phone rang. I liked my phone's ring. But in this setting, the reggae beat beach tune sounded stupid. Hawkins raised my purse in the air to eye level and stared at it.

"Hawkins, can I get that?" I asked.

He thrust a hand into my bag and pulled out the phone. He looked at the screen and said, "Oh, don't worry about it, Mullet. It just says 'Travis cell' is calling." The ringing stopped and he pressed a couple of buttons. "And it looks like this is about the twelfth time he's called in the last fifteen minutes. Hunh, when I heard that before I thought the jerking of the gears was firing off a CD in your car." He laughed, tossed the phone back in my bag. "If he called that many times, he'll call again."

"Could you at least call him and let him know where I am?"

Hawkins tilted his head to the side. For a brief moment, I thought he was seriously considering my request. "Nah, he'll keep. It's best if you keep men guessing, Mullet."

I was hustled into a dingy little room where cheap plastic, molded chairs in a putrid shade of orange flanked the sides of a long, scarred table.

"We'll take your cuffs off now, Mullet. But if you act up, we'll fasten you to the chair or to that ring in the wall back there."

I bit off the smart-ass retort I wanted to fling in his direction and focused on the relief of having my hands free again. The two men left the room, pulling the door closed behind them.

Hawkins returned right away—my cell phone in his hand. I thought he was going to let me make a call after all and stretched out my hand for the phone.

"Oh, no, Mullet. No. No. No." He propped one foot in a chair and rested his elbow on his knee. He punched in a number.

"KSAT-12? Good. Can I speak to Gina Galaviz, please? Thank you." He grinned at me while he waited. "Look, Gina. I thought you might want to know that the investigator for the defense in the Bobby Wiggins case was just picked up today by the Hays County Sheriff's Department for questioning as a person of interest in the homicide of Happy Parker." Hawkins grinned at me again while he listened. "Oh, yes. I did say homicide." He pushed a button disconnecting the call.

"You are a pig, Hawkins. What do you expect to accomplish with this little farce?"

Instead of responding, he smiled and stabbed another number into the phone. It just amazed me that he could get those chunky fingers in the right place on those tiny buttons. "KGNB? Good. Is this David Ferguson? Great. David, I thought you would want to know that an ex-cop from your 'hood who's investigating the Bobby Wiggins case for the defense has just been picked up in Hays County as a person of interest in the murder of Happy Parker." He terminated the call and turned to me. "Any more questions, Mullet?"

I sat mute.

"Thought not. See ya later."

My eyes followed his back as he left the room. I was alone again. At first I was content to sit still and rub life back into my reddened wrists. But as the minutes crawled by, my anxiety grew.

What was happening in that courtroom? I was certain that Dale Travis was about to be ambushed by the prosecutor. I wanted to warn him. But there was no telephone in sight and no place to hide one.

Why was Hawkins calling Happy's death a homicide? There must be an autopsy report—at least a preliminary one. They must have rushed that through this morning. And if it was a rush job, there had to be something obvious overlooked at the scene. The Medical Examiner did not bow to law enforcement pressure to announce conclusions unless there was no room for doubt.

And does all this mean Heather is right? It must. Faver and Parker's murders had to be connected. If so, it had to boil down to that bloodstained T-shirt Happy found in his kick drum. Did the police find that? They couldn't have or I would not be sitting here right now. I've got to find that T-shirt. I wonder if Heather knows where it is. If she does, she may be the next to die. I've got to get out of here. Lost in thought, I didn't realize I was on my feet pacing and rubbing my right arm until the door banged open.

"Ms. Mullet," the deputy barked. "If you cannot retain your position in your seat, you will force me to restrain you again. And rubbing on that ugly tattoo ain't going to make it disappear."

My butt hit hard plastic at the speed of light. The deputy glared at me as if daring me to defy him.

I smiled and put the sweetness of a sugar bowl into my voice. "Sir, when do you think Mr. Hawkins might come back and talk to me?"

"When he's good and ready," he said as he slammed the door.

Another perfectly good smile wasted on a man with no appreciation for the finer things in life.

CHAPTER TWENTY-NINE

Dale Travis lived by the philosophy that a person is late when not fifteen minutes early. People were a perpetual disappointment to him. When the courthouse bell tolled at half-past two and there was no sign of Molly, he was irritable.

He punched in Molly's number on his cell. No answer. For the next fifteen minutes, he paced the hall and called her number at the end of each lap. At 2:45, Thelma Wiggins stepped out of the elevator and into the hall, heading toward the courtroom.

"Molly's late, Thelma," he said.

"And hello to you, too. Dale. Nice to see you again," Thelma replied.

Chagrined, Dale held out his arms for a hug. Thelma took two steps back. "Sorry, Thelma. I forgot," Dale said. "Listen, I need Molly but I've got to get into the courtroom. Here's my cell. Can you keep calling her until the hearing begins?"

"Sure, Dale. Go on inside. Molly will be here."

By 3:00, Thelma was concerned, too. This was not like Molly. Molly was prompt. Molly was dependable. The hot glow of hope that brought her bouncing to the courtroom today faded to a flickering light. Something was wrong. With great reluctance, she turned the cell phone off, walked into the courtroom and slid into the row behind the defense table.

Dale turned to her with a question on his face. She shook her head. His jaw tightened. His lips pursed. He spun around in his seat.

From afar, it sounded like sleigh bells coming down the hall. As the noise neared, the clanging grew harsh and the whispered shuffling of shackled feet scraped on Thelma's heart. A chain of orange jumpsuits linked at the waist came through the side door. Deputies led them across the courtroom and seated them in the jury box.

Bobby looked bewildered and distressed as he sat with his fellow prisoners. Then his eye caught his mother's and he smiled. He lifted his cuffed hands to give her a thumbs-up. In the process, he jostled the man next to him who gave him a quick, hard elbow into the side. Bobby winced. Another little piece of Thelma died. The chains struck up another discordant symphony as the prisoners stood when the judge entered the room.

Dale argued his case for the dismissal of all charges against Bobby Wiggins for the murder of Rodney Faver. When he finished, the judge turned to the prosecution.

"Your Honor," District Attorney Ted Kneipper intoned, "the state believes this motion is premature. The investigation into the death of Happy Parker and his possible involvement in the murder or Rodney Faver is ongoing."

Judge Krause bowed her head and studied the papers before her. Travis used this lull in the proceedings to study his opponent. There was a reddish tint high on his cheekbones—he was excited about something. Not a good sign. His jawline was pink and stubble-free. That shave was less than an hour old. That was even worse—the man obviously had plans to strut before the TV cameras. *What surprise is he going to pop on me now?*

The judge broke Dale's reverie. "Motion denied," she said.

Dale Travis sprang to his feet. "Your Honor, we request a ruling on our second motion."

"Proceed, Mr. Travis," she said with a nod of her head.

"Your Honor, we ask that you reconsider the denial of bail for our client in light of these recent developments. The appropriateness of the charges against Bobby Wiggins has been seriously brought into question by Happy Parker's written deathbed confession to the crime with which Wiggins is charged. The presumption of the innocence of my client demands that he be released pending further investigation."

Ted Kneipper was on his feet. "Your Honor?"

"Yes, Mr. Kneipper."

"The State would like to submit to the court a copy of the Medical Examiner's report regarding the death of Happy Parker."

"Objection, Your Honor," Dale Travis barked. "The defense has never seen this document. In fact, we were unaware of its existence."

"With apologies to the court, Your Honor, the State only received this report moments ago."

"We're not at trial, Mr. Travis. Objection overruled. You may submit the report, Mr. Kneipper."

Kneipper handed a copy to the bailiff. "Your Honor, you will see from this autopsy report from the Bexar County Medical Examiner's Office that the manner of death was homicide."

"Objection, Your Honor."

"Overruled."

"As you see, Your Honor," Kneipper continued, "despite the presence of a suicide note and the conclusions of the officers at the scene, Happy Parker's death was not caused by injuries sustained in a motorcycle accident, whether intentional or not. There is a bullet lodged in Happy Parker's skull. And since no weapon was recovered at the scene, the assumption is clear:

Happy Parker did not pull the trigger. A person or persons unknown fired that fatal shot."

"Do you have a suspect, Mr. Kneipper?"

"No, Your Honor, but the investigators are questioning a person of interest up in Hays County as we speak."

"Your Honor," Travis said, "the presence of a person of interest in Hayes County is even more reason to grant my request for bail."

"On the contrary, Your Honor," Kneipper said. "Investigators have found nothing to link the murder of Rodney Faver to the Happy Parker homicide."

"The note is a clear link," Travis argued.

"At this time, investigators suspect that the person of interest may have played a role in Parker's death for the sole purpose of diverting suspicion from Mr. Travis' client," Kneipper explained.

An unpleasant thought formed in Dale's mind. He turned and scanned the courtroom. Molly Mullet was not there. *Of course not. Molly Mullet is the person of interest now in custody one county north of here.*

"That is an outrageous allegation, Your Honor," Travis protested.

"Motion for bail denied, Mr. Travis. If you have no further business for this court, we will move on to the next case."

Dale retrieved his cell phone and bolted out to his car. Thelma stayed in her seat, unwilling to leave while Bobby was still there. She felt broken and hollow. But she turned toward Bobby, stuck her thumb in the air and smiled.

CHAPTER THIRTY

An hour passed. Then an hour and a half. Toward the end, I was entertaining myself by looking for bunnies, dogs and people in the peeling paint—sort of like the childhood game of looking for shapes in the clouds, only a lot more depressing.

Finally, the door eased open and in walked Lieutenant Hawkins looking very pleased with himself. "Sorry to keep you waiting, Mullet."

Yeah, right, I thought. But I smiled and said, "No problem, sir."

"I was wondering if you could tell me where you were on the night that Happy Parker died."

"How about you tell me where you think I was, Hawkins. That will save us some time. And after you do that, I would like to call my attorney."

"You're not under arrest, Mullet. You don't have a right to call anyone."

"Well, then, if I'm not under arrest, then I think I'll just go on home." I placed my palms on the table and pushed myself to my feet.

"Sit, Mullet. I'm not joking around with you here. This is serious."

I slid back into my seat and stared at him. "What's troubling you, Lieutenant?"

"You were out at Happy's place before his murder. You were out at Happy's place after his murder. I want to know where you were in between."

"I'm at a disadvantage here. You keep calling Happy's death a murder, but the cops on the scene said it was an accident. I don't know why you are saying otherwise."

"Sure you don't. Look at you, Mullet. Your face. Your arms. You want to explain how that happened?"

"I'd love to. But first I need to talk to my attorney."

"You need to talk to an attorney? You were a cop, Mullet, you know how this works. Asking for a lawyer is like waving a red flag with 'guilty' written on it in big, bold white letters. If you didn't do it, what do you have to hide?"

"Lieutenant, have you ever for one moment considered that Happy's murder and Rodney Faver's murder are connected?"

"It's crossed my mind."

"Do you realize that means Bobby Wiggins could not be responsible for Rodney Faver's murder?"

"I ran that thought up a flagpole and saluted it a time or two."

What is it with this guy? One minute he's spitting out ghetto slang, the next he's recycling phrases from my grandmother's trash bin. "Then why aren't you out there looking for who killed them both?"

"I am, Mullet."

I laughed. He must be kidding. He made me for both homicides? But I looked in his eyes and saw no amusement lurking in the shadows. "You think I killed them?"

"Just the other day, you spent a considerable amount of time target shooting. And you were damned good."

"Did Eddie tell you that?"

Hawkins did not respond.

"Oh, come on, Hawkins. Get real. If I killed Faver, why in heaven's name would I be working to get Bobby Wiggins off the hook?"

"Stranger things have happened, Mullet."

"Be logical, Hawkins."

"I am being logical. Perps often insert themselves into an investigation to find out what we know—what we're thinking."

"If that were the case, Hawkins, it would be pretty stupid of me to be working on the side of the defense, wouldn't it?"

"Perps are stupid. That's why they're perps."

"I'm going home, Hawkins."

"No, you're not. Make one move and I'm cuffing you to the chair."

Outside of the ratty little interview room, a tempest was brewing. Loud voices struggled to talk over one another. In the midst of all the din, I heard the welcome voice of Dale Travis.

"You stay right here, Mullet," Hawkins said as he opened the door and left the room.

With the door ajar, the voices outside the room were now distinct. "I demand to see my client immediately," Dale shouted.

"She's not your client. She works for you," Hawkins said.

"The two are not mutually exclusive, officer. I do not discriminate on any basis."

"Are you implying that I do?" Hawkins asked.

"I'm sure your record speaks for itself. I demand to see my client now."

"Your client is not under arrest and therefore she is not entitled to an attorney at this time," Hawkins countered.

"Then charge her or let her go," Dale insisted.

"She's a person of interest and I have not finished questioning her."

"Hawkins!" Ted Kneipper's voice rang out from the doorway.

I peered out the crack of the door to make sure it really was Kneipper. It was. Something very odd was going on if he came all the way up here to tug on Hawkins' leash.

"The attorney is within his rights," Kneipper said. "Release his client."

The look Hawkins shot at Kneipper was lethal. I was sure glad he was not looking at me. With clenched fists, Hawkins turned and stomped out of the room.

Travis put his arm around my shoulders, plucked my purse from the property desk and escorted me outside. The media frenzy instigated by Hawkins' telephone calls was in full tilt in the parking lot. Microphones poked in our faces. Flashes burned circles on our retinas. Video cameras followed our every move. Each shouted question was answered by a "no comment" from Dale.

I huddled deep under his arm, my head hung low. I now understand why so many people made the futile gesture to cover their faces as they struggled through hordes of hungry reporters.

Dale deposited me in the passenger seat of his car, walked around and climbed behind the wheel. The pack moved in and surrounded us. Dale popped his car into reverse and eased backwards, scattering reporters and cameramen in his wake.

"How many points do I get if I hit one? Do I get double if they're carrying heavy equipment?" Dale laughed.

I couldn't believe it. I'd been tormented and harassed and he was grinning ear to ear. "Dale, what about my car?"

"Don't worry. Oops, almost clipped that one. My paralegal is driving your car back to New Braunfels."

"But does she know how to work a stick?"

For a moment, his grin faded. "I don't know. I never thought to ask."

Oh, my poor car.

CHAPTER THIRTY-ONE

I was under strict instructions from Dale Travis to lie low today while my name and face were splattered across the news. "The furor will die down if you become invisible. Screen all your calls through the answering machine. Do not even set a foot outside of your house."

I was only joking when I asked if I could go out and get my mail. But Dale was not joking when he said, "Absolutely not. Stay behind closed, locked doors and pulled drapes every minute of the day."

I hated the thought of leaving my mail out in the box all day for anyone to rifle through it while I wasn't looking. I suppose that was a bit paranoid, probably a bit egocentric to even think anyone would be interested in rifling through my mail. But it still bothered me.

Who could I trust to retrieve my mail? Lisa? Yes, Lisa. I hadn't returned her last call. I could call her now and invite her over for lunch. I dialed her number at work.

"New Braunfels Police Department. Lisa Garcia speaking."

"Lisa, this is Molly."

"Molly. Molly. Molly. *Pobrecita.* What is going on? Where are you? When can we get together? I tell you, Molly, I gave that Lieutenant Hawkins a piece of my mind—not that he would know what to do with it. What was he thinking? That man is *loco.* How are you? Are you okay?"

"I'm fine, Lisa. I'm just lying low today."

"Hah! I bet that Hawkins wishes he could lie low."

"Were you that hard on him?"

"Yes. But he deserved it. And I wasn't the only one. The Hays County Sheriff called up here throwing a fit. Seems like Hawkins played his little game up there without notifying anyone in major crimes. And the Texas Rangers are beside themselves, too. Called Hawkins a hot dog."

"Really?"

"Yes, *Mija*. He has been called on the carpet so many times today, he's worn a hole in it. Now, what can I do for you?"

"Would you come over and have lunch with me?"

"Of course. I would love to."

"And could you grab the mail out of my box on your way in?"

"Oh, are you afraid of your mailbox after what happened the other day? Poor Molly. *Pobrecita.*"

I tried not to let her hear even the slightest taint of irritation in my voice—but jeez, I'm not a ninny. "No, Lisa. I am not afraid of my mailbox. I just . . ."

"That's okay, Molly. I understand. It will be our little secret."

I suppressed my growl.

"Do you want me to pick up lunch on my way?" Lisa asked.

"Oh, no, Lisa. I'll fix lunch for us. No problem."

"See you at noon."

I stood in front of the refrigerator with "no problem" ringing in my ears. It seemed as if I'd spoken too soon. I had the supplies I needed to make grilled cheese sandwiches, but that was about it. In the pantry, I found a lonely can of Campbell's tomato soup—the bright red and white can, refuge of the desperate. Okay. Grilled cheese and tomato soup. Simple. Homey. Could be a lot worse.

The sandwiches sat on the counter waiting to grill. The soup simmered on the stove. I looked out the front window and saw a blond woman in high heels and sunglasses walking down the street. She stopped at my mailbox, opened it and extracted my mail.

I was ready to launch myself out the front door when the blonde turned and started up my sidewalk. There was something about her walk that looked familiar. That little strut in her step. I've seen that before. Lisa? I cracked open the door and whispered, "Lisa?"

"Shush. Shh. Shh. Shh. Shush." She mounted the steps and squeezed through my front door.

"Lisa?"

"This wig itches," she said, pulling it off of her head. She tossed her real hair and prinked it with her fingers.

"Lisa?" My mental turntable was stuck in a groove.

"Yes. Yes. Yes. What? What? What? You've never seen a wig before?"

"Yes. But where did you get a blond wig?"

"I've had it for ages. You never know when it might come in handy."

"You've used it before?"

"Many times," she said, twirling it on her finger. "Many, many times. It is very useful for spying on boyfriends."

"Boyfriends?"

She nodded and gave me an enigmatic smile. "And it is a good thing I wore it today. I parked a couple of blocks away to case your house. There is a man sitting in the car two houses up staring in this direction."

"What?"

"Look," she said pulling back the edge of the drape with one index finger and pointing with the other.

"Is it a cop?" I asked.

"Don't know. He put a newspaper in front of his face when I

got near. But cop, reporter or killer, Molly, whoever he is, he's bad news."

Great. I grilled the sandwiches, ladled the soup and served our lunch.

"Grilled cheese and tomato soup," she gushed. "My favorite. How did you know? You should not have gone to so much trouble."

I didn't have the heart to tell her I had no choice. I updated her on everything that had happened since I picked up the fingerprint powder from her in the parking lot.

"I'll go to work and get back in Lieutenant Hawkins' face."

"It seems like he's got his hands full already, Lisa."

"I won't be happy until he turns in his badge."

"Isn't that a little harsh?"

"After what he's done to you, how can you even ask that? *Madre de Dios,* Molly, you are too softhearted. You need someone watching over you twenty-four/seven. Unfortunately, I have to work for a living."

Lisa wiggled the wig back over her hair. "Call me," she said as she walked out the door.

The phone rang all afternoon. It was a mixture of hang-up calls and messages from the media begging me to return their calls. I almost did call Gina Galaviz but knew Dale would seek the death penalty if I did. At 5:30, the answering machine picked up on a different kind of call.

"Hey, Molly. This is Stan Crockett calling to see how you're holding up today."

I snatched the receiver, pressed the stop button on the recorder and said, "Stan, I'm here."

"Good. Glad I got you. Seems like you've been having a rough day. Thought maybe somebody ought to take you out to dinner."

"Sorry, Stan, I'm on strict orders not the leave the house."

"You're under house arrest?"

"Not exactly. My attorney has ordered me confined to quarters."

"Maybe you ought to get another attorney."

"What makes you say that, Stan?"

"Seems to me like he has a serious conflict of interest."

"Don't be silly."

"I'm not, Molly. I'm just thinking of you. If these murders are pinned on you, his first, primary client walks out of jail and Dale Travis is a hero. And you are left holding the bag. I only say this, Molly, because I care about what happens to you."

Talk about conflicting emotions. His suggested suspicion of Dale's motive churned my stomach. But Stan's concern for me brought a flush to my cheeks and sent tingles up and down my arms. Stan Crockett may be odd-looking, but, I swear, he has the most seductive voice in the world.

In a near whisper, he said, "So c'mon, Miss Molly. Come dance with me by the light of the moon."

I felt the edges of my resolve eroding like the sand on a stormy beach.

"Dale Travis will never know."

That remark snapped me back to the reality of my situation. "Maybe not, Stan, but someone will. There's a car two doors down with someone inside of it. It's been sitting there all day."

"So we wait until it's dark and you slip out the back door."

"If one snatch of video is shot, if one photo is snapped, Dale Travis will have my head."

"So, we go down to San Antonio to some raucous, jumping place and get lost in the crowd. Or better yet, we'll go some place secluded and intimate where it'll feel like we're the only two people in the world."

My knees and my will both weakened. The beep of call waiting straightened my spine. "Sorry, Stan. I've got to stay in tonight. I've got another call. I'll talk to you later." I pressed the button to the other line before he could tempt me again. "Hello."

"I thought I told you to screen all of your calls."

"I have been, Dale. I was on another line and forgot."

"Don't forget again. You've been inside all day?"

"Yes." Good grief. He's worse than my father.

"Good. You're being watched."

"I know. I spotted the car up the street. Who is it?"

"I'm not sure. There are a lot of rumors going around, so you probably have more than one watcher."

"Is one of them paid by you?" I felt like an ungrateful wretch the second those words were out of my mouth.

"I'll ignore that comment, Molly. You've been through a lot the last couple of days. I doubt that your spies will last through the night. But if you want to go anywhere tomorrow, first take a walk around the block and make sure no one is demonstrating any interest in you."

"Will do."

"Get some rest tonight. And, Molly?"

"Yes, sir?"

"Be careful."

Those last two words were not a comfort.

I checked the locks on every window and door at least five times. I checked the chamber in my gun at least twice as many times as that. When I lay down in bed, I thought about getting a dog again. I'd feel safer. And I wouldn't be all alone.

But thoughts of a dog always turned to thoughts of Charlie. I fell to sleep with tearstains on my face and dampness on my pillow.

CHAPTER THIRTY-TWO

There was a side of me that longed to indulge in a couple of days of feigned agoraphobia, but the restlessness that inhabited the other side vetoed that notion without hesitation. Today I would try to wrap up some loose ends in Austin. Thank heaven for Austin—where jeans and T-shirts are acceptable apparel almost anywhere and at any time. I slid into my most comfortable pair, topped it with a Leon Russell T-shirt and was on my way.

First of all, I needed to talk to Trenton Wolfe. Since he wouldn't return any of my calls, I would drop in on him at home. Then there was that keyboard player—what was his name? I flipped through my notes. Oh yeah, Fingers—Fingers Waller aka Francis Xavier Waller. I had an address for him in South Austin. Finally, there was Jesse Kriewaldt. I had no clue where to find him, but I knew a few places to look.

After an hour on Interstate 35, I headed out Ben White to Capital of Texas Highway and into the rolling hills of far west Austin. Expensive homes sprouted on this hill with the same prolific abandon demonstrated by the dandelions in my backyard.

I drove down roads designed with artful curves and lined with manicured lawns. I rang Trenton Wolfe's doorbell and waited. I pressed the buzzer again and turned to survey the view. It was breathtaking. One rolling hill followed another as the land fell down into a valley where the skyline of downtown

Austin beckoned with the magic promises of Oz. I rang one more time and gave up. I jotted a note on the back of a business card and stuck it in the doorframe.

Time for South Austin, a funky enclave of hipsters and polished rednecks. A deeper contrast to far west Austin couldn't be found. It was the only place in the city where pick-up trucks outnumbered SUVs, the area with the lowest percentage of houses with air conditioning and largest percentage of people who used human-powered push mowers instead of the polluting kind. It was the birthplace of slogans like "Keep South Austin Weird," "South Austin—too cool to bulldoze," and—my personal favorite—"South Austin—we're all here because we're not all there."

I tooled down the main drag, South Congress Avenue, past two fabled landmarks, the Continental Club and Allen's Boots, to a little side street that looked seedy even by South Austin standards. Here was the last known address of Fingers Waller.

I rang the bell, heard nothing and knocked on the door. I heard a woman's voice yelling, "I'm coming. I'm coming." I could only hope she was talking to me and not expressing her ecstasy under the ardent ministrations of Fingers Waller.

The door swung open. "Yeah?" the woman said.

The first thing I noticed about her was her eyes. They were dark and flat with no light reflected in their depths. Then I noticed her hair—long and blond, stringy and matted, as if two weeks had passed since its last encounter with a bottle of shampoo.

"Hi, I'm Molly Mullet," I said handing her a card. "I'm investigating the murder of Rodney Faver and I'd like to talk to Fingers Waller."

"Who wouldn't?"

"Is he here?"

"Get real. Do I look like a woman living in domestic bliss

with the man of my dreams?"

"Do you know where I could find him?"

"For all I know, he's tinkling the ivories at some Holiday Inn off the interstate in Nebraska."

"Nebraska?"

She rolled her eyes and audibly exhaled while shaking her head. "A figure of speech. Okay?"

"When's the last time you saw him?"

" 'Bout a week before Faver bit it. Good ole Francis Xavier tucked his keyboard under his arm, called me a few choice names, shoved me to the floor and walked out the door."

"You haven't seen him since?"

"Nah. He did call a couple of times that first week, but I was still pissed off so I hung up on him."

"Do you have any idea where he might have gone?"

"Probably bunking with Wolfe. He always goes whining to him when he has a problem." She sneered.

"I thought all the guys went to Stan Crockett?"

"Crockett? Shit. He's not the saint everybody makes him out to be."

"What do you mean?"

"Listen, I only know what Fingers told me and Fingers is not here. I don't know where he is and I don't care anymore. Just go away and leave me alone."

The door slammed in my face.

I headed next for a daytime hangout in South Austin for musicians and the wannabes who wanted to see them: Ruta Maya Coffee. Behind many businesses in Austin beat the heart of an idealist. Ruta Maya was no exception. The company was founded on the principle of returning a fair portion of the profits for the producer of the coffee. Their goal: to empower the Mayan farmer as a viable economic force in his community. As a result, they offered only shade-grown coffee beans from a cooperative of organic producers in the highlands of Chiapas, Mexico. At Ruta Maya, even black coffee was served with a heaping teaspoonful of righteousness.

It was more spacious than the chain coffee shops. Its industrial ceiling with exposed pipes and ductwork loomed over partial walls painted in bright colors and covered with an ever-changing exhibition of artwork. At night, Ruta Maya transformed into an eclectic venue for music and poetry readings. It was so Austin, it was surreal.

When I walked in, I spotted Ray Wylie Hubbard tucked in a corner with a couple of friends. Once the wild child of progressive country music, best known for writing "Up Against the Wall Redneck Mother" and his rowdy stage shows, Ray and his music have matured. Blues overtones colored his latest releases, making him one of the most esteemed songwriters and performers in American roots music. His warm, weathered voice and shaggy, unassuming demeanor was a recognizable presence throughout Texas and beyond.

To Ray, Jesse Kriewaldt was, in all likelihood, just another drop in the ocean of unsung songwriters that dogged his steps daily, handing off CDs and looking for a big break. Those were the people I wanted to meet.

I scanned the room, looking for faces filled with more desperation and hunger than Ray had known for years. I spotted a trio of prospects at a table in the middle of the room. I grabbed a cup of coffee and approached them.

"Hey, guys. Do any of you know Jesse Kriewaldt?"

"Why?" said a pencil-thin young man with pitch-black hair and skin as white as a subterranean worm.

"I'd like to talk to him."

"Why?" he asked again.

"I'm an investigator on a murder case down in New Braunfels and Jesse knew the victim."

"So?" the worm said.

"Ease up, Gordon," said the blond ponytailed occupant at the table. "Yeah. We know Jesse," he said to me as he stroked a straggly goatee. "Are you a cop?"

"Nope. Investigator for the defense."

Blondie pushed a chair out with his foot. "Have a seat. Are we talking about the murder at Solms Halle?"

"Yes. You know something about it?"

"Just rumors, man, nothing more. But, hey, I haven't seen Jesse for days. Usually see him here two, three times a week. Expected to see him here today. What the hell did you do to your face?"

The question took me by surprise. I'd been avoiding my reflection to put the injury out of my mind. My hand flew to my face and an itching sensation crept across my skin. Beneath my fingertips, I felt long streaks and scabs. It was all I could do not to yield to the urge to scratch the wounds bloody. "Oh, that," I said. "I tripped over a dog."

"And he attacked your face?"

"No. I landed on my face."

"Ouch. You know, my sister was real clumsy, too. My mom sent her to special classes to teach her how to fall without hurting herself so much."

Clumsy? I am not clumsy. Well, maybe a little. I smiled a puny smile and changed the subject. "Do you know where Jesse lives?"

"Don't know that he exactly has a regular place."

The silent member of the trio spoke up. He was spared the wormy whiteness of his friend by the random fate of being born Hispanic—but he was the palest Latino I've ever seen. "He crashed at my place all last month. But I don't know who's putting him up now."

Ponytail darted his eyes around the room, leaned forward and whispered, "You know, Jesse wrote that song 'Bite the

Moon,' Wolfe's big hit. Trenton Wolfe stole it from him."

"I heard Jesse claimed that," I said.

"Well, it's true," Ponytail insisted as the other two provided a back-up chorus of affirmation.

"How do you know?"

"We heard the CD," Gordon the worm spat out as if daring me to call him a liar.

"You did? Interesting. Do you have a copy of it?"

The three looked at each other then turned to me and shook their heads and sighed. Rats.

"But he was supposed to see the dead guy up in Solms that day before the show. Did you know that?" Ponytail asked.

"Did he meet with him?"

"Don't know. But he said he was going to work out a deal with the dead guy. He was going to get paid *and* he was going to get attribution. And trust me, it's easier to get cash than to get songwriting credit when somebody steals your work."

"Have you seen him since that day?"

"Yeah. But he didn't want to talk about it," the pale Latino said. "When I brought it up, he acted pretty weird. Like he had bugs crawling under his skin or something."

"Really? Do you think he could have killed Faver?"

They looked at me with disgust and horror. Their distaste could not have been more intense if they caught me desecrating the statue of Stevie Ray Vaughan down at Town Lake. One by one, they popped to their feet, stuck their hands in their pockets and filed out the door.

Jeez. Two for two. My tact needed some serious work.

CHAPTER THIRTY-THREE

I headed over to Lamar to check out another daytime haunt of
local musicians, South Austin Music Store. The neon guitar
perched atop the long, flat-roofed building made it impossible
to miss. The sign on their lot said "Musicians Parking Only." I
chose to ignore it and pulled into an available slot. If questioned,
I'd sing. It wouldn't be pretty, but then again, nobody around
here was expecting a diva.

It was a bit difficult to walk around inside South Austin
Music. The place was packed tight with gear. Guitars hung
from endless racks on the walls. Basses stood in a cluster as if
seeking warmth. Folk instruments gathered together in a corner
without ethnic distinction. And, of course, there were amps, accessories, spare parts and a repair shop, too.

I asked around and did find a couple of people who knew
Jesse—sort of. But none could remember when they last saw
him or knew where he might be now. After running into two
stone walls today, I was feeling a bit on the stubborn side and
stuck around for a couple of hours talking to everyone who
came in and feigning interest in musical paraphernalia when the
need arose.

Stars had replaced the sun by the time I headed toward
downtown. I grabbed a Thunder sub on the way and ate it in
my car. I traveled past the downtown area into the adjacent
campus of the University of Texas. There, I went to the Texas
Union building, home of the Cactus Café.

For more than twenty-five years, this venue has built an acoustic music tradition and gained national recognition in the process. Many singer-songwriters like Lyle Lovett, Lucinda Williams and Robert Earl Keen kicked off their careers on the Cactus Café stage. Their success was a magnet for those who wanted to follow in their footsteps.

I hung out, listened to some good music and chatted up as many people as I could. The guy behind the bar and all the waitstaff knew who Jesse was—but that was all they knew.

When weariness set in, I called it a night. Earlier in the day, I'd planned to make a detour into San Marcos on my way back home. I wanted to pay a visit to the Cheetham Street Warehouse. If anyone knew Jesse, owner Kent Finley would. But I was just too beat. As I drove past the city on the interstate, I made a mental note to find out which night was open mike and drive back up here then.

All in all, a wasted day. I was whipped, mentally and physically. When I pulled into my driveway, I sat in my car for a few minutes until I found the energy to move.

I trudged up to the door and froze. Light from the street lamp glinted off of something on my doorknob. I whipped out my keys. For the first time in three months I was grateful for the little key chain light my brother-in-law picked up for me at a soybean convention. I shone its little beam on the knob. A loop of guitar string winked back at me.

I pulled my gun and took a step back. A rush of adrenaline washed away my fatigue in a flash. I was on high alert. Gun on the ready. Ears fine-tuned. I edged my way to the back of the house.

I shone my little light on the back doorknob. Nothing there. I eased the key into the lock and shoved the door open. It banged hard into the wall.

With bent knees and extended arms, I worked my way

through the house room by room. A wave of nausea swept over me each time I threw open a closet door, a shower curtain, a large cabinet. I found no one.

I went back through the house again, looking for any indication that someone had been inside in my absence. I searched for anything moved, disturbed or missing. I checked all the windows, making sure they were locked. I pulled all the drapes. I examined every opening to my house for signs of forced entry. Nothing was damaged. Nothing was out of place. I exhaled my relief.

I made a cup of chamomile tea and sipped it in the silence of my living room. Listening. Thinking. Rubbing on my arm. Wondering what I was missing. Where was the key to open the door to Bobby's jail cell? And why couldn't I find it?

Who killed Rodney Faver? Trenton Wolfe, who made an art of avoidance? Jesse Kriewaldt or Fingers Waller, whose absences made the heart grow full of suspicion?

What about Rodney's ex-wife in a murder-for-hire scheme? Stan Crockett? Mike Elliot? The only person I could scratch off my list was Happy Parker—and I sure couldn't credit my outstanding investigative skills for that.

And what about Heather? Unlikely, but not impossible. But why? Killing Happy was an easy fit. Relationships hide fatal bedfellows in ways that no one can imagine from the outside looking in. But what earthly reason would she have to kill Rodney Faver?

And then there was me. I wasn't on my own list of suspects. But I topped Hawkins' list. Oh, man, I had to shut off my mind.

I wanted to take a shower to wash off my body's adrenaline-induced stench, but I was too edgy to confine myself behind a shower curtain with water thundering in my ears. I stood in front of the sink and used a washcloth to clean myself up as best as I could.

I didn't know if I could sleep. But I would try. I pulled back the bedspread. My eyes were tricking me. I closed them tight. I shook my head. I opened them. It was still there. Another coil of guitar string rested right on top of my pillow.

CHAPTER THIRTY-FOUR

He hunkered down across the street, concealed from view. He enjoyed seeing the rigidity that snapped into Molly's body as she approached her front door.

He savored her anxiety as her gun flashed in the glow of the streetlight. He watched her edge carefully around the house. He had a childish urge to sneak up behind her and shout, "Boo!"

She disappeared from sight. Then he saw lights going on in the house one by one. He saw glimpses of her stiff body as she passed by the front windows.

He shifted his weight, uncomfortable and impatient, as she sat still as a sleeping cat sipping from a cup in the chair in front of the window.

She left the room and his sight for an interminable period of time. His thighs cramped. He stood, stretched and shook them out, taking care to remain hidden.

Her bedroom was at the front of the house, but her blinds were drawn. Nonetheless, he could see the shadow of her passing. He knew she was going to bed. All the rest of the house was now dark.

He knew she was about to find the memento he left for her. He wished she would scream when she did. But he knew she would not.

He consoled his disappointment with the knowledge of her fear. He knew it rippled through her body like a striking snake.

Ripping at her gut. Pounding in her heart. Stealing her breath. He knew she was afraid. And her fear made him smile.

Chapter Thirty-Five

I didn't get to sleep until daylight. I slept until my telephone rang midday. I pick up the receiver without thinking.

"Is this Molly Mullet?"

"Yes, it is."

"This is Bart Seidell. I am an attorney representing Trenton Wolfe. I am calling to warn you that your harassing phone calls to my client will no longer be tolerated. And you must stop stalking him immediately. One more incident and we will file charges."

"I have not made harassing telephone calls."

"Twenty-two calls in a week is harassment in my book, Miss Mullet."

He did have a point. "But I am not stalking him."

"The note you left when trespassing on his property indicates otherwise, Ms. Mullet."

"Trespassing?"

"Yes, Ms. Mullet. I advise you to cease and desist at once."

"Just what is your client hiding, Mr. Seidell? Is he trying to cover up the role he played in the death of Rodney Faver?"

"I will not dignify that with a response. You have been warned. Stay away from my client. I am filing a restraining order request this afternoon."

"A restraining order?"

"Goodbye, Miss Mullet."

Clunk.

He insulted me, threatened me and hung up on me. I felt my anger rising, but stomped it down. I was exhausted, and fuming is not conducive to sleep. I drifted off with visions of Trenton Wolfe in handcuffs dancing in my head.

A couple of hours later, my doorbell rang. I peered out my bedroom window but could not see enough of the person on the porch to do me any good. Then I looked out on the street—a florist truck.

I sprinted to the front door and took delivery of a beautiful bouquet—swollen yellow rosebuds pregnant with promise, cheery white daisies with egg yolk centers and a whole bunch of other beautiful flowers whose names eluded me.

I pulled out the little white envelope and opened the card. "Since you would not let me feed your body, allow me to feed your soul. Stan."

My, my, my, Mr. Crockett. One lunch, a couple of phone calls and already you're sending flowers. I could get used to this. I picked up the phone to express my gratitude. When he answered, I did so—profusely.

"So what is my super-sleuth up to now?"

My super-sleuth. He said "my" and in that voice of his. I tried to keep the melting of my heart out of the tone of my voice. "I've been trying to find Fingers Waller."

"Fingers? Should call him 'Fists' the way he knocked around his girlfriend. Aside from his keyboard playing, I have no use for the man. And I told him so on more than one occasion. I wanted Trent to dump him. He wasn't so great that we couldn't find a replacement, maybe one with more talent. But Trent thought it could jinx us—throw us off track.

"And I think Trent believed Fingers when he said his girlfriend was a lying druggie. But I'd seen her black eyes and the fingertip bruises on her arms. So what if she was into drugs? That didn't make her Fingers' personal punching bag."

"Do you know where I could find him?"

"Did you go to his girlfriend's place? Last I heard he was living with her."

"Yes and no. He hasn't been there for a couple of weeks."

"Really? Well, I haven't seen him since our gig at Solms Halle."

"So, you're saying he's a violent man?"

"Maybe. Maybe not. He was violent with the women in his life. But I can't say I ever saw him raise a hand or pick a fight with anyone else."

"But you would think he was capable of it, wouldn't you?"

"Maybe. Maybe not. Why don't you forget about Fingers and just relax at home and enjoy the flowers? Or better yet, let me take you to dinner tonight."

"When all this is over, Stan, I'll be glad to take you up on that offer. Right now, I need to keep focused on this job."

"You know what they say Molly, all work, no play . . ."

"I'll keep that in mind, Stan." Mercy, that man was a serious temptation. Who knew where this might lead?

I went outside and pulled the mail out of my mailbox. An electric bill, a gas bill and a letter. I ripped open the flap of the letter with my thumb as I walked back in the house.

I read the first few words, "Trenton Wolfe is responsible for the death of his sister," and stopped dead in my tracks. The letter continued, "You ought to look into this amazing coincidence. His sister, Megan, was asphyxiated when Trenton was just seven years old in their fancy old house in the Park Cities of Dallas. He was the only other person in the house at the time. He was institutionalized for a while. And the police turned a blind eye.

"Rodney Faver's murder sounds like a natural progression to me."

The letter was unsigned and undated. There was no return address. The letter was typed. The envelope typed. Or printed.

And now my fingerprints were all over it. Crap.

I called the office of Bart Seidell. "Mr. Seidell, please."

"May I ask who is calling?"

"This is Molly Mullet."

"I am terribly sorry, Ms. Mullet, but your calls are not welcome in this office. Mr. Seidell specifically told me not to forward any call from you. Good day."

She hung up. Good freakin' grief. Another Ms. Arbuthnot. Did lawyers clone these women in a secret factory somewhere?

I redialed. "Don't hang up on me this time, ma'am. Just tell Bart Seidell that Molly Mullet received a letter today and she now knows at least one of the secrets his client is hiding."

"I will not, Ms. Mullet. Mr. Seidell is not interested in any communication from you."

"Fine. I'll give him until tomorrow at noon to change his mind. Then, I'm contacting every media source I can find."

This time, I hung up. Man, that felt good for a change.

CHAPTER THIRTY-SIX

My doorbell rang early the next morning. Unlike the previous morning, I'd already been fortified with two cups of coffee and was ready to greet the day. I peered through the curtain on my door. Out on my porch was an absolutely gorgeous specimen of a man. Tall, broad shoulders, dark hair, mustache—you'd think I ordered him from my fantasy catalogue. When he realized I was staring at him through the window in the door, he flashed his badge. Damn. Another cop.

I opened the door. "Yes, sir. May I help you?"

"Sergeant Barrientos, ma'am, with the Austin Police Department. Could I please come in and speak with you for a moment?"

How could I say no? I led him to the sofa and offered him coffee, tea, but stopped short of me. How could I even think that? I am one sick woman.

"Ms. Mullet, I understand you were up in Austin earlier this week looking for Jesse Kriewaldt."

"Yes, I was."

"Have you been up to Austin since?"

"No. Have you found Jesse?"

"Yes. Well, no. Actually, Leslie found him."

"Leslie?"

"You know, Leslie."

"No. Can't say that I do."

"Oh, that's right. You don't live in Austin. If you did, you would. Can't miss her—him—a regular feature of downtown life."

"Wait a minute. Do you mean Leslie, everybody's favorite transvestite?"

He grinned. "The one and only."

"How did Leslie find Jesse? And what the heck is Jesse doing?"

"Jesse's not doing much. You see, Leslie was out looking for a friend of his—hers—and saw a piece of cardboard with a couple of feet sticking out down the alley. He—she—thought the shoes looked familiar and lifted up the cardboard. Instead of his friend, he found Jesse—or the remains of Jesse. By the time Leslie got to the police station, she was a mess. He came hobbling in—a heel broke off on the way over—and her wig was askew."

"I don't think I have ever seen Leslie less than impeccable."

"Neither had we. It took a while to figure out what had Leslie in such a state of acute distress. Then we went out and recovered Jesse's body. So I have to ask again: have you been up to Austin at any time in the last forty-eight hours?"

"Oh, not this again."

"Don't worry, ma'am, I'm no Lieutenant Hawkins."

"You heard about that?"

"It's pretty well known over a twenty-county area. It's even spun off a whole new take on every blond, Polish or lawyer joke you've ever heard. I do, however, need to eliminate you, since so many people knew you'd been hunting Jesse down. If you could give me a list of everyone you saw yesterday or talked to on your land phone and the time of each encounter, I'll be on my way."

"Sure. But what happened to Jesse?"

"It appears as if he was strangled."

"With a guitar string?"

He gave me a measured look through hooded eyes. "How did you know that?"

"Didn't. I was on the scene of the Rodney Faver murder."

"That's right. I knew that. It just slipped my mind. Could you make that list for me now? And if you could, jot down any contact information you might have by each name. It would save me a lot of time."

I grabbed a pad of paper and a pen and sketched out my timeline. As I wrote, I took as many surreptitious looks at the officer as I dared. I didn't think he had noticed. Then I looked at him one more time, and he was staring me straight in the eye with raised eyebrows. My lips formed an asinine excuse for a smile and he laughed. Good sign.

I finished my list without looking up again. As I handed it to him, I said, "I'm sorry I can't give you a verifiable alibi for the whole time. I spent quite a bit of it alone."

"Only guilty people can manage to account for their time minute to minute over a two-day period."

"Thank you for that."

"Just telling it like it is. Well, here's my card. If you think of anything that could help me—anything at all—let me know."

"You are looking into a connection with the other two murders, aren't you?"

"Of course. But we don't have anything definitive yet. Are you holding something back, ma'am?"

I thought about handing over the guitar strings to him right then and there. But he was a cop, and even though he said he wasn't another Lieutenant Hawkins, I was not in a real trusting mood. "No, sir," I said.

Chapter Thirty-Seven

The phone rang and I snatched it up and tensed. I thought it'd be Bart Seidell. I was wrong.

"Good morning, Molly. How are you today?"

"Eddie. Eddie Beacham. You rat."

"What?"

"Don't play innocent with me, Eddie Beacham. You ratted me out to Hawkins."

"Molly. I'm an officer of the court. I had no choice."

"Oh, give me a break, Eddie."

"Really, Molly. It was an untenable situation."

"Bite me, Eddie!"

"Ooooh, that sounds quite tempting."

"Stuff it, Eddie. Why are you calling now? What else does Hawkins want to know? What else do you want to pin on me?"

"Oh, Molly, please. Let's talk about this over lunch."

"Drop dead, Eddie." I slammed down the phone. I've got to do this more often. Hanging up on people can really be gratifying.

The next time the phone rang, I took a deep breath and exhaled loudly before I picked up the receiver. "Molly Mullet. May I help you?"

"Ms. Mullet. This is Ms. Graceton."

I waited for more but it was not forthcoming. Graceton? Graceton? Didn't know. "Yes?" I said.

"I did speak to Mr. Seidell since you issued your threat . . ."

"That was not a threat, ma'am. That was simply a deadline."

"Humpf. I considered it so threatening that I contemplated calling the police before I spoke to Mr. Seidell."

"You what?"

"Nonetheless, Ms. Mullet, I did speak to Mr. Seidell. And he is willing to talk to you at this time."

"Is he there?"

"Yes, he is."

"May I speak to him, please?" I said through clenched teeth. This woman might even be worse than Ms. Arbuthnot.

"First, Ms. Mullet, I need to inform you that I do not like it one little bit when someone hangs up on me. So, quite frankly, if you want to talk to Mr. Seidell, you will have to call back on your own dime." Clunk.

She hung up on me. She hung up on me again. Damn. Call on my own dime? How old is this battle-axe anyway? Battle-axe? Jeez. Now, *I'm* recycling my grandmother's discarded phrases.

When she answered, I smothered my annoyance and in my sweetest voice said, "May I please speak to Mr. Seidell, please?"

"May I ask who's calling?"

I knew she knew who this was. And I knew she knew I knew it. I stuffed those thoughts down and in the most saccharine voice I could muster said, "Why certainly, madam, this is Ms. Molly Mullet of New Braunfels."

"One moment, please."

Seidell came on the phone and without a polite greeting said, "Read the letter to me."

I complied.

"Fine. Mr. Wolfe and I will meet with you in my offices in Austin this afternoon at two p.m. Please be prompt." Clunk.

He hung up on me. I wanted to call back so I could hang up

on him. Or at least on Ms. Graceton. Instead, I accepted the inevitable. Miss Manners was right. Rudeness was a loser's game. And I just lost again.

I might be heading up to Austin but I knew with an address of the eighteenth floor, I dared not visit Mr. Seidell's office in blue jeans. Once again, I lamented the tragedy of my wardrobe and settled on a black-and-white flowered dress that Charlie used to love.

That thought put me in a morose state of mind—not the best attitude for dealing with Interstate 35. The ride to Austin was always stressful once you hit the city limits. Sometimes construction or an accident made the agony start sooner. At least in the middle of the day, it would not be as bad as it would be during drive time.

I found a parking meter just a block and a half from Seidell's high-rise. I clunked in eight quarters. I probably would not be there more than an hour, but I didn't want to risk another parking ticket. This town counted violations in seconds, not minutes.

The elevator doors opened onto a lobby that reminded me a lot of the one in Dale Travis' office in Houston—same awesome view, just a different city, similar layout with a slightly different color scheme and at the front desk, my new nemesis, Ms. Graceton. She looked a lot like Ms. Arbuthnot—except older and more vindictive.

When I told her my name, her face twisted into a pained expression and without a word, she picked up the receiver, pressed a button and said, "That Ms. Mullet is here."

She looked in my direction without really looking at me and said, "The conference room is down that hall, the fourth door on your right."

The door was open. Trenton Wolfe and Bart Seidell, on the side of the table facing the door, stared at me when I entered.

Seidell asked me to close the door and invited me to take a seat.

As soon as I did, Wolfe did not waste time with niceties. "Let me state for the record: I do not like you. In fact, you make me sick. But I am complying with your blackmail . . ."

"Wait a minute. Blackmail?" I said as I pushed away from the table.

"Ms. Mullet, please be seated. You did threaten media exposure. And, I presume, you do want to know the whole story. Am I correct?"

"Yes, but . . ."

"Then you are going to have to allow Mr. Wolfe to say his piece first."

I can't say that I liked it. But I'd started this game, and I was going to have to deal with it. I sat and pulled my chair back up to the table.

"As I was saying," Wolfe continued, "I am complying with your *blackmail* in the hopes of sparing my mother the grief a rehashing of these events in public would cause. The note you received was correct on a couple of points. My sister Megan did die when I was seven. We did live in Park Cities. But the innuendo beyond that was not based on fact."

Trenton Wolfe entered the world with luck on his side. A luxurious family home in a wealthy neighborhood. Loving parents and no knowledge of want. His sister Megan, four years his senior, doted on him—most of the time. In true older sibling tradition, though, there were those times when she regarded him as nothing more than a pest.

A heavy freeze rocked Dallas one late November night in 1981, leaving a chilly day in its wake. Trenton's father Bill went off to work as usual that morning. After breakfast, his mother Jillian went out in the backyard garden to cut away the frost-damaged growth. Usually, seven-year-old Trenton and eleven-year-old Megan played outside while their mother worked among her beds of flowers and herbs. Today, though, it was just too cold.

They took advantage of the absence of adults in the house by reveling in the forbidden act of sliding down the banister of the elegant, sweeping staircase in the front foyer. They swooshed down to the bottom and raced back to the top, all the while listening carefully for the return of their mother, giggling at their own brazenness.

When their rumps were too sore to slide again, they segued into Trenton's favorite fantasy game: Trent Wolfe, Bronco Buster. Megan, of course, played the part of the bronco. Trenton stood in a bow-legged stance, and swung his lariat in the air in a desperate attempt to mimic the beautiful, erect, round hoops of the cowboys he saw at the rodeo. As a rule, however, his were misshapen and floppy. He threw the rope with all his strength and skill hoping to drop it perfectly around his sister's neck. It was a pathetic attempt that fell far short of its target. But Megan—on days like this when she was feeling fondness for her little brother—helped the rope along pretending the mighty cowboy had performed a perfect lasso.

On all fours, she reared back, her hands clawing the air in an imitation of flashing hoofs. She turned toward him, pawing the "hoofs" in the air near his face.

"This horse is loco," he drawled in his best cowboy voice imitation. "I need to get me some help to tame this here one." Trenton raced down the stairs to fetch Billy Spurs, his imaginary friend.

Megan reared up again and raced after him. The rope around her neck snagged on the baluster where the banister turned toward the landing. The rope snapped taut and jerked her off her feet. She landed on her back on the banister and started to slide down—tightening the rope even more. She grasped the slippery, waxed wood surface, struggled to gain purchase, teetered and slipped over the side. Impotent fingers brushed the railing as she fell and hung by her neck kicking and choking.

"Megan! Megan!" Trenton screamed as he raced back up the stairs. His awkward, small fingers fought to pull the rope up and off of the carved chunk of wood. But the rope was too tight and he was too weak. He pulled up on the rope, trying to drag her back on the stairs. All that did was squeeze the loop around her throat even tighter. Megan's face turned blue.

Trenton blanched and screamed her name again. Sobbing and choking on his tears, he shot down the stairs and pushed up on Megan's feet. Her knees bent—nothing more. He dragged a wooden chair out of the dining room and placed it under her legs. He climbed on the embroidered seat and wrapped his arms around her legs just above her knees. He pushed up. She did not budge.

He raced outside stumbling and choking, nearly crawling to his mother. Her back was to him, the earplugs for her pocket radio blocking out his cries for help. He tripped on a hump in the grass and hit the ground screaming, "Mother!"

Jillian heard a whisper of his scream and spun around. She dropped her pruning shears and flew to Trenton. She reached out to comfort him but he was on his feet running at a full gallop back to the house. She kicked off her garden clogs and chased after him.

In the front hallway, Trenton stopped. Panting and pointing, he wailed out his sorrow. Jillian jumped onto the chair and boosted her daughter up while she lifted the rope over her head. She climbed down and sat cross-legged on the floor. She put a hand on the side of Megan's face and pressed her cheek against her own. With her other arm, she hugged the limp body tight to her breast. She rocked back and forth, moaning and oblivious.

Trenton stood speechless and confused. Then he picked up

the phone and pressed 9-1-1. He could not speak. He could only sob.

The heart-wrenching sobs of a child were enough to throw emergency response teams into gear. Their sirens filled the air of the Park Cities. But their arrival was far too late.

Trenton no longer spoke. He refused to eat. He looked no one in the face. Jillian took him to a counselor for weeks with no improvement. Then, one day, she found him in the kitchen. He had removed every knife from the wooden blocks on the counters and from out of all of the drawers. He lined them all up on the counter, side-by-side. He walked down the row of lethal blades giving each one an affectionate touch.

Jillian committed Trenton to a child psychiatric facility. She could not bear the thought of losing her second child, too.

Trenton told his story with visible anguish. My heart was touched, but my mind wondered why the look of anger never left his face. Why, in the aftermath of this emotional release, did he still scowl at me with defiance in his eyes?

Emotionally, I wanted to believe that this experience in the past left him incapable of squeezing the life out of another human being. Logically, though, I knew that the scars of childhood bore fruit in adult lives and some of that fruit was laden with poison.

"Trent, do you have any idea who killed Rodney Faver?" I asked.

He looked at his attorney, turned back to me and said, "No."

"Do you know how a bloody T-shirt got in Happy's kick drum?"

One side of his upper lip raised in a nasty sneer. "Did Happy Parker do that to your face before he died?"

I rose to my feet. I had had enough.

"Yeah, leave, bitch, and leave me the hell alone."

I spun around and pulled open the door but before I could cross the threshold, Bart Seidell was by my side. "Look, I know my client's been rude. But I know his mother. She is a sweet, fragile woman. If you take this to the press, you'll rip her world in two."

I would commit to nothing until I knew who killed Rodney Faver. And Happy Parker. And Jesse Kriewaldt. "Good day, Mr. Seidell."

"At the very least, Ms. Mullet, please give me a heads up first so I can prepare Jillian for the onslaught."

I nodded my head and walked down the hall.

CHAPTER THIRTY-EIGHT

I pulled out of my parking space regretting the wasted quarters. I drove half a block to a red light. As I waited for it to turn to green, I realized that I never asked the most important question.

I circled the block, hoping to regain my quarter-rich parking slot but someone beat me to it. She beamed at the meter, dropped her change back into a purse and bounced down the street. I growled and went hunting for another empty space. I found one, a block farther away with a whole two minutes left in the meter. I sacrificed more quarters to the City of Austin coffers—another reason to like New Braunfels. A few years back, the city fathers removed all the parking meters downtown, deeming them a detriment to the tourist industry.

I power-walked to Seidell's building. I chastised myself with every step for my emotional reactions during the interview. If I'd been more detached, more professional, I would have remembered all the important questions. Was I capable of developing that skill? I didn't know. But I would try.

When the elevator doors opened, I almost went straight to Ms. Graceton's desk to ask for permission. Screw that. And her. I strode past her without a glance in her direction.

"May I help you?" she shrieked as I passed her. "Excuse me. Excuse me, miss. Where do you think you are going? You cannot go back there without being announced."

I walked faster. I reached the doorway to the conference

room and stopped on the threshold. Both men were still there, their backs to me as they looked out the window. Wolfe's hands were jammed in his pockets. The tension of his anger was written across the rigid muscles of his back. Seidell stood to his left, one hand resting on the other man's shoulder. The low rumble of his voice was constant, but his words were inaudible.

Ms. Graceton snapped at my back, "I'm going to have to ask you to leave."

Both men spun around at the sound of her voice. Before they could echo the shrew's sentiments, I blurted out: "I forgot the most important question."

"What the . . . ?" Wolfe sputtered.

Seidell grabbed his forearm and said, "Wait, Trent. Thank you, Ms. Graceton."

"Sir, I did not give her permission . . ." Ms. Graceton began.

"Ms. Graceton, I said, 'thank you,' " Seidell repeated.

She gave me a look I had seen before. The last time I saw it, it was contorting the face of a friend's cat who was plucked mid-lunge on its way to a lizard—not a pretty sight. At least, Ms. Graceton did not growl.

"What is your question, Ms. Mullet?" Seidell asked.

"Who could have written that note?"

Seidell looked at Wolfe, who shrugged and turned away.

"Think. Please. Someone wanted me to think the worst of you. Who?"

Wolfe turned back toward me, shrugged again and shook his head.

"You've got to have suspicions. Who? Why? Does the writer really think you're guilty of killing Faver? Or does he just want me to think you are? Who knows your past? Who hates you enough to reveal it, Trent?"

He would not look up—not at me, not at his attorney. He just shook his head. But I knew I'd hit home. He slumped into a chair and turned towards me at last. Bewilderment smoothed away the angry edges on his face. "That's a good question," he said. "But I don't know the answer."

"C'mon, Trent. The name of someone must be racing through your head."

The anger was gone, but there was something else in Wolfe's face that made me uneasy. He was hiding something. I could see it in the depth of darkness in his eyes, in the clenched muscles of his jaw, in an awkward twist in the corners of his mouth. He knew something.

"Maybe it's all more byzantine than I thought, Trent. Maybe I just haven't given you enough credit—enough respect. Maybe you orchestrated this whole encounter. Maybe you sent the note to me, to bring me here, to manipulate my sympathy and make me look elsewhere."

The anger streaked through Wolfe's face like a bolt of lightning. He sprang to his feet, turned his face to the window and barked, "Get that bitch out of here."

"I presume you know your way out," Seidell said.

I'd asked the important question. As a result, I now had more questions than answers. And doubts—big honkin' doubts—about Trent Wolfe. And about myself.

CHAPTER THIRTY-NINE

On the way back from Austin, I thought I'd detour over to Wimberley and pick Heather's brain about the guys in the band and see if she knew anything about a bloody T-shirt. Then I thought about little Crapper and almost changed my mind.

I stopped at a grocery store in Buda to prepare for my visit. For Pete and Labia, I bought a two-pack of large bone-shaped treats that promised hours of chewing pleasure. I doubted it would take the two Pyrenees more than five minutes to finish them off. For Crapper, I got a bag of small tempting tidbits.

I pulled up to the cabin. Pete and Labia treated me like an old friend. They took their bones and moseyed off with wagging tails to demolish them. Crapper greeted me with all the enthusiasm and warmth of a hungry shark. I ripped open the bag of treats and Crapper's body language altered into alert subservience with the first whiff. I popped a treat in his direction and he snatched it out of the air. I palmed another treat and he followed me, whimpering with every step. I tossed him two or three treats on the way to the front door. He didn't miss a catch.

Heather pulled open the door and spotted the slavish dog at my feet. "Aw, you and Crapper have made friends."

Who said money can't buy you love? The buck-ninety-nine I'd forked over for that bag of yummies was the best investment I ever made. "Heather, I need your help."

"Anything, Molly. I won't feel right till we find out who killed

Happy." She burst into a wail. I suppressed my negative reaction and gave her a hug. She apologized for losing it, and we sat sideways and cross-legged on opposite ends of the sofa. Crapper sat between us, beaming a constant look of adoration in my direction.

I related my visit to Seidell's office. Wolfe's childhood trauma was news to Heather. "It does explain a lot about him, though," she said. "He always held something of himself back. No one I know of ever felt they really knew him."

I was now convinced that Wolfe's anger was more the reaction of an innocent man than a guilty one. The real mystery remained. "So who could have sent me that note, Heather? Who hates Wolfe that much?"

She shook her head slowly. "Got me. I didn't know anybody who actually hated Trent. They got annoyed with him. Called him a diva behind his back. But hated him? Well, there was some bad blood between him and the keyboard player—what's his name?"

I drew a blank, too.

"Whatever," Heather continued. "There was no love lost between the two of them. Lots of times, Trent introduced Happy and Stan to the audience—sometimes even the one-night stand back-up musicians and vocalists. But never once do I remember him introducing that keyboard guy. Don't know what was up that. Did you talk to him?"

"Can't find him," I said. "Nobody seems to have seen him since the Solms Halle gig."

"That's suspicious."

"I thought so, too, at first. But then there was Happy. Then there was Jesse. I really think whoever killed Faver killed them all. If Fingers did it—yeah, that's his name, Fingers. Fingers Waller. Anyway, if Fingers did it, he had to hang around for days to do the other two murders and somebody would have seen him."

"I told you that right away. I told you whoever killed Rodney killed Happy, too." Her voice cracked and flew into another wail.

My impatience rose to the surface and with it came a flash of insight about myself. I was uncomfortable with her tears because her anguish dredged up the shadows of my first few days without Charlie. With that revelation, my empathy overrode my irritation and I rocked her in my arms until she ran out of tears.

"Heather, are you okay now?"

She nodded her head and sniffled.

"Can I ask you about something else?"

She nodded her head again, blew her nose and said, "Anything."

"Did Happy ever say anything to you about finding a bloody T-shirt in his kick drum?"

Heather's lower lip quivered, "A bloody shirt? In his kick drum? No. I don't think so. I would remember that if he told me."

"Stan told me he found one. If Stan's right, what could Happy have done with it?"

"Let's check the laundry room," she suggested.

We searched through the mound of dirty clothes, closely examining each T-shirt in the pile. A choking noise scratched Heather's voice every time she picked up a piece of Happy's clothing, but she stuffed down her emotions and focused on the job at hand.

We moved to the bedroom and went through Happy's dresser drawers, pulling out, unfolding and looking closely at each T-shirt. Then we folded them back up and stacked them on the bed.

We shone a flashlight under the bed but only found two dog

toys and a convention of dust bunnies. In the walk-in closet we slid hangers one-by-one, looking for the suspect garment with no luck. We pulled over a step stool and cleaned everything off the top shelf. We sat on the floor and went through every item we found up there. No T-shirt with even a trace of blood.

We finished and just sat there lost in thought. In the far corner of the closet I spotted a pair of red-and-blue boots covered with an elaborate design that included a big white lone star of Texas on the front of each one. "The boots?" I asked.

"Happy's," she said, and a rueful smile lazed across her face. "Happy loved those boots, but every time he wore them, he complained that they made his feet sweat. Didn't stop him from wearing the boots, though."

I crawled over to the corner and looked inside. One boot was empty. The other was not. I unbent a wire hanger and used it to fish out a wadded-up, light-gray T-shirt. There along the neckline was the telltale dark rusty stain of dried blood.

Heather gasped. "That's Trent's."

"Are you sure?"

"Look at the front of it. I'm positive it's Trent's."

The design on the front was a wolf, his neck craned back in a howl. Above him shone a full moon, as golden as sunlight lying low on the horizon. "Get me a bag," I said. "A paper bag."

I stood with my arm elevated, holding the T-shirt in midair on the bent hanger. I was empathizing with Moses by the time Heather returned with a small lunch sack. "Is that the best you can do?"

"Sorry."

"No paper grocery bags?"

"All plastic."

"Okay. Open it up, place it on the floor and hold it steady."

I guided the shirt to the small opening and slid it off the hanger. Part of the shirt slouched over the top. I shook it down, taking care not to touch anything but bag. I folded down the top, taped it, dated it and initialed it. I'd never seen real evidence collection firsthand but, heck, I'd watched plenty of episodes of *CSI*. Oh, jeez, I must be the most pathetic investigator on the planet.

But I did have evidence—real, hard forensic evidence. And it pointed to Trenton Wolfe. This afternoon's visit to Seidell's office ran in fast-forward speed through my mind. I felt naïve. And manipulated. And more than a little ticked off.

CHAPTER FORTY

Paranoia sat beside me and laughed as I drove back to New Braunfels. Before I left Happy's place, Heather dug around the cabin, looking for something that would contain an unadulterated sample of Happy's DNA for comparison with what was found on the T-shirt. As a result, I was driving down the road with a joint, hand-rolled and sealed with the spit of Happy Parker. I took great care to abide by the speed limit.

I also left with a commitment from Heather to visit Trenton Wolfe and return with a sample of his DNA. I thought it was a good idea when we talked about it, but now I was having second thoughts.

There was no denying that Heather's chances for success were high. The role of grieving girlfriend was natural and required no artifice. But what if Wolfe saw the motive that lurked beneath the surface? Would Heather be the next to die?

When I pulled into the driveway, memories of the night I found the guitar string on the doorknob rampaged over me like flood waters. I was afraid to get out of my car in front of my house and walk to my door. Quite frankly, that pissed me off. I should not have to fear coming home.

I flung open my car door, balanced my evidence bags in my left arm, and with my right hand held my gun down by my thigh. I realized there was a flaw in my organization when I reached the front door. I needed a free hand for the keys. I set the bags down on the porch and manipulated the key into the lock with my left hand. It was a clumsy effort made even worse by my anxiety about being out on my porch after dark.

I placed the bags on the kitchen counter and searched through the house. I was thorough, but nothing was amiss. I was still too edgy for a shower—just thinking about it conjured up images of Norman Bates armed with a guitar string—and drew a bath instead. I waited outside of the bathroom to listen for any suspicious sounds until the tub was full. I luxuriated in a long soak. My gun rested within reach on the top of the toilet seat.

Even after that, falling asleep wasn't easy. When I did, my dreams were haunted by Keystone Kops busting me for possession of pot while canned laughter roared in my ears.

The next morning after sufficient caffeine fortification, I considered my options for DNA testing. Probably the most sensible thing would be to drive my evidence down to Houston and turn it over to Dale Travis. What would Travis do with it? He could turn it over to the cops. Nope. Not without a court order. He could send it out for testing. Not that either. He could sway the jury more with innuendo than with a T-shirt obtained in a dubious chain of custody. He could accept it, smile at me, say, "Thank you," stick it in a drawer and forget about it. Bingo.

Scratch Dale Travis. I sure couldn't take it to the cops. Hawkins would find a way to use it against Bobby. Only one option left. I had to find a lab and take it there myself. And pay for it myself. I wasn't wild about that part. I called Lisa.

"New Braunfels Police Department. Garcia speaking."

"Lisa, this is Molly . . ."

"*Mija!* How are you? Where are you? What are you up to? Have you found the killer yet?"

"Fine. At home. Been pretty busy. Not yet. I think that covers them all."

Lisa laughed at me and at herself. "What can I do for you?"

"If you wanted to get some DNA profiles run, where would you take them?"

"To the police department, of course. And they'd send them up to the state lab in Austin for testing. What are you up to, Molly?"

"Okay. So, what if I didn't want to take it to the police?"

"*Mija,* if you have evidence, you must turn it over to the police."

"Evidence? Who said I had evidence?"

"Molly?" she said in a motherly tone of disapproval.

"What would I be doing with evidence?"

"I am not joking. Obstruction of justice is a serious charge."

"Aw, c'mon, Lisa."

"You can bring it in here, Molly. Hawkins has been chewed on by everybody in the department with teeth. He wouldn't dare mess with it or step out of line in any way."

"Is Hawkins still on the force?"

"Well, yes. But the rest are good cops here."

"I know that, Lisa. I worked there. Most of them are great cops. But I don't exactly trust my instinct anymore to judge which is which. Besides, I work for the defense. Dale Travis probably frowns on his investigators volunteering evidence to the other side."

"Aha! You do have evidence."

"There are all kinds of evidence in this world, Lisa. It's not all criminal. There's evidence for a paternity case. Evidence for a malpractice suit. Evidence of a bug inside my drive-in window hamburger bun. Evidence. It's everywhere. Help me, Lisa. Please."

With a sigh big enough for a person ten times her size, Lisa gave me the name, address and phone number of a lab in San

Antonio. I just had to wait for Heather to return from her mission.

I spent the day running down the list of people who ever knew Trenton Wolfe. I got more hang-ups than anything else but I did talk to a few people. All the information I got from them, though, was vague, old or irrelevant. I probably would have had a better luck with a list of strangers who bought his CDs.

Several times that afternoon, I considered calling his mother, Jillian. Each time, I changed my mind before I finished dialing the number.

At last, Heather rescued me from phone duty. She arrived with pink cheeks, twinkling eyes and a purse as big as Houston. She pulled out the first paper bag. "Beer bottle," she said.

I looked inside. "There's still beer in it."

"Well, if I let him finish it first, he might have thrown it away before I could grab it. He went for a leak. I made my move."

"Didn't he wonder what happened to his beer when he came back?"

"Yeah. Sure. But I played dumb. He wandered around for a while looking for it. Then he gave up and got a fresh one out of the fridge."

With fingertips barely touching the next bag, she elevated it from her purse, swiveled and dropped it on the counter, her face squeezed tight with distaste. "And this. This is disgusting."

A crumpled up tissue lay in the bottom of the bag. Disgusting? A wadded tissue? Oh, man, I sure hoped it wasn't what I was thinking. "Uh, Heather, besides being disgusting, what is it?" I held my breath praying I was wrong.

"Spit. He has allergies. Sinus drainage. He spat in it." Her whole body shuddered with revulsion.

What a relief! "Could be worse, Heather."

"Ha. If it weren't for Happy, I wouldn't have had it next to me in the car for that hour-long ride."

"Anything else?" I asked trying not to laugh at her.

"Yes," she beamed as she tilted the next bag in my direction. "A joint."

"You ripped off his pot?"

"Oh, Molly, of course not. I just asked him for one for the road. He rolled it. He licked it shut. I held out the bag and he dropped it in."

"Didn't he think it was odd that you had him put it in a bag?"

"Listen, he already thought I was odd. I cried the whole time I was in his house. He would have gone along with most anything just to get me out and on my way."

I shook my head. My stash of illegal substances doubled instantly. Heather just faced off the man who she thought killed her boyfriend without batting an eye. Amazing.

"Heather, did you notice anyone else around the house while you were there?"

"No. I didn't think there was anyone but Trent."

"No signs that somebody else might be crashing there?"

"Like who?"

"Fingers Waller."

"The keyboard player? Why would he be there?"

"His girlfriend mentioned the possibility. I was trying to tie up loose ends."

"Okay, I'll go back up there tomorrow and search the house."

"Heather, you can't just knock on someone's door and search his house."

"Of course not." She plucked up a strand of her hair. "This blond stuff. It's not real. My real color is mousy brown. So, guess what? I do have a brain. Ta-da."

For a second she had me. I thought I'd offended her. But no, she was making fun of me. It was good to see her upbeat about something—even if it was at my expense.

"And you know what? I can add. Without a calculator! Isn't that incredible?"

"Okay, Heather." I laughed. "You made your point. So what's your plan?"

"I ask for a tour of his house."

"You'll ask for a tour? Oh, that is so girl, he'll never fall for it."

"Wanna bet? If he doesn't, I'll start crying again. He'll do anything to get me to stop."

I laughed. Oh yeah, I'd known men like that. And women who knew how to use them. I always acted offended when a woman resorted to that trick but, secretly, I was envious of their easy on/off faucets and willingness to do anything to get what they wanted.

"So, do you want me to go back to Austin tomorrow?" Heather asked.

"You did good today, Heather. Let's see where this DNA leads before you take any more risks."

"If you change your mind, you've got my number. See you around, Molly. And thanks—really—for letting me help." A tear threatened the corner of her eye. She brushed it away and she was gone.

I putzed around the house the rest of the evening. Read the newspaper. Watched the news. Played solitaire on the computer. Wrapped it all up with an episode of *Forensic Files* on Court TV.

I was heading for bed when the phone rang. I almost picked up the receiver but pulled back just in time to let the answering machine take it.

A distorted singsong voice filled the room: "This little piggie went to Solms Halle. This little piggie took a big fall. And this little piggie had no home. Now here's piggie number four. Is she afraid to walk out her front door?"

A childlike laugh rang out, followed by the sound of ragged breathing and a slurp of melting Milk Duds. The answering machine clicked off. I stood rooted in place. Was there something else in my mailbox? Another present on my door-knob? A booby trap outside my front door? Or was there noth-ing—nothing at all? Nothing but the fear of something hidden—the unknown lurking in the darkness?

Staying out of the line of sight of the windows as much as possible, I went room to room turning off all the lights. I stood to the side of the windows, peering out in every direction. I saw nothing.

I feel asleep in a chair near the front window, gun in my hand, sweat on my palms.

CHAPTER FORTY-ONE

He smiled as the lights snapped off one by one. Her fear was so strong, he imagined he smelled it. He sniffed the air and inhaled deeply.

He felt a twitch and a throbbing in his pants. She was far more exciting than the three men before her. He never anticipated this thrill, this sexual charge. The others were quick and efficient—necessary kills but nothing more.

Toying with her was an experience beyond comparison. The anticipation had been such an intense pleasure. The kill would be exquisite.

Would curiosity get the best of her tonight? Would it propel her outside and into his arms? The possibility that tonight would be the night was exhilaration as well as a disappointment. He knew he would miss the game when it was done.

He saw fleeting shadows of her movements through the house. He ached to be inside with her, watching each cautious step, seeing the soft trembling in her hands, feeling the adrenaline course through her veins.

His breathing grew labored. His heart beat a tattoo in his chest. He reached down and rubbed himself. He jerked his hand back. Not here. Not now.

Then, for a long time, he saw no sign of life in the house. Every unidentified sound made him tense with longing. He waited until the hope that she would step outside died a natural death.

He crept around to the back of the house and dismantled the rifle he had rigged to the back door. Had she opened it, a dummy round would have struck her in the chest. It would not kill her, but it would knock her off her feet, giving him time to move in on her.

Tonight was not the night. He sighed. But that night was near.

CHAPTER FORTY-TWO

I sipped on my second cup of coffee, trying to recover from a night spent in the chair. A quiet knocking broke the morning's silence. I approached the front door wondering if it might not be a better idea to crawl in bed and pull the covers over my head. A young woman with long brown hair pulled back and clasped at the nape of her neck stood on my porch. Her face glowed with an aura of serenity, the kind of peace won only after hard battles with personal demons. She looked far too young, though, to have made that journey.

I eased the door open a crack. She spoke at once. "Hello. I'm Jenny Kriewaldt. Are you Molly Mullet?"

How did she know my name? And in knowing my name, how did she know where I lived? Was she related to Jesse? He had a sister. Could this be her?

Before I could ask, she added, "I'm Jesse's twin sister. I understand you're looking for whoever killed my brother."

"How did you know that?"

"We stopped in Austin before we came here," she said as she fumbled in her purse. "And we spoke to him," she said, flipping a business card in my direction.

It was Sergeant Barrientos' card. "And he told you where I live?"

"Oh, no. He said he couldn't do that."

That was a relief. "So how did you find me?"

I found your address on the Internet and got directions from

Mapquest. Or I should say *he* did, she said, pointing to a car parked at my curb.

I looked out and saw a shadow behind the tinted glass. Unease roiled my stomach. "Who is he?"

"Just a friend. He drove me up from College Station. Say, can I come in and talk to you for just a minute?"

I felt comfortable with Jenny, but a stranger lurking outside my door made me edgy. Then again, a stranger lurking inside my house wasn't on my list of favorite things, either. But at least I could keep my eye on him. "He can come in, too, if he'd like."

"No. That's okay. He'd rather sit in the car and smoke."

With reluctance, I invited her inside and offered her a seat. I sat in the chair that offered the best view of the car and her "friend."

"Do you know anything about Jesse's murder?" I asked.

"No. Not really. But I thought it might help if you knew something about Jesse."

"Tell me about your brother." I doubted if she had any significant information to offer, but if she needed to talk, I could do my good deed for the day and listen to what she had to say.

"Jesse and I are orphans. We were sixteen when our parents died in an automobile accident on an icy road. Our dad was a state employee. He worked for the comptroller's office for twenty-two years. Mom was a teacher—elementary school—third and fourth grades.

"When they died, everyone who knew them pulled together to help us finish our schooling. Between scholarships, grants and contributions, every penny of expense at a four-year state school was covered for both of us. I chose to attend Texas A&M. I really wanted Jesse to come out to College Station with me. But he said he had to be in Austin, the live music capital of the world. He enrolled at the University of Texas. I didn't know it for months, but he dropped out of UT after six weeks. He said it distracted him from his music. He said he had to devote himself to his muse. He was such a dreamer.

"After he moved out of the dorm, he never had a real place to live. He crashed on one friend's sofa, then another. Sometimes he slept in the streets. I hoped in time he would get this songwriting stuff out of his system and settle down to the business of life." She paused and flashed a rueful smile. "When I said stuff like that to him, he said I sounded like Dad and asked me when I'd start crunching numbers for the comptroller. I'd remind him that I was a genetics major, and he'd say I couldn't deny my genetic destiny. I'd end up at the comptroller's office one day. The numbers called to me from my blood."

She blew a blast of air up from her bottom lip, flaring the loose strands of hair on her forehead. "Anyway, I worried about Jesse a lot. Then, one day, I stopped worrying. He gave me this CD," she said, handing it to me. "When I listened to it, I knew he had the touch. I knew he had the talent to make a living with his music. Not as a performer, of course. Jesse's singing left a lot to be desired. But I knew he was good enough to make a decent living writing songs.

"When 'Bite the Moon' hit the charts, I recognized it right away. Jesse had no phone number I could call, so instead of leaving messages with his friends, I drove down to Austin to celebrate his success. That's when I found out that Trent Wolfe didn't buy Jesse's song. He stole it. I was angry. I told Jesse not to let Wolfe get away with it. I told him to hire a lawyer. But Jesse had to go it alone."

An involuntary sob escaped. Her body shook for a moment and I rose to offer her my arms. She waved me away, straightened her back, folded her hands in her lap and continued. "He called me on a Saturday afternoon. He was so excited he could hardly talk. 'I saw the band manager,' he said. 'He's going to fix everything. I get credit for the lyrics. I get credit for the composition. They'll put ads in the trades and correct all future CDs in production.' 'But do you get money, Jesse?' I asked him.

" 'Yeah, I get a lump sum and royalties, too. But hey, my name, Jesse Kriewaldt, will be out there. I made my bones at last.' I never spoke to my brother again. He said he would call in a couple of days but he didn't. I called some of his friends. They hadn't seen or heard from him either. Then I knew why." She hung her head. Her shoulders rose and fell with a big sigh.

"Anyway, I wanted you to have a copy of the CD, and I wanted you to have this," she said, pulling a small photo album out of her purse. "I made reprints of my favorite pictures of Jesse and made a bunch of these. When I heard about you, I wanted to you to see him. I wanted you to be able to visualize him while you worked. Jesse was the only family I had. And now he's gone. And I'm on my own. I'm having a hard time accepting that."

I said, "Thank you." I wanted to say so much more, but could not find the words. She seemed so centered for one so young, but she'd certainly paid a high price to get there.

"Well, I've got to run. My phone number and e-mail address are in the front of the album. Let me know if you find out anything."

She stuck out her hand and I took it between both of mine. "Thank you, Molly," she said, and I felt blessed. When she smiled at me, she looked like one of Botticelli's angels.

After she left, I slid in Jesse's CD. Jenny was right about his singing, and just as she did, I recognized the song right away. I played the Wolfe Pack CD next. When Wolfe's voice sang Jesse's words, I felt the raw power of Jesse's poetry. The full band added more instrumentation, giving the composition greater depth. There was a slight variation in the rhythm, but there was no denying it: this was the same song. The song Jesse lived for. The song Jesse died for.

I played Jesse's CD again while I looked through the pages of photographs his sister left me. A toddler Jesse with a plastic guitar dragging in the dirt behind him. A ten-year-old Jesse holding a full-sized guitar like a sub-machine gun. An early adolescent Jesse, hair hanging in his eyes as he struggled to look soulful and worldly slouched in a beanbag chair, a guitar draped across his lap.

All of the snapshots hit me with a painful poignancy, but none as much as the most recent shot. There Jesse smiled and his eyes met mine. His face was a reflection of Jenny's, with a sharper jaw and a hungrier look—a face too soft, too sweet, too pure to last.

Until today, Jesse had been merely the third of three unsolved murders. Now I could see him, hear him, ache for him. He was a real person. I had to make sure he was not forgotten.

CHAPTER FORTY-THREE

I didn't know where to turn next. I needed to review what I knew and what it meant to me with another set of eyes and ears. I could bounce it all off of my quasi-employer, Arnie. I was sure he'd give me time and attention. But I wanted face-to-face interaction, and the thought of driving to Houston made my fingers twitch. It was like playing Russian roulette, and the gun was being held to the body of my little car.

So, of course, my thoughts turned to Lisa. In her weird little way, she had a great knack for cutting through the crap. She agreed to grab a lunch along the way and meet me in Landa Park.

It was my favorite place in New Braunfels. In one corner, the waters of the Comal River bubbled up from underground—clear, clean, cold water. The baby river ran under the road and split. One branch of the path of blue—incredibly blue—water raced in a beeline to the small lake. The banks were flat and low, nearly level with the surface of the fast flowing water. Overhead a canopy of trees—trees that in other regions of the country would tower like prehistoric giants—were squat and gnarled here, struggling to find nutrients in the rock-strewn soil. Every inch grown was a valiant triumph of determination over the elements.

The other branch of the newly spawned river meandered through the park, artificially widened at one point for a kiddies' wading pool and tapered back to a narrow six feet where a small, flat footbridge connected the two sides. Not much farther down, the distance was fifty feet and spanned by a graceful, arcing bridge. Then that branch, too, fed into the lake.

On the lake, geese, mallards and teal floated and squawked while black swans drifted by, adding dignity to the noisy chaos. Egrets and herons of all kinds high-stepped on the banks, hunting for food. On the islets in the lake, black cormorants gathered in the trees, their wings spread wide to soak up the sun.

The lake fed a naturalized community pool, then collided with a small dam and cascaded into a wide, deep, clear-as-glass river. During warm months, the river filled with tubers who floated on the steady stream of moving water, exiting just before the Comal crashed into its wilder, longer sister, the Guadalupe River.

Between all this water lay huge swaths of green, the tortured shapes of ancient live oak trees and scatterings of picnic tables. On holiday weekends, the park was packed with families who reserved their tables in advance, and chock-full of huge barbecue grills towed in by truck. The smell of mesquite and the squeals of children filled the air, and for a brief span of time, the people outnumbered the squirrels.

On this early spring day in the middle of week, the park was a peaceful place. A few people sat on benches contemplating the lake, singles and couples walked here and there and the squirrels ruled. I sat down and opened up my lunch, but only had time for one bite before Lisa joined me.

After a little small talk—Lisa talked, I listened—I pulled out a piece of paper. "This is the suspect list I drew up early on in the investigation. I wanted to see what you think about all these people. Who should I eliminate? Who should remain?"

"Who you need to add?" she asked.

"If you think of someone, sure."

Lisa looked at the sheet I laid on the picnic table. "You can scratch two names off right away. If you're right and the murders are connected—and I think you're right about that—then none of the crimes were committed by Happy Parker or Jesse Kriewaldt."

I started to draw a line through Happy's name, then I stopped. "Unless one or both of their deaths were a revenge killing for a previous murder."

Lisa scrunched up her face and shook her head. "Too complicated, *Mija*. The simplest solution is the right solution."

I scratched them off the list. "Now, I hate to divert us from the task at hand, Lisa. But what you said reminded me of something else. You know how you always call me '*Mija*'?"

"Yes, *Mija*," she said with a smile.

"Well, I checked with a Mexican-American woman I know down at the courthouse. She said that it is literally a contraction of 'my daughter,' but if a person is fond of any younger girl or woman, it is appropriate. She said that no one uses it for someone older—it would be disrespectful."

"Oh, *Mija*, please, that is so rigid. I am not being disrespectful. Even though you are older, I look upon you as a little sister—my little sister. I love you like a little sister. Does that make you feel better?"

I said, "Yeah," but I wasn't really sure. I had a feeling it did not reflect well on the level of my maturity. There was nothing to do but change the subject before I thought about it for too long. I pointed to Teresa Faver—now Tess Holland—and looked at Lisa.

"The ex-wife?" she asked.

I nodded my head.

"Killing Rodney makes sense. But the other two? She wasn't sleeping with them, was she?"

"You sure have a jaded view of relationships, Lisa."

"Please. It's always money or sex—without them, murder

would be rare. So what's the verdict, was she—could she have been—sleeping with them?"

The picture of Tess I found on the Internet flashed before my eyes. I wouldn't put it past Tess—but Jesse or Happy *with* Tess? Nah. "Not likely," I said.

"Mike Elliot?" she asked pointing to his name. "Why would you ever have his name on here?"

"There's a natural friction between the manager of a venue and the manager of the band. It seemed logical."

"Friction, sure. But the murder of Faver wasn't friction. It was white-hot passion."

"Who knows what passion can erupt in a heated argument?"

"*Mija*, Mike does not have that much passion. If he saved it up for years, he couldn't accumulate that much passion."

"Lisa, that's not a nice thing to say about any guy."

"I'm talking murder here, not sex. But, now that you mention it, there probably is a synergy there. Or maybe it's a life-style choice. Murder or sex. One guy takes one road, the other is great in bed."

I rested my forehead in the palm of my hand and shook it back and forth. Heaven knows, I'd never be bored around Lisa.

"Molly, look at me. I'm not joking. I would *not* joke about passion. You weren't thinking of Mike as a possible boyfriend, were you? Look at me, Molly."

I raised my head. I felt the heat of a blush in my face.

"Oh, *Mija*. No. No. No. It will never do. He will never be able to satisfy you. Trust me on this."

"Oh, c'mon, Lisa. What is this routine? 'I'm a *Latina*, I know all about passion, *Gringa*.'"

"Just because it's a stereotype doesn't mean it's not true. We have a gift."

I couldn't argue with that one. I scratched Mike off the list.

"Fingers Waller? Who is he?" Lisa asked.

"The keyboard player."

"Oh, that's his name. What about him?"

"He disappeared right after the Solms Halle gig and I haven't found anyone who has seen him since."

"He could be dead."

"Or he could be a prime suspect," I said. I put an asterisk by his name.

"Trenton Wolfe?"

"He fed me a story about childhood trauma that was supposed to make me believe he was incapable of killing Rodney Faver in the way he was killed. But I don't know. He's an angry man. And he claimed credit for a song Jesse Kriewaldt wrote."

"Okay. That could be a motive for killing Jesse. Why would he kill Happy Parker?"

"He knew something about Faver's murder, maybe?"

"All right. Why Faver?"

"He made a deal that afternoon with Jesse. But he hadn't the time to do anything about it yet."

"Prime suspect number two," Lisa declared.

I put an asterisk by his name.

"Heather? Who's Heather?"

"Happy's girlfriend," I said.

"Another Tess?"

"Pretty much. But not exactly. Unlike Tess, she was broken up about Happy's murder—or at least acted as if she was. And, unlike Tess, she knew Jesse. But I just can't see it."

"Scratch her?"

"Yeah," I said. One more down.

"Stan Crockett? Is he the one that looks too skinny to be alive?"

"Yeah." I laughed. "That's Stan. But he really is alive."

"Are you sure?"

"Yes. He sent me flowers."

"Put an asterisk by his name, too."

"You must be kidding. I'm going to scratch him off the list."

"No, you can't. Are you blinded by flowers? By lust? By love?"

"No," I snapped. I worried that there might be a bit of truth—a little, tiny, miniscule bit—in her judgment of my conclusions about Stan.

"Put an asterisk," she insisted again.

"Lisa, he's the only member of the band who approached me and talked to me. And he did it without a lawyer and without a hassle."

"Asterisk," she said again with the stubbornness of a toddler.

We compromised. Stan Crockett got a check mark next to his name.

"Bobby Wiggins is not on your list?"

"Bobby? No, of course not," I said.

"Have you really, really examined the possibility of his guilt?"

"Aw, c'mon, Lisa. You know how I feel about Bobby."

"You must be objective, *Mija*. The key was, after all, in *his* pocket."

"Lisa," I whined.

"Write his name down. But you can give him a check mark, not an asterisk. So there you go. Two prime suspects—Trenton Wolfe and Fingers Waller. And two maybe suspects—Stan Crockett and Bobby Wiggins."

I winced when she said Bobby's name.

"What do you do now? What are your next steps?"

"I don't know, Lisa. I'm fresh out of ideas."

"No, you're not. You've laid out clear priorities here. Number one: locate Waller. Number two: find out everything you can about Wolfe. Have you called his mother?"

"No," I admitted.

"Why not?"

"She won't be objective."

"Of course not, but she might drop a tidbit of information you can use."

"I would just dig up her old pain."

"Think about calling her anyway. What is a few minutes of her pain compared to Bobby's lifetime? Think about it, *Mija*. Priority three: find solid, concrete evidence to eliminate either Crockett or Bobby or both. If you can't, you need to consider upgrading those checkmarks to asterisks."

I nodded in agreement.

"And when you finish this case, *por Dios*, take the time to get that ugly thing off of your arm."

In response my hand flew up and landed on the sleeve over my tat. "How did you know about that?"

"*Mija*, everybody—*everybody*—knows about that."

"You're kidding."

"Hawkins has called you cow-pie behind your back for years."

"Oh, man."

"And everybody—*everybody*—knows he is talking about you."

Lisa had to get back to work, but I decided to walk around the park a bit before heading to my car. I was too deep in thought to realize trouble was heading my way until it ran into me.

When it did, I landed butt-first in the wading pool. Sprays of water shot high up in the air, eliciting screams from the children gathered there, some in fear, some in delight. I heard hurried apologies punctuated by heavy panting. I brushed the wet hair out of my eyes.

A spacey little woman in a flowery spring frock and heels—heels in the park?—switched her weight from one foot to another. A large, goofy-looking Great Dane strained and tugged at the end of the leash in her hand. I worried that any minute he would jettison her through the air, head over heels, and she'd land in my lap.

More than anything, I just wanted her to go away. "No problem," I said with a smile.

No problem, my ass—literally. It's hard to be inconspicuous walking through the park with wet jeans, straggling hair and a broad swath of mud across my rump.

I'm an investigator, for Pete's sake. Where, oh where, is the glamour?

CHAPTER FORTY-FOUR

I took Lisa's advice, plodding through the list of priorities but getting nowhere. Day followed day. Week followed week. If I wasn't running in place, I was running in circles.

The DNA test results on the T-shirt came in. It was no surprise that the DNA in the bloodstain matched Rodney Faver. I wasn't sure, though, how they knew that at the lab. I told them I thought it was Rodney Faver's DNA, but I didn't give them a sample. They must have pursued some underground voodoo DNA network.

They confirmed that they found Trenton Wolfe's DNA in the sweat stain in the armpits. I expected that. They did have a surprise for me, though. Wolfe's DNA was intermingled with an unknown DNA sample.

"What does that mean?" I asked.

"It is consistent with the T-shirt having been worn by more than one perspiring individual."

Hunh. I was even more confused after that call than I was before it. The thought that more than one person wore that T-shirt that night didn't make sense. Unless . . . unless what? I pulled the pinball lever in my head and let the ball fly. After ricocheting from one thought to another, it finally scored. Unless someone wore the shirt to implicate Wolfe. Then stuffed it in the kick drum where he knew it would be found. But he wasn't as cool and calm as he thought. He was sweating, and that sweat left an undeniable ID card. And maybe that's how

Fingers Waller fit into the picture.

Or maybe I'd got it all wrong again. Maybe Wolfe got someone else to wear the shirt first, knowing that person would leave trace evidence behind. Then he put it on to commit the murder, knowing an analysis of the shirt would lead to confusion instead of clarity. My head was spinning out of control. Too many what ifs. Too many maybes. Too little time.

I called Sergeant Barrientos to check on the status of Jesse Kriewaldt's case. He had run out of leads. I suggested Trenton Wolfe and Fingers Waller.

"It's like Waller fell off the face of the earth," he said. "No credit card activity. No bank transactions. He did make a large and suspicious withdrawal the Friday before Faver's murder, but since then nothing.

"We had no trouble finding Wolfe, but his alibi is solid for the most likely time frame for Kriewaldt's murder."

"Are you sure?" I asked.

"It all checked out. The only thing we have to go on now is an unknown DNA sample from under Kriewaldt's fingernails. A few skin cells were found there. We think they could belong to his killer. We ran it through the national data base, but got no hits."

I came very close to offering up my DNA results for comparison to his. A match might answer both of our questions. As much as I wanted to do that, though, I knew I had an obligation to wait until after Bobby's trial.

I called Mike Elliot to see if he'd picked up any useful gossip from the musicians who played at Solms Halle. Mostly he complained about the increasing difficulty in making new bookings and the suspicious looks that the performing artists gave to members of his staff.

"Everyone is pretty much convinced of Bobby's guilt," he said.

"What about you, Mike?"

"No. I've tried. But I just can't picture it. No matter how many arguments I hear from people who believe Bobby did it, I can't picture the Bobby I know as a killer. But, then again, I have my doubts, too. Maybe I really don't know Bobby as well as I thought I did."

Great. An old friend having doubts about Bobby did not bode well for the outcome of the trial.

Every couple of days, Thelma Wiggins called. There was the lilt of hope in her voice when she said hello. But when I had nothing new to offer, she said goodbye in despair.

I fended off four more dinner invitations from Stan Crockett. And hung up on Eddie Beacham at least three times—maybe more. Would he ever get the hint?

I was discouraged—so discouraged. I still had not found Fingers Waller, dead *or* alive. Was his DNA the unknown profile on the T-shirt? Three people were dead. Was Fingers responsible? Or was it Trenton Wolfe? Or was it someone else altogether, who I was too dense to imagine. Every lead led to a dead end. And every dead end felt like failure.

Unless Fingers was the killer, I had surely talked to the killer at one time or another. If it was not Wolfe, then women's intuition was an illusion and my investigator's sixth sense bankrupt.

For better or worse, the end of Bobby's legal ordeal was near. Jury selection started tomorrow. With his client behind bars, Dale Travis had pushed the trial through, accepting the first date the prosecution offered.

I saw Dale early in the morning at the historic Faust Hotel, a couple of blocks from the courthouse, where he'd moved for the duration of the trial. I pleaded with him to get a postponement and give me more time to find the perpetrator. He told me to relax. My job was done and done well. He said I'd dug up enough reasonable doubt to bewilder a dozen panels of jurors. Dale Travis was satisfied. But I was not. I had to find more. The killer of Rodney Faver and Happy Parker and Jesse Kriewaldt had to pay. But what if I was wrong about that, too? What if I'd been searching for the one person complicit in all the crimes when they weren't connected at all except by serendipity and coincidence? Killers instead of a killer? Had I not found an answer because I was asking the wrong question all along?

Still, I had to do something. I'd make one last visit to Bobby—one more attempt to jog something useful out of his memory. The bloody key was in Bobby's pocket. That meant he came in close contact with the killer for at least a fleeting moment in time. I needed him to remember that moment. I had to help him isolate it and extract it.

Chapter Forty-Five

"Bobby?" I asked holding a photo of Rodney Faver in front of me. "Did you kill this man?"

"No, Molly. I didn't. I swear."

I pressed the picture up to the glass. "Bobby, did you tell the police you killed this man?"

"No, Molly," Bobby said hanging his head and swinging it back and forth.

"Bobby, look at me."

He raised his winter-sky blue eyes to meet mine. "Yes, Molly?"

"Mr. Travis told you about the tape, didn't he, Bobby?"

He nodded with vigor, but his eyes did not waver from my gaze.

"You told them you killed this man, didn't you, Bobby?"

"No! No!" He shook his head in short jerks.

"No?"

"No. I told 'em I killed that man, but not this one. But I didn't kill no man, I swear. I just told 'em I did 'cause I wanted to see Mama. 'Cause I wanted to go home." His hands worried each other. He clutched his left hand with his right and then switched back again. "You gotta believe me, Molly."

"Wait a minute, Bobby." I reached across the table and placed the palm of one hand flat against the glass, hoping to soothe and to help him concentrate. "I do believe you. I'm just confused. You did tell the police you killed a man?"

"Yes, Molly. I told 'em, but I didn't do it. Honest."

"I know, Bobby. I believe you. But this man," I said, tapping my finger on the photograph, "this man is not the man you said you killed?"

"No. It was the other man."

"What other man?"

"That man that was messin' in my closet."

Holy crap. "Who was that, Bobby?"

"You know. The skinny man."

"Skinny man?"

"Yeah, Molly. That one in the band. The one that plays the low-down guitar."

"Low-down guitar?"

"Yeah, you know, he plays like this," Bobby said, putting his arms in the classic bass guitar playing position. "Doh, doh, doh," he sang in a descending scale.

"The bass guitar player, Bobby?"

"Bass guitar?" His eyes shot back and forth and then he smiled. "Yeah. Yeah, that's what they call it. Bass guitar."

"Was it Stan Crockett you said you killed, Bobby?"

"I'm not sure, Molly. I think he said his name was Stan. But they can let me go home, Molly, 'cause Stan ain't killed. I know he ain't killed."

"Because you didn't kill him?"

"Yes. No. I mean, I knowed I didn't kill him, Molly. But I figured somebody killed him on account of they thought I killed him. But he ain't killed. I know he ain't killed," Bobby said.

"How do you know that, Bobby?"

"He visited me."

"He did? Did you put him on your visitors' list?"

"No. He had a buddy that works here, so he got to visit me. And he told me how he was helpin' you. He told me everything would be perfect. I told him to tell the police he ain't killed."

Stan Crockett—that Godforsaken pig. "What else did he tell

you, Bobby?"

He hung his head and swung it side to side. "I don't remember, Molly. I was so happy he wasn't killed and all . . ."

"That's okay, Bobby." I patted the glass with my open hand. "Hey. Bobby?"

"Yeah?"

"I saw a pair of fawns today in the woods across from the elementary school."

His eyes sparkled like those of a child on Christmas morning. "How many spots?"

Melancholy washed over me like floodwaters. Bobby and I used to sit real still and try to count the spots on fawns when we were kids. If I didn't find proof, Bobby might never see a fawn again. The trial started tomorrow. The rest of Bobby's life hung as heavy as a waterlogged woolen blanket across my chest.

"I don't know, Bobby. I couldn't get a good count without you."

I didn't have Dale Travis' faith in the power of reasonable doubt. I could see a Comal County jury viewing his whole presentation as smoke and mirrors, another sideshow from a fancy, big city attorney, created to obscure the truth, not reveal it.

I sensed all along that somewhere in Bobby's confession there had to be a truth we were all missing. I watched that tape so many times but never could find it. Now, I had it. Bobby caught Crockett making a dry run in the closet. That's when Crockett finalized his plans. That's when he decided to pin it all on hapless Bobby Wiggins. I knew the truth now. But what was I going to do with it?

CHAPTER FORTY-SIX

I went by the Faust Hotel on my way back from the jail. Stepping through the front doors was like stepping back in the past, a funky flashback to 1929. Designed and decorated in the ornate art nouveau Spanish renaissance style, it is filled with fine wood period furniture and adorned with the appropriate accessories for the time. The most impressive feature of the lobby is the tile floor. Its Persian rug pattern was designed for exclusive use in this hotel. It is rumored that the hotel's first owner, Walter Faust, Jr., still rode the elevator and walked the halls, a blue aura outlining his every step.

It was quaint and comfy, like an imaginary stroll through your great-grandmother's life. I loved that hotel. I wish I could say the same for the reception I got from Dale Travis. I was excited about my conversation with Bobby. Dale was exasperated.

"What can I do with this information, Molly? I can't introduce it at trial unless I put Bobby on the stand. How do *you* think he'd hold up under cross?"

"It's not too late to get a postponement, Dale. I'll take all the information I have to Barrientos at the Austin P.D. I think with what I have, he'll be able to connect Stan Crockett to Jesse's murder in no time. Then the prosecutor's flimsy case will blow away in the wind."

"How many times do I have to tell you, Molly? I am not requesting a postponement. Both Bobby and Thelma die a little more every day Bobby is behind bars."

"I know," I agreed with a sigh.

"Listen, Molly, I admire your idealistic desire for perfect justice. But that is not my job. And it is not yours. Your job is done. I have what I need to get an acquittal for Bobby. If I were actually concerned about the outcome, I'd clutch at any straw you offered. But I am not. If I were paying you, I would have ordered you to stop pursuing this line of inquiry weeks ago. As it is, I cannot tell you what to do on your own time.

"I do know what I would like you to do over the next couple of weeks. I want you to be in the courtroom. I could use your perspective and knowledge of the prosecution witnesses. Your insight into them would be a valuable tool for me as I conduct my cross-examinations. So valuable, in fact, that I would like to pay you out of my pocket to serve as my consultant throughout the trial."

"Really?"

"Yes, of course. Just be there in the courtroom, listen intently and give me the feedback I need to ensure a win. Will you do it?"

"Yes, Dale. I'd be glad to do anything I can."

"But do not distract me during the trial with any more raggedy-ass theories about who may or may not have killed Rodney Faver. Understood?"

I nodded. I wasn't happy with that raggedy-ass reference, but I let it slide.

"I need to stay focused on one thing and one thing only: my client. Is that clear?"

"Yes sir, it certainly is."

"Good. I'll see you in the courtroom tomorrow morning."

Conflicting emotions tore at me like two birds over one scrap of bread. On the one hand, I was elated that Dale regarded my skills highly enough that he was willing to pay for them. I might have a future as an investigator after all.

On the other hand, I despaired that he was indifferent to my quest to put the real killer behind bars. I wouldn't have any help or support from him to make that happen. He wouldn't even buy me a little time to do it all on my own.

Maybe I was an idealistic fool, but I knew I would not rest easy until the deaths of Faver, Happy and Jesse were resolved—until Stan Crockett or whoever did it was arrested, convicted and serving time.

There was one way to connect it all to Stan, or perhaps even clear him despite my suspicions. I needed a sample of Stan's DNA.

CHAPTER FORTY-SEVEN

At home, I picked up the phone and dialed before I could change my mind. "Hey, Stan, Bobby Wiggins' trial starts tomorrow. I'm all antsy and need some diversion."

"Just what did you have in mind?" he asked, seduction etched on every word.

The sound of his voice had a different effect on me now. Instead of eliciting chills up and down my arms, every syllable formed a hard, cold lump in the center of my chest.

"I thought you could come on over to my place tonight and I would fix dinner."

"Sounds delightful, Miss Molly. Can I bring a bottle of wine?"

"Why not? I'm partial to white merlot."

"White merlot it is then. See you this evening."

One step down. A minefield ahead. Now I had to plan dinner, run to the grocery store and get busy. I was scratching down my list for the store when the phone rang. *Please don't let it be Stan calling to cancel.*

"Hi, Molly. It's Lisa."

"I'm so glad it's you," I said without thinking.

"Thank you, Molly. That's so sweet."

Not really. But why ruin her day with honesty. "Well, you know me. What's up?"

"Monica and I were thinking that we needed to save you from yourself tonight. We both know you're a nervous wreck with everything kicking off in the courtroom tomorrow. So, we are going to come over, pick you up, take you to dinner then find someplace fun for a few mind-numbing drinks. And we won't take no for an answer."

"Gee, Lisa. *That's* really sweet. But you all are going to have to take 'no' for an answer, because I already have a dinner date."

Dead silence on the other end of the line for five, then ten, seconds. "Date, Molly? Did you say date? You are not just saying this so we'll leave you at home to fidget in peace?"

"No, Lisa, really. I have a date. Honest."

"This is the first one since Charlie . . . uh . . . since Charlie's been gone, isn't it?"

"Well, sort of. But to be honest, it's kind of work, too."

"*Mija,* what are you up to now?"

"I need a DNA sample. The easiest way to get one is to invite the subject of my curiosity to dinner."

"A DNA sample? Molly, is Wolfe coming to your house for dinner? Oh my! I know he might be a killer, but he's a star. He's hot. And a star. And he'll be in your house?"

"Lisa. Pull yourself together. I didn't say it was Wolfe. I didn't say who it was, and I want to leave it that way."

"Oh. Did you find Waller?"

"Lisa, I'm not naming names."

"Okay. Fine. Don't tell me. But obviously you think that whoever you are inviting to dinner is a murderer. Right?"

"Well, yeah, possibly."

"*Mija,* that could be very dangerous. Let me connect you to Lieutenant Padgett. You need back-up."

"No, Lisa. Absolutely not. I do not want the police involved. I shouldn't have even told you. Please don't screw this up for me."

"But, *Mija* . . ."

"No, Lisa, no."

"Okay. Okay. No SWAT team. But how about some quiet,

unassuming, undercover back-up?"

"Lisa, if one police officer shows up at my door, or even in my neighborhood, in uniform, in plain clothes or in no clothes at all, I swear I will never—never—speak to you again."

"But, *Mija* . . ."

"I'm serious, Lisa. I'm a big girl. I have a big gun. And—I know this sounds corny—but I know how to use it."

"Okay. Okay."

"Promise?"

"I promise. I shouldn't. But I promise."

I ran to the grocery, returned with food and supplies and got busy in the kitchen. I marinated the steaks, scrubbed the potatoes and rubbed them with olive oil, fixed a big Caesar salad. In the cabinet underneath the sink, I stood up open paper bags, ready to receive glasses, utensils or any other harborer of DNA I could pick up before, after or during dinner. Then I waited like a spider for the tug on my web.

CHAPTER FORTY-EIGHT

Stan could not keep his eyes off the clock. He checked the time far too often. He was doubling his anxiety level with this neurotic vigilance, but he could not help himself. The minutes oozed by slower than a slug. The anticipation was so intense, it was painful.

He took a long shower. With the showerhead turned to pulse, he stood under it as the water beat his tension way. By the time he dried off, though, it had returned. He felt its tightness in his shoulders and neck. He struggled to ignore the throbbing in his groin.

He willed his hand not to reach down and rub. He won that battle, but found himself, without thought, pressing against the arm of the sofa, the back of a chair, anything to ease the insistent hammering beat from below.

He dressed with slow deliberation, attempting to chew up as much time as he could with that mindless activity. He stood before the bathroom mirror and combed his hair. He stopped and leaned forward to check his teeth and make sure no foreign objects were stuck between them.

He knew he was a peculiar-looking man, but he also knew that when he spoke, women would forget about his appearance. He cultivated the timber and tone of his voice with the same devotion he used to cultivate his career. Both were worth the effort. He could charm the pants off the shyest virgin and he was now a star. He wasn't a pretty boy like Trenton Wolfe, but he did okay. He longed to get back on the road again. But first, he had to clean up his mess and replenish the band.

He was amazed that Mullet was making this so easy for him. He did not have to plot and plan their encounter. He did not have to sneak into her house. She invited him there. She'd open the door and welcome him with open arms.

Life is good, Stan Crockett, he said to himself, *but death can be even better.* He laughed out loud at his play on words.

In the bedroom, he slid a coil of guitar string into each of the back pockets of his jeans. He opened a dresser drawer and pulled out a small revolver. He checked to make sure it was loaded and pushed it down into the specially crafted holster on the inside of his boot. He wondered if he needed to bring a knife, but then decided if he wanted one tonight, Mullet's kitchen would be open for business. And he smiled.

Timing was the all-important factor here. When should he make his move? If she was a lousy cook, he'd jump after the first bite, he thought. Again, he laughed out loud at his cleverness.

He hoped she was an incredible cook. It would be exquisite to savor the taste of well-prepared food and the intense anticipation at the same time. To look across the table and watch her chew and sip, knowing all the while that she was enjoying the final pleasure of her life.

He shuddered, rubbed himself and headed for the door. It was time.

CHAPTER FORTY-NINE

The baked potatoes were five minutes from done and the coals burned red hot in the grill on the back porch, when the doorbell rang. I slid the gun into the back waistband of my jeans and made sure my oversized T-shirt concealed it from view. I considered wearing more feminine attire, but none of my dresses had a good place to conceal a weapon.

Satisfied that I was as ready as I'd ever be, I opened the front door and invited Stan into my home. I felt kind of creepy doing that. I hoped I could erase his presence from my memory when all this was behind us.

I poured two glasses of wine, handed one to Stan and said, "Have a seat. I'll go put the steaks on the grill." As I dropped the meat on the hot metal grate, I thought I saw something moving a few yards away. I blinked away the smoke and rising steam and looked again. Nothing. Probably my jumpy nerves imagining things, or a just a neighbor's cat streaking through the yard.

I joined Stan in the living room, where he entertained me with stories of his life on the road. He slipped in a lot of tales brimming with sly sexual innuendo. It was embarrassing but I had to admit, a couple of weeks ago, I would have been flattered by his obvious attempt at seduction.

Now I was immune to his voice. I listened to his big-star bull crap and saw right through it. But I smiled just the same, acted amazed and begged for more. Each minute was more irritating than the last.

As we ate, he complimented the food often, which was nice even coming from a possible cold-blooded killer. I felt some discomfort, though, at the way he stared at me when I chewed and concentrated on my lips when I took a sip of wine. It was as if he was hungry, his plate was empty and the only pleasure he could get from food came from watching me consume it.

After dinner, I stashed his wine glass and fork into bags under the sink. Once again, I caught something outside the window from the corner of my eye. I looked but saw nothing. Relax, Molly old girl. The danger is not in the backyard, it's seated on your sofa. I walked back into the living room with two big mugs of coffee.

"All we've been doing tonight, Molly, is talk about me," Stan said. "I don't know a thing about you."

Thank God for that, I thought with genuine gratitude. "Oh, I've had a boring little life, Stan. Just a small-town girl. Never done much. Never seen much. Never been much of anywhere. I'll probably die in the same state at some ripe old age—unlike poor Jesse Kriewaldt."

His eyes turned to dark slits. "Who?"

Jeez, what was I doing? I needed to put on the brakes or change direction. I knew I shouldn't continue with this, but I couldn't help myself. I was careening downhill and out of control. It was as if, since I no longer had any interest in flirting with Stan, I felt compelled to flirt with danger. I rubbed my back against the chair to feel the comforting lump of my handgun in the small of my back. "Oh, you know Jesse. He's the guy that wrote 'Bite the Moon.' "

"That punk. Sorry wannabe songwriting loser. You can't believe everything you hear, Molly."

"Really, Stan. Have you heard this?"

I crossed the room and turned on the CD player. The thready

voice of Jesse Kriewaldt filled the room. Before I could turn back around, I felt Stan's hot breath on the back of my neck and a line of sharp pain across my throat. *Damn you, Molly Mullet. How stupid. Why did you ever turn your back on that man?*

I reached back for my gun. His hand was there first. He batted my hand away, pulled out the gun and tossed it. It bounced on the sofa, hit the floor and skittered across the floor.

I gasped, but could not breathe. I clawed at my throat. *Oh, dear God, don't let me die.* I felt pain cut deeper into my skin. I struggled to maintain consciousness. My head was light. My knees wobbled. I threw my hands up and back. I tried to dig into his eyes, but I couldn't find them. I'd lost all sense of where my body ended and his began. *Oh, Charlie, this is it. Open the door. I'm coming home.*

I thought I heard shattering glass. And then I fell forward. The sound of a gunshot pulled me out of the black abyss. My face was pressed to the floor. I had no idea of how I got there or how long I'd been there. I turned my head in time to see something large hit the floor in front of me. It was Stan. Did I do that?

No. Lisa was on his back. He reared up on his arms and tried to throw her off. She hung on like she was super-glued in the saddle. All the while, she held a huge coffee table book in her two hands and rained down blows on his head again and again.

Monica sat on Stan's legs as calmly as if she was on her front porch in a rocking chair. She was talking on her cell phone as a thread of blood twisted and turned on its way down her arm.

If it weren't for the searing pain around my neck, I would have sworn I was dreaming. I blacked out again, but it couldn't have been for long because Monica was still on the phone when I woke up. I brought my fingers to my throat and felt a sickening slickness. I held out my hand to look at my fingers, but I couldn't focus, and everything was in black and white. Where did the color go? It must be a dream. I brought my fingers to my lips and licked their tips. The rusty tang of blood raced through my taste buds. I never remembered taste in any other dream I'd had. This was real. I needed to get up and help Lisa and Monica. Before I could make a move, I was gone again.

The next thing I knew, I was in a bright room that hurt my eyes. I was lying flat on my back instead of on my face. A guy in a white jacket loomed over me. It was hard to focus on his outline because everything was so white. I was either in a hospital or in heaven. I'd be pleased with either option.

The guy leaned closer to me. Man, he was cute. Or maybe not. I either almost died or actually died and was probably delusional either way.

Then he spoke. "Hi. It's time for you to say, 'Where am I?' and then I'll say, 'You're in the hospital.' "

"Oh." I was alive. Good. I'd kinda gotten used to living my life that way. I reached up and felt the bandage on my neck.

"You'll be okay. We had some repair work to do, and you'll probably have a scar. But I suppose in your line of work, a scar will add character, credibility and a bit of gravitas to your persona. And it will offset the absurdity of your cow-pie tattoo. So I wouldn't worry a bit about it."

Oh, man. That freakin' tattoo might as well be on my face. I changed the subject fast. "Shouldn't you be saying, 'Young lady, you're lucky to be alive'?" My voice was so raspy I didn't recognize it.

"You really shouldn't talk unless necessary. But no, you're lucky you have friends like those two girls who kept it from being a closer call."

"Where the heck did they come from?"

He laughed. "Got me. You'll have to ask them about that."

"Well, where did they go?"

"The bossy one gave the officers and deputies a hard time

243

because she wanted to stay with you. She was clutching some oversized book that she claimed was for your protection."

I smiled despite the pain it caused. "Must be Lisa."

"I don't know. I wasn't sure if I got their names straight. But anyway, they hustled her off to the police station, or maybe the sheriff's office, to take her statement."

"Monica?" I asked.

"The quiet one is still here. She fought us for a while. She wanted to stay by your side. Finally, we convinced her to let us treat her bullet wound."

I lurched up to a sitting position. "Bullet wound?"

"Nothing vital was hit. The bullet side-scraped a bone and exited out her back. She'll have a sore arm and shoulder for a couple of weeks. Otherwise, she'll be fine."

"What about . . ."

"The guy who attacked you?"

I nodded and a pain seared from one side of my neck to another.

"He survived, unfortunately. But he is under arrest."

"For murder?"

"No, attempted murder." He laughed. "You really didn't die. Honest."

"I need to get out of here," I said. I tried to move my legs to throw them over the side of the bed, but they wouldn't budge. A soft touch from the white-coated guy was all it took to put me flat again.

"Not hardly," he said. "You need some rest. You lost a lot of blood."

I started to object, but then I was gone again.

CHAPTER FIFTY

I knew there was a lot of activity in and out of my room throughout the night and into the early morning. I couldn't say who or why those people came into my room. All I knew was that when I was aware of someone's presence, I tried to wake up and speak, but my eyelids fluttered and slammed shut each time.

No one was in the room when my eyes snapped to attention, and a sense of panic shot adrenaline through my bloodstream. At first, I didn't understand the reason for my alarm. Then I remembered. I was due in court this morning. What time was it? I looked around. No clock in sight.

I threw my legs over the side of the bed and steadied myself as a wave of nausea struck. I put a hand over my mouth and breathed deeply. When the sickness passed, I slid off the edge of the bed and onto my feet. I grabbed the nightstand as my head spun and my knees turned to weak pudding. I opened the top drawer of the little table and spotted my watch. Flecks of blood dotted the crystal. The time was 9:15. Crap.

I eased over to the closet, tossing aside my hospital gown as I walked. I pulled out my day-old panties and slipped them on. Then I grabbed my jeans. The waistband was dark and crusty with dried blood. The stain extended down to midway on the pockets. I swallowed my revulsion and slipped them on. It was my own blood, after all. With any luck, my T-shirt would cover up the worst of it.

Then I looked for my bra and T-shirt, but they weren't there. A shadow of a memory crossed behind my eyes. Someone in white cut off both articles of clothing while I drifted in and out of consciousness. Crap. Crap. Crap. I slid my hospital gown back on and went in search of a shirt.

I went down the hall, sticking my head in one room after another. I was greeted by puzzled looks from the bed-bound residents. I smiled and said hello. Finally, I looked into one room and instead of meeting another pair of eyes, I saw a lump under the blanket. Even the head was covered and the back was turned toward the doorway.

I crept into the room and eased open the closet door. Crap. It was a man. Oh well. I pulled off my hospital gown, took the plaid shirt off the hanger and slid my arms inside. Yikes. It was a very large man. The shirt went down to my knees. I looked like a derelict. On the bright side, the shirt covered the bloodstain and my misbegotten tattoo, plus it was baggy enough that no one would notice that I was braless. I whispered "Thank you" to my sleeping donor and tiptoed out the door.

I tried to look nonchalant as I scurried up the hall, down the hall and out of the building. A lot of people noticed, though. I returned each odd look with a smile.

On the sidewalk, it dawned on me. I didn't have a car. I didn't have a cell phone. Damn. A taxi pulled up the circular drive by the front door and disgorged a passenger. I hobbled up to the driver and asked if he could give me a ride to the courthouse. Through suspicious eyes, he scanned me head to toe. He sighed, shook his head and said, "Get in."

Three blocks away from the hospital, I remembered I did not have my purse. I dug in all my pockets but, as I suspected, I didn't even find a spare penny. I asked the driver to take me to the law offices of Edward Beacham instead.

After explaining to the driver that I'd be back with the seven-dollar, fifty-cent fare and a healthy tip, I burst through the front door of Eddie's office. "Sara, loan me twenty bucks."

"What the hell happened to you?"

"It's a long story. I'll explain later, Sara. I promise. I've got to pay the cab driver and get to court."

"You're going to court dressed like that? Our worst client looks better than that. You gotta at least comb your hair."

"Please, Sara, just give me a twenty."

She shook her head, opened the petty cash box and handed me the money. As I grabbed the bill from her fingertips, Eddie emerged from the back office. "Molly?"

"Hi, Eddie," I said as I headed for the door.

"What's up with you?"

I didn't stop to answer.

"She's late for court," Sara said.

"Dressed like that?" I heard Eddie say as the door shut behind me.

I handed the money to the relieved driver and told him to keep the change. I walked a block and crossed the street to the courthouse. As I slipped into the courtroom, Dale Travis spoke in an earnest voice to the group of prospective jurors, asking questions and jotting down responses.

I slipped up the aisle. He turned toward me just then. His eyebrows shot up so high, I thought they might fly off. I smiled. He scowled. He turned back to the jury. I sat in the bench behind the defense table. I whispered a condensed version of the night's events into the assisting attorney's ear.

She scribbled a quick note and held it up in front of her chest. Dale glanced at it and waved her off. She extended her arms and pushed the note toward him and shook it.

Dale blew an exasperated breath and turned to the judge. "Your Honor, may I have a moment, please, to consult with my colleague?"

"Yes, you may, Mr. Travis, but make it quick."

"Thank you, Your Honor."

He put his arms on the table and leaned forward, casting a disgusted look at me in the process. I smiled. He listened to the other attorney and looked up at me with wide eyes and a gaping mouth. He spun around and said, "Your Honor, may we approach the bench?"

"Certainly."

Dale and Ted Kneipper whispered to the judge. Dale was calm but forceful. Kneipper's arms flew in every direction when he spoke. Abruptly, the two men turned back around and walked toward their respective tables, Dale with a slight smile hiding in the corners of his mouth, Kneipper with a furrowed brow and clenched fists.

Curiosity buzzed through the rows of onlookers, causing Judge Krause to slam her gavel. The crowd noise ended as if she'd pressed a mute button. "Deputy, please escort the prospective jurors to the deliberation room."

The men and women who'd responded that morning to the call of justice shuffled across the front of the courtroom and out the side door. When the last one disappeared from view and the deputy nodded at the judge, she said, "Court is adjourned for fifteen minutes," and slammed her gavel again.

"Gentlemen, I'll see you in my chambers," she said looking from Kneipper to Travis. She rose with a judicious swish of black robes and descended the steps. She paused then and turned to face me. "Miss Mullet, you'd best join us."

She exited the courtroom, the two attorneys fast on her heels. I trailed behind them, and as I pushed the wooden swinging door, I heard loud voices in the back of the courtroom. I turned to find the source of the commotion and saw the red face and agitated demeanor of the Comal County Sheriff. By his side, a pale chief of police barked back at him as they entered the double doors.

I stepped into the judge's chambers, and the clerk pulled the door closed behind me. Dale gestured to an empty chair and I slid into it.

"Dale, this best not be another of your fancy courtroom hijinks."

"No, Your Honor. Trust me, I save all my hijinks until after the jury is empanelled," Dale said with a laugh.

The judge glared at him. She was not amused.

"Don't trust him, Judge," Kneipper said. "Travis is as full of weasely moves as a barn full of ferrets."

"You all are both lawyers, and I am one, too. Based on my many years of experience with this species, I do not believe it is wise for me to trust either one of you. But why don't we try you on for size, Ms. Mullet. Just what is going on here?"

I pulled one side of the bandage loose from my neck, wincing with each tug.

"Oh my," said Judge Krause. "I don't think even Travis would go this far for a bit of courtroom drama," she said to the prosecutor. To me, she asked, "Who did this to you?"

"Stan Crockett, ma'am."

"And you think this same man also committed the murder we are about to try Mr. Wiggins for?"

"Yes, ma'am."

A buzzer blared on the judge's desk. She pressed a button and said, "Yes?" A loud pounding on the door drowned out the response at the other end.

Dale rose, cracked open the door, looked out, and then pulled it wide open to reveal the sheriff and the police chief. Both looked agitated now.

"Sorry for barging in like this, Your Honor, but your clerk didn't want to let us in," the sheriff said.

"She was just doing her job, gentlemen. Now what's on your mind?"

"We arrested the guy who did that," the sheriff said, pointing to me.

"There's a possibility that he also killed Rodney Faver," the police chief added.

"Possibility? Your Honor, Stan Crockett killed Rodney Faver," the sheriff contradicted his cohort.

"We don't know that with certainty yet, Sheriff," the police chief argued.

"The man confessed. What more do you need?"

"So did Bobby Wiggins," the police chief retorted.

"So you claim," the sheriff snapped back.

"Gentlemen, gentlemen," the judge interrupted.

"Sorry, Your Honor," both men mumbled in unison.

"Ted, do you think a withdrawal of the charges against Wiggins might be in order?"

The district attorney looked like he'd taken a punch in the gut. His eyes blinked in a staccato rhythm, his mouth opened and shut like a landed fish. He looked at the judge as if he didn't understand a word she said.

"Ted? Pay attention," the judge ordered. "It looks as if Ms. Mullet here just flushed your case down the proverbial toilet. Should I save the taxpayers a few dollars and dismiss this case?"

Kneipper swallowed hard. "Dismiss without prejudice, Your Honor?"

"With prejudice, Your Honor," Travis countered. "There's no reason to keep Wiggins hanging on the hook on these groundless charges."

"Without prejudice," the judge pronounced. "At least until we sort this mess out."

"Yes, Your Honor," Dale responded.

"Let's go back into the courtroom, gentlemen, Molly."

We filed out and took our seats as the judge ascended to the bench. She called for the deputy to bring the jury pool back into the room. When they were seated, she thanked them all for their willingness to serve and sent them on their way.

Then it was time for the two attorneys and the judge to complete their official last waltz. When all the proper steps were executed, the judge slammed down her gavel and said, "Court adjourned." She then turned to Bobby and said, "Mr. Wiggins, you are free to go."

For a moment the courtroom was as silent as a church in prayer. Then a roar erupted. The prosecution team left the room by the back door to avoid the press.

Thelma, sobbing and laughing at the same time, hugged Bobby. Still holding one of his hands, she threw one arm around Dale Travis and pulled him tight against her. Her eyes met mine over the top of Travis' shoulder.

Thelma moved in my direction, tugging Bobby behind her through the crowd of backslapping well-wishers who smothered the defense table. She sat down on the bench beside me and pulled Bobby down next to her. "Thank you, Molly. We can never repay you."

"Thank you, Mrs. Wiggins. There's no need."

"I must say though, when I saw you creep in here in that outfit, I thought you must've been drinking." She tilted her head and examined my neck. "From the looks of it, girl, I'd say a hangover would have been a blessing."

She dropped Bobby's hand and with a touch lighter than butterfly wings pressed my bandage back in place. Even with her gentleness, a searing pain streaked across my throat.

Next to Thelma, Bobby's expression bounced between a grinning pleasure to that of a lost and bewildered boy and back again.

"I need to get Bobby home," Thelma said. "Praise the Lord,

that sounds so sweet. He needs some quiet time to understand what happened here this morning."

I nodded and winced.

Thelma patted my cheek and rose. "Come on, Bobby, let's go home."

"Home?" Bobby asked.

"Yes, home, Bobby," his mother said.

Bobby followed her for a few steps. Then he stopped, turned and retraced his path. He threw his arms around me, pinning my arms to my sides. "Thank you, Molly," he said, and we both burst into tears.

CHAPTER FIFTY-ONE

A deputy gave me a ride home at last. I stepped up on my porch where the tattered remnants of yellow crime scene tape, once tied to the railing, now flapped in the breeze. I opened the front door with only one thought on my mind: a hot cup of chamomile tea followed by a nice, long nap.

The chaos in the living room stunned me as I stepped inside. An occasional table lay on its side. Beside it the shattered remains of my great-grandmother's lamp, ruined beyond repair, the hand-painted windmill on its pottery base no longer recognizable.

One corner of the Oriental rug in the center of the room was stained a rusty black with what I assumed was my dried blood. The poor rug looked like a lost cause. Beside the rug, more blood soaked deep into the grain of the wood on the boards of the oak flooring. Hopefully, a light sanding would restore it.

In the kitchen, I turned on the teakettle and surveyed the damage. Someone had swept a pile of glass to the side of one cabinet. Here and there I spotted the twinkle of missed pieces strewn across the floor. A scrap piece of plywood fastened by big, ugly nails hung over the missing pane in the door. Next to the door, a square hole in the sheetrock revealed the skeleton of the house—in all likelihood, the spot where the bullet lodged after passing through Monica.

I opened the cabinet doors under the sink. My paper bags were untouched and now worthless. As the teakettle whistled, the telephone rang. I splashed water over the tea bag in the waiting mug and picked up the kitchen phone.

"Molly?"

"Yes."

"This is Sergeant Barrientos—Rick Barrientos—Austin P.D."

"Hello, Sergeant."

"I understand congratulations are in order."

"Yes," I said with a smile. "Bobby is out of jail."

"And Stan Crockett's behind bars."

"Have you charged him with Jesse Kriewaldt's murder?" I asked.

"Not yet. Crockett confessed to Faver's murder and claimed it was self-defense. He insisted, however, that he didn't do Parker or Kriewaldt."

"You believe him?"

"No. Not at all. Right now, I'm waiting for word on a search warrant. When I have it, we'll get hair and blood samples from Crockett to compare with the evidence we found at the murder scene.

"The Hays County Sheriff's Department doesn't buy his claim of innocence in the Parker case, either. They're all over at Crockett's house now, and a team of evidence techs is on their way there from Austin. What they hope to find is the weapon he used to shoot Parker, but so far no sign of it."

"Do you know about the DNA on the T-shirt I took to a lab in San Antonio?"

"Yeah, your attorney called me about that. Kind of weird, getting an assist from a defense attorney. But this whole case has been pretty weird. I called the Texas Rangers' office down in San Antonio. They've got someone going over to pick up the evidence from the lab. The way I figure it, Crockett put on Wolfe's T-shirt and pulled on the orange poncho. From his dry run, he knew the gap around the neckline might leave blood on the shirt underneath, so he had to wear someone else's shirt and picked one of Wolfe's. He left the poncho on the body, but he discarded Wolfe's shirt in the kick drum where he knew it would appear hidden, but someone would find it and turn the investigation away from him. But, Molly, there's another reason I called."

"Yes, Sergeant."

"Well, uh, this isn't exactly business, so Rick would be more appropriate."

"Okay, Rick."

"I'd like to see you again—unofficially. How about dinner sometime?"

"Sure," I said with a grin. We made plans. He'd pick me up Saturday night at 7:00.

I hung up the phone with a smile engraved in my face and finished preparing my cup of tea. In the bedroom, I exchanged my stolen shirt for a large faded T-shirt, soft, worn and still bearing a fading scent of the dryer sheet that hugged it as it spun dry. I slipped off my crusty jeans and two-day-old panties and eased my battered body under the covers.

I sipped my tea, propped up in bed, grinning like a schoolgirl. The phone rang again. It was Mike Elliot.

"I thought you'd want to know that Susan Tedeschi is playing here Thursday night."

"Oh, man, that's right. It kinda slipped out of my mind. I would love to see her."

"I thought so. I, uh, put your name on the list at the front desk. I was hoping you'd come as my guest. I'll be working that night, but I'll still be able to find some time to sit with you. That is, of course, unless you want to bring someone else with you. I could put another name on the list if that's what you want."

"Of course, not, Mike. I'll be *your* guest. That'll be great."

"I'll see you Thursday night, then."

"See you then. Thanks, Mike."

My, my, my. A wounded, bandaged neck. A few stray scabs still decorating one side of my face. And go figure. I've never been more popular. I fell asleep feeling like the queen of the ball.

I'm not sure how long I lay there, lost to the world, when the doorbell rang. I pulled off the covers and swung my legs out of bed. Every muscle in my body screamed in protest. Grunting with the effort, I picked my jeans up of the floor. Yuck! I dropped them again in disgust.

I walked over to the dresser to find a clean pair and the doorbell rang again. "Just a minute. Just a minute," I shouted.

I shuffled to the front door while each creaking joint responsible for my mobility begged me to lie back down. There on my porch was Trenton Wolfe, and by his side was Bart Seidell. I was speechless and wary.

Seidell broke the silence. "May we please come in and have a word with you, Ms. Mullet?"

I pulled the door all the way open and gestured them inside. "Please do," was all I said.

They sat side-by-side on my sofa. Seidell looked comfortable. His face bore that serene—albeit obnoxious—one-day-I'll-be-a-judge look that influential and successful lawyers often wore. Wolfe, on the other hand, fidgeted with discomfort.

Seidell poked Wolfe with an elbow and flashed a smile at me.

Wolfe swallowed a couple of times and spoke. "I owe you an apology, Ms. Mullet."

Yes, you do, buddy. And it's killing you, isn't it? I thought as, in the back of my mind, my mother's voice badgered me to be gracious. I was not in the mood. I could still feel the sting of his name-calling like a fresh slap in the face. Although I couldn't force myself to be the forgiving hostess, I could follow my mother's other maxim: if you don't have anything nice to say, don't say anything at all.

After an awkward silence and pointed looks from his attorney, Wolfe continued. "And I owe you an explanation, too." He cleared his throat.

I sat imperious in my chair with regal posture and my hands in a proper but prissy pose in my lap. I'm not proud to admit it, but I enjoyed watching that man squirm.

"You see," Wolfe said, "the night we wrote—uh, I thought we wrote—'Bite the Moon,' I had indulged in a lot of wine, marijuana and other illegal substances." He turned to Seidell with a question on his face. Seidell nodded and Wolfe said, "I really don't remember much about that night. I just remember the next morning, Stan said, 'Let's run through it again.' And I said, 'What?' And he said, 'The song we wrote last night.' And I said, 'What song?' "

Seidell rolled his eyes and shifted his weight on the sofa.

"Then he pulled out the lyrics he said I wrote and he typed up," Wolfe continued, "and the melody he said he composed and then scored after I passed out."

"And you believed him?" I asked.

"Well, yeah. And after we did that first run through, I thought maybe I should get wasted more often. This was really good stuff," he said with a chuckle.

"Get to the point," Seidell interrupted.

Wolfe shrugged. "So, anyway, after all this came down, I went digging."

Seidell sighed.

"Uh, Mr. Seidell went digging and found a copy of Jesse Kriewaldt's CD. And we knew the truth. I never wrote those lyrics. Jesse did. I knew Jesse had been around that day we did the gig at Solms Halle. And he looked real happy when he left. At the time, I just figured Rodney stroked his ego and gave him encouragement for his future. You know, the rah-rah, you'll be a great songwriter someday speech. Rodney always had a soft spot for those sad sacks. Looking back, though, I imagine what really happened is that Rodney made him a belated offer for the purchase of the rights to 'Bite the Moon.' I guess Rodney then confronted Stan about stealing the song. And you know the rest."

"All this for one song?"

"It wasn't just the royalties. Our whole rep was built on that song. And Rodney was fielding commercial offers to use the song to push product."

I closed my eyes and swallowed. One song. Three deaths— almost four, I thought as my hand brushed across the bandage on my neck. I opened my eyes when Seidell spoke.

"We are on our way to the police department here in New Braunfels. We thought we owed you an explanation first. After we make a statement here in town, we'll stop at the Hays County Sheriff's Department and then continue north to the Austin Police Department. Once again, we deeply regret any inconvenience or affront we may have caused." He rose to his feet and stuck out his hand.

Inconvenience? Affront? Jeez! I thought about leaving Seidell's hand hanging in mid-air, but years of Miss Manners' indoctrination pushed my hand forward to grasp his.

Seidell shot Wolfe a hard glance.

"Oh, yeah," Wolfe said as he thrust out his hand. "We're really sorry."

I shook his hand, too, although I was certain the only real source of his remorse was that he had to apologize at all.

Once again, I was alone. I felt hollow in my empty house. Now that I was up and about, I figured I might as well get started on the cleanup. First priority: the broken window glass on the kitchen floor. I went to the bedroom for my slippers. I sure didn't need cut-up feet to add pain to my already tortured body.

I slipped them on where they sat right inside the door. I heard a small noise and froze in place, listening, my body rigid with the strain. I heard nothing more. Probably nothing in the first place. I was such a paranoid freak.

Creaking and moaning with every bend of my body, I swept the biggest pieces of glass into a dustpan, then went to the hall closet for the vacuum. I paused again, thinking I heard the sound of breathing. If my imagination didn't calm down soon, I'd have to see a therapist. How stupid.

I lifted the vacuum. It felt much heavier than normal as I carried it the short distance down the hall. I had to lean on it to recover for a moment before I turned it on. I ran it over the whole area and stood back to examine the kitchen for any telltale glints that betrayed the threatening presence of a missed sliver.

CHAPTER FIFTY-TWO

He crouched beneath her open bedroom window and listened to her breathing. The rhythm was steady and slow. He knew she was deep in sleep.

He thought about easing the screen off, leaning in the window and shooting her where she lay. Even if she heard him removing the screen, she would be dead before she was really awake. It would be so easy. Too easy.

He yearned to have his hands on her as she gasped for her last breath. To fight her as she struggled in vain. To smell her fear. To see the wet stain spread on her pants as her bladder released. To hear the rustle of vulture wings. To feel her life fade away.

I am a dead man, he thought. *I can wait.*

By the time she roused in response to the ringing doorbell, his knees were stiff and throbbed with pain. He moved with quick precision and grace just the same. He removed the screen as soon as she left the room. He pulled his body over the windowsill and slithered inside. He stepped into her closet, pulling the door almost shut behind him. He buried himself behind her hanging clothes.

He inhaled her scent and the familiar throbbing beat resurrected in his pants. He rubbed its source, urging patience as he listened to the murmur of voices from the other room. Soon the visitors would be gone. Soon he and she would be alone. When she returned to the bedroom, he'd make his move.

He was a walking dead man, but before his song ended, he would watch her die.

CHAPTER FIFTY-THREE

The phone rang. I picked it up and regretted it the second I heard the sound of his voice.

"Mullet. This is Hawkins."

"I have nothing to say to you, Hawkins. Leave me alone. Forever. And drop dead." I slammed the phone down. I smiled.

The phone rang again. I snatched it off the cradle. "Hawkins, I'll get a restraining order."

"Shut up, Mullet. There's a squad car on the way to your house."

"I can't believe you are doing this again, Hawkins, you stupid jerk. I am calling my attorney right now. Goodbye."

"No. Don't hang up, Mullet. Listen. Please."

The desperation in his voice gave me pause.

"Another prisoner jumped Crockett. They took him to Mc-Kenna. At the hospital, the deputy was reattaching his cuffs. Somehow, he got her gun. The deputy is dead. One nurse may be dying. And we don't know where Crockett is."

The tingle of rushing adrenaline teased my cheeks and raced down my arms and legs. "Please, Hawkins. Please tell me this is your idea of a sick and stupid joke."

"Mullet, unless all your doors and windows are shut and locked, you better get out of the house right now."

Crap. Crap. Crap. I couldn't think.

"Mullet. Mullet. Are you still there?"

"Yes," I hissed as the image of the breeze blowing through

my bedroom window stirred in my mind. "My window is open."

"Get out of there."

I froze. My eyes searched every corner of my room as they filled with the tears of panic. My gun, where is my gun?

"Mullet? Do you hear me?"

"Yes," I exhaled.

"Go! Get out of there! Go now!"

I set down the phone. I had to have my gun. What if he was just outside of the door? Hiding on my porch? Beside my porch? Behind the tree? I had to have my gun.

I raced to the nightstand beside my bed and jerked open the drawer. It wasn't there. Where was it? Then, the memory swept through me. I saw the gun's sparkling arc as it bounced on the sofa and skittered across the floor. Was it still there? Under the chair? No. The police must have confiscated it when they processed the scene. Damn. I inhaled a deep breath and took just one step. My closet door flew open and slammed like thunder against the wall.

There stood Crockett in his orange prison garb. The brightness of his clothing drained the last sign of life from his face. Dark rings outlined sunken eyes. Cheekbones threatened to erupt through the skin of his face. A cuff dangled from his left wrist. His right hand gripped a gun.

"Stay right there, girl," he said.

He stepped between me and the bedroom doorway. "I don't know why you found me more expendable than your idiot friend, Ms. Mullet. It was a bad choice."

He took a step toward me. I glanced with longing at the open window on the other side of the bed. I entertained a brief fantasy of scrambling across the mattress and lunging out the window. But I knew I'd be dead before I reached the other side.

There was another window on this side of the room. But it was closed. Locked. Curtains drawn. I backed up to it just the same. Crockett moved another step closer.

"Stand still, Molly Mullet. I really don't want to have to shoot you."

"There's a squad car on the way, Stan."

He shrugged. "I can kill you long before it gets here."

"If you kill me it will just be that much worse on you," I said. I couldn't believe I said that. Here I was, about to die, stealing dialogue from a cheap thirties gangster movie.

"Maybe. Maybe not," he said. "I killed a deputy earlier today. Don't really think anyone will care about you one way or the other. But, as I said, I don't want to shoot you."

I exhaled a ragged breath of relief. "You don't?"

"No, Ma'am. I want to hold you while you die."

Cold sweat popped up on the nape of my neck and in the palms of my hands.

He patted his orange pants. "Darn. No pockets. Guess I'm fresh out of guitar strings," he said with a grin.

He took one more step in my direction. I backed my rump up against the windowpane. Charlie, I thought, please make my stupid plan work or let me die fast and quick.

"This time, I'll have to use my hands. I wouldn't have to squeeze too hard to pop open that fresh cut on your neck. It'll make it all a little messy but I won't mind too much. Will you?"

"Maybe. Maybe not," I said. I braced my legs and pushed my body off the floor and into the windowpane with all my strength. My body flew backwards. My rump slammed into the glass. For an eternal moment, it resisted my attack. Then it cracked. Yielded. And I tumbled through.

I heard a gunshot. I hit the porch on my back. Jarring pain bounced through my head. I didn't know if I was hit or if my agony was all from impact. I didn't take the time to figure it out. On all fours, I scurried across the porch, down the steps and into the flowerbed beside the house. Another shot fired. I smelled the cordite burning in the air. I heard the pounding of his feet inside the house.

Keeping low, I darted from the flowerbed to the far side of my car. As I ducked down, another shot rang out. It missed me. It hit my car. A sound like cracking ice echoed in my ears as a spider web of fissures traveled across my windshield. Oh, my poor car.

After that, there were so many sounds I could not always tell where one began and the other ended. Sirens, shouts, gunfire, running feet. I had no idea what was happening, and I dared not expose myself to find out.

"Mullet. Molly Mullet."

It was Hawkins. I never thought I'd be glad to hear his voice. But there you go—how sweet a sound.

I rose to my feet and he rushed to my side.

"You're bleeding, Mullet."

I put a hand to the bandage on my neck and felt stickiness oozing through the gauze.

"Let's get you into one of the ambulances," he said, throwing an arm around my shoulders.

I squealed. It was like little tiny knifes digging into the flesh of my back.

"Oh shit, Mullet. I'm sorry. You threw yourself through that window, hunh?"

I nodded and tried to smile through clenched teeth. Hawkins escorted me to the ambulance and instructed the EMTs to put me face down on the stretcher. They slid me in and I shouted, "Hawkins."

He stuck his head through the back doors. "Yeah, Mullet?"

"Did you kill the bastard?"

"Naw. He took one in the shoulder, one in the hand, and another in the knee, but he'll survive. So, don't worry, you'll still be the star witness for the prosecution, girl."

"Thanks, Hawkins. Thanks a lot. You might need to visit the firing range a little more often."

He just laughed and walked away. I could still hear him laughing as the doors were shut and we drove off.

CHAPTER FIFTY-FOUR

At the hospital, they cleaned and rebandaged my neck. There was a little pulling on the stitches but no real damage. I suffered through the indignity of an exposed backside as nurses plucked slivers of glass out of my body from the top of my shoulders down to the top of my thighs. A gaggle of doctors strolled by making jokes at my expense. The nurses tried not to laugh at me, but their strangled snorts gave them away.

A deputy came to my rescue again and gave me a ride home in the brightness of a fresh morning. This time, I tilted my body to the side in the seat. It wasn't very dignified, but it was far less painful. I'd be sleeping on my stomach for days.

I stepped onto the porch and saw that someone had enhanced my décor with another ratty piece of plywood—this one hammered over my busted bedroom window. I sighed and let myself in.

I hurried through the living room, not wanting to look at the damage still there. In the kitchen, I fixed a tuna sandwich and ate it standing over the sink. A sink-feeder having a tuna sandwich for breakfast. Pathetic.

Do I go to bed? Or do I clean up the disaster zone of blood, broken pottery and tumbled furniture. I walked into the living room and surveyed the war zone. My answering machine light blinked a samba beat distracting me from the task at hand. I pressed the button and listened. A call from Gina Galaviz at KSAT-12. Another from Brad Messer's producer at KTSA. One from David Ferguson at KGNB. I shut the machine off. To hell with the rest of the messages. I was going to bed.

I almost made it. But the doorbell rang. I toyed with the idea of ignoring it, then trudged to the door. Eddie Beacham stood on my porch. In his arms was a wiggling ball of fur. I fought the urge to smile—no sense encouraging Eddie. I folded my arms across my chest. "Cute puppy," I said.

"He's a real sweetheart. I think you'll like him. And he's AKC registered, one-hundred-percent Shetland Sheepdog."

"Funny. I didn't think I'd see you with a Sheltie. You look more like the pet rat type to me."

"Still holding a grudge, Molly?" He tsked at me. "Things turned out well just the same. Seems like, under those circumstances, you could let it all go."

My hand flew to my cut throat. "No thanks to you, Eddie."

"That's cold, Molly. And I sure am sorry I caused you problems, even if they helped lead you to the solution. Mind if I set this little guy down? He's squirming so much, I'm afraid I might drop him on his head."

"Suit yourself. What's his name?"

The puppy gamboled toward me and I squatted down to greet him. He wriggled his rump, wagged his tail and licked my fingers. Again, I forced down the smile I did not want Eddie to see.

"The name's up to you, Molly," Eddie said.

"You want *me* to name *your* dog?"

"It's your dog. Call him a peace offering."

"That would be a stupid name." I grimaced, knowing I was being difficult and obnoxious.

Eddie sighed. "Whatever, Molly. It's up to you."

"Eddie, I can't accept this."

The puppy lifted himself up on his hind legs and licked my nose. I was melting. I had to act fast. I scooped him in my arms, stood up and held him out to Eddie.

"He's yours, Molly. You love dogs. It's time you had one again."

"It's more complicated than that, Eddie."

"I know. It's all wrapped around your grief for Charlie. It's been five years, Molly. It's time to move on."

"I can't."

"Yes, you can. And this little guy can help you do it."

I looked into the puppy's eyes and warm tingling surged to my fingers and toes. No. No way. "Eddie, here. He's your dog." I sat him back down on the floor and made shooing motions in Eddie's direction. Instead of moving toward Eddie, the puppy plopped down on his rump and stared at me with adoring, begging eyes.

"You know how irresponsible I am," Eddie said. "How could you sleep at night not knowing if I remembered to give this poor, defenseless puppy his dinner?"

I bit my lower lip. "You are irresponsible."

"Yes, I am."

"Undependable."

"You know it."

"The poor thing could starve to death."

"That's a fact." Eddie grabbed the doorknob and added, "I'll leave you two to get acquainted." He pulled the door shut and we were alone.

"I could name you Chase." A sharp pain stabbed my heart as memories of the dog who'd died far too young struck me hard again. I looked down at my new dog and said, "Bad idea. You don't need to walk in a past pet's shadow, do you?"

He yipped and his rump bounced on the floor.

"I know. How about I call you Jesse?"

He threw back his head and let out a half-howl that sounded a lot like Jesse when he sang.

I smiled, wrapped my arms around him and inhaled deep gulps of his sweet puppy smell. "Welcome home, Jesse."

ABOUT THE AUTHOR

Edgar Award finalist **Diane Fanning** is best known for her true crime classics about serial killers, wife murderers, fake doctors and desperate women. She uses that real-life knowledge to bring the pages of her fiction to life. Author of *Through the Window, Into the Water, Written in Blood, Gone Forever, Baby Be Mine, Under the Knife* and *The Preacher's Wife,* Diane lives in the Texas Hill Country where she is now at work on *Light My Fire,* the next Molly Mullet murder mystery.